All We Have Is Now

Also by Robert Taylor

The Innocent

All We Have Is Now

Robert Taylor

St. Martin's Press ✹ New York

www.stmartins.com

Library of Congress Cataloging-in-Publication Data

Taylor, Robert
    All we have is now/Robert Taylor— 1st ed.
      p.cm.
    ISBN 0-312-28481-0
    1. Gay men—Crimes against—Fiction. 2. Murder victims' families—Fiction. 3. Trials (Hate crimes)—Fiction. 4. Trials (murder)—Fiction. 5. Grandmothers—Fiction. 6. Gay actors—Fiction. 7. Texas—Fiction. 8. Grief—Fiction. I. Title.

PS3570.A9516 A79 2002
813'.54—dc21

                                           2001048994

First Edition: June 2002

10 9 8 7 6 5 4 3 2 1

For Helen Yglesias
and
Constance Hunting,
friends and mentors

and for
Theodore Nowick,
always my love

With heartfelt gratitude

- to my terrific agent, Malaga Baldi
- to my wonderful editor, Keith Kahla
- to John and Susan Daniel, who made my first
  venture into publishing such a satisfying and
  rewarding experience
- and to all those who have given me support and
  encouragement through the years, among them
  Hetty Archer, Barry Berman, Peggy Bryant, Beverly
  Gologorsky, Doris Grumbach, Bruce Mallonee,
  Nancie Monteux-Barendse, Eric Price, Phoebe
  Prosky, Harold Shaw, and Chandler Williams

All We Have Is Now

Prologue

Our revels now are ended.

—William Shakespeare, *The Tempest*

Trevor's death was a long time coming, slow and agonizing, but it still seemed sudden to me. Because he was so young, I guess. We both were. Young and unprepared for such a thing. Looking directly at our own mortality thirty, forty years too soon.

After he died, I was sure I'd never be able to love anyone that much again. Never have the strength. Or the courage. I know that sounds dramatic, but . . . why not? I'm a very dramatic man. Dramatic is what I do best.

My closing up so completely was a tribute to our love, in a way, to its depth and intensity. But it was more than that. It was also the result of having to watch him die. Sitting there, helpless, as he faded away. Little by little, relentlessly, for almost three years. Kaposi's sarcoma, we discovered, is a cruel and merciless killer. Those ugly sores creep across your body, making you crazy. And the pains never let up. Not ever.

When we'd met, Trevor was a striking man, strong and vigorous. He'd loved tennis and volleyball. Especially volleyball. And he ran every morning, early, his wavy brown hair flying out behind him, his silky shorts showing off his firmly rounded rear end and his long, muscular legs.

I loved lying in bed, naked, waiting for him to come back—all sweaty, breathing fast, exhilarated. As he was throwing his running shoes and socks on the floor of the closet, I'd get up and kiss him, pull his wet T-shirt over his head, slide down his shorts and jockstrap. We'd walk, arm in arm, to the bathroom and stand under the shower, soaping each other, slowly, tenderly. Some mornings, when he got back early enough, we'd turn off the water and race to the bedroom to make love—but not always. There were times when just being together like that, close and utterly at peace under the stream of water, was all we could have wanted.

Then we found out, and nothing was ever the same again. As his strength ebbed and he became too weak to stand for long, I had to help him into the tub and bathe him there. When even that got to be too much, I'd carry a basin of warm water to the bed and wash him with a soft cloth. Sex for us, then, was mostly by hand. Gentle, loving, but a far cry from the erotic romps of earlier years. My tests kept coming back negative—so ironic, the randomness of that fickle disease—and we knew what not to do. It wasn't fear, therefore, that limited us, it was Trevor. Willing, but nowhere close to able.

I found myself missing so many things. Concerts and movies, dinner out at a nice restaurant, walks along the Potomac. Ordinary things, too. Things we'd always done together. Shopping for groceries, folding the laundry, one of us tossing a salad while the other broiled a piece of fish. But most of all, most of all, I missed those mornings, standing with Trevor under the shower, arms around each other, our closeness the only thing that mattered.

Still, even though we had very little left, we did have each other. Every night before we slept, I lay beside him and held him in my arms. And every night I felt him growing thinner and weaker. He couldn't hold me the way he always had before, strong arm across my chest, strong hand gripping my side. I had to lift his arm and put it across me. It just lay there, his fingers barely able to caress my skin, and that made me sadder, somehow, than anything else that was happening. It was such a sure sign of the inexorableness of his slipping away.

Near the end, he was all shriveled up, muscles gone, hair gone, his body covered with sores, the light gone out of his eyes. It hurt me to look at him, but I kept on smiling, kept holding him, soothing his tired wreck of a body till it was over.

Trevor worried a long time, at the beginning, before he told his parents, the banker and the Women's Club president. His fears, we soon saw, were justified. They turned their backs on him. His own parents. Cut him out of their lives completely. To be fair, a part of it surely was the suddenness with which the complacent little world they lived in was shattered. Finding out, all at once, that their son was gay— and that he was dying.

They told him he'd brought it on himself, living the way he had, so he could just find his own way of dealing with it. And they meant it. They packed up the things he still had at home—wearing gloves the whole time, I have no doubt— and left them for him in cardboard boxes piled out by the front curb. We drove all the way up to Pittsburgh from Washington to get them. One hot, steamy weekend in July. He didn't quite have the courage to go ring the doorbell—they'd been so remote and unyielding on the phone—but he was very much afraid this might be his last chance. We ended up hanging around for a while, standing there beside the car after we'd loaded his things, feeling a little foolish. But no one came out of the house. No sign of movement at any of the windows we could see.

His older brother called once from California, I'll give him that, in response to a note from Trevor. Said he wished he could get away but he couldn't right then. Really couldn't. Big push on some new software he was just finishing up. He'd be in touch, though. Check in to see how Trevor was getting along. We never heard from him again. Trevor called twice and left messages on his answering machine, but he didn't return either of the calls.

I have no family—I'm an only child, and my parents are both dead—which means I know a lot about loneliness. But that was my first experience with flat-out rejection.

And Trevor's boss? The tough, no-nonsense congressman Trevor had worked for, loyally, brilliantly, all those years, eased Trevor out as soon as he realized what it was Trevor had. Replaced him the second time he went to the hospital, and let him show up at work when he got out, only to find there was no place for him anymore. The congressman was shocked, he said on the phone when Trevor finally got through. Shocked and disappointed. That wasn't the real problem, though, Trevor told me. Not all of it, at any rate. An election was coming up (for congressmen, I'd learned, elections are *always* coming up), with an especially tough challenger this time around. So Trevor's old boss wasn't taking any chances. Wasn't about to give his opponent some-thing *this* juicy to use against him. He lost the race anyway, so who says there's no justice in the world?

Trevor's friends on Capitol Hill—who, of course, still had their jobs—let caution win out over loyalty and affection as well. They kept saying they'd get by to see him, but only a couple did. And only a time or two. Practical politics at work, Trevor told me with a sad smile. The only thing he was able to hang on to, after eight years of hard work, was his health insurance. Not even *those* profiles in courage up on the Hill were willing to risk the repercussions of denying him that.

Our gay friends, bless them, were our salvation. They pitched in and did what they could, and groups all over town, made up mostly of gays and lesbians but not entirely, started banding together, looking for ways to be useful. They brought meals by, visited with Trevor, helped us deal with a medical establishment that, we soon realized, was as unsure of how to cope with it all as we were. Unfortunately, by then, the mideighties, so many around us were getting sick, more and more all the time, that both friends and helpers were spread pretty thin. That meant a lot of the time it was just us, Trevor and me.

Capitol Rep, though, was wonderful about it all. I was well established there by then. Had worked my way up to leading roles in at least a couple of plays each season and had made a favorable impression on the audiences. Regulars told me they looked forward to seeing *Ian McBride* on the cast lists when they were announced. You don't get to be a star when you stick with a repertory company, not in the Broadway sense, but I was as close to that as anyone can be at Capitol Rep. So when Trevor got sick, the management did what they could for me. Gave me less demanding, less time-consuming roles for a while and let me skip plays entirely when I needed to. I loved them for that.

Having the whole summer off between seasons helped, too. That first summer we rented a little beach house at Rehoboth and had a happy time walking along the shore and wading in the surf. The lesions all over his legs and his back made Trevor so self-conscious he wouldn't wear a bathing suit, even inside the house. Wouldn't go into the water above his ankles. But he enjoyed the sun and the breezes. And the quiet. By the second summer, he didn't have the strength to go anywhere, and we sweltered together through a particularly humid Washington August.

The third summer he died.

Although I tried hard not to, I found myself closing up. Building a wall around me that would protect me from feeling that much pain ever again. I'd loved Trevor so much. Had counted on being able to love him for years and years. And have him around to love me. But . . . the Fates are capricious and laugh at what we wish for. They took him away and left me, alone and uninfected, to mourn him.

The shell I built around me was tough and formidable, able to keep out all possibility of affection or attachment that threatened to require too much of me. I still saw my closest friends, spent time with them, now and then—dinner parties, bridge games, a weekend or two in New York—but I didn't let myself make any new ones. When the cat Trevor and I had loved so dearly got old and infirm and had to be put away, I wouldn't even consider getting another.

I was lonely a lot of the time, especially at first. Trevor

and I had, after all, not been apart for more than a few days for almost eight years, and I was determined to preserve the memory of that closeness. Before long, though, my body rebelled as this self-imposed celibacy sent my hormones into overdrive. I started going out to the bars, occasionally, having casual but prudent sex often enough to keep from going entirely crazy.

As the months, then years, went by, I got used to being alone, or at least convinced myself that I had done so. I believed my loneliness was the price I had to pay in order to be safe. More and more, I retreated into the world of books, the safest place I could think of. Whenever I wasn't rehearsing, or performing, or meeting social obligations, I read. The classics, recent fiction, biography, memoirs, Greek drama, anything, everything. Way into the night often, hoping, I believe now, that I'd be so tired when I turned the light out I wouldn't be overwhelmed by the emptiness on the other side of the bed. Sometimes it worked; mostly it didn't.

Many of my friends, the ones I stuck with in the midst of my solitude, kept trying to 'fix me up.' I didn't mind, really. I thought I would, but I didn't. I met some interesting men that way and enjoyed brief affairs with a number of them. Brief, more often than not, because of my aloofness whenever real intimacy was about to intrude. I was determined not to cross that line, ever again.

I was tempted, from time to time, I have to admit, but the smallest hint of genuine interest on either side put me instantly on alert and sent me into full retreat. One way I protected myself was to limit even the briefest of liaisons to those on the peripheries of male attractiveness—on the one hand, stunningly gorgeous men who, I was sure, could never manage to actually include someone else within the circle of their self-absorption and, on the other, those not quite handsome enough to please my highly developed aesthetic sense.

For a long, long time, all this seemed just fine to me. My elaborately constructed defenses were keeping me safe.

Ariel

If of life you keep a care,
Shake off slumber, and beware.
                    Awake, awake!

I

Those twelve or so years, interestingly enough, were a time of enormous success for me in the theater. I was still trim and fit. Still attractive, in an increasingly mature way, wrinkles only around my eyes, a bit of gray at my temples the only real sign of advancing years. Still able to handle leads that didn't absolutely require a fresh-faced male ingenue. Several performances—especially Hickey in *The Iceman Cometh* and the father in *All My Sons*—received such widespread praise that friends and colleagues kept pushing me to break loose from Capitol Rep, go to New York, and try for the big time. I wouldn't do it. I felt comfortable right where I was, secure in the familiarity of my surroundings, however hermetic and closed off from the rest of life they may have been.

To my delight, Capitol Rep, undaunted by the Folger Theatre just up the hill, began a systematic assault on the works of Shakespeare, a play a year off into the foreseeable future.

The timing was perfect. I was at the peak of my form, leavened by pain, eager to tackle these most desirable of roles. Makeup and years of experience made me appear youthful enough for Benedick and Hamlet, I was just right for Theseus and Macbeth, and I was able to age convincingly for King Lear.

Then came Prospero, a role I'd wanted to play ever since I was a child and first read *The Tempest,* whose spirits and monster and aura of make-believe had captivated me. Through the years, I'd come to understand the play's layers upon layers of complexity—which take it far beyond make-believe into profundity—and thereby to admire it all the more.

As soon as the cast was announced, I went right home, poured myself a glass of wine, took my copy down off the shelf, sat in the easy chair in my study, and read the play straight through. I was struck, again, by the depth and power of Prospero's journey. Banishment. Life on a not-quite-deserted island. His enemies brought within his grasp. An unexpected move toward understanding and forgiveness. Quite a story.

I looked forward even more than usual to the first week of rehearsals, a time I've always loved. Meeting the players I don't already know, beginning to forge the intense bonds of community that are essential if the play is going to succeed, hearing the director's view of the play and plans for bringing that view to life.

The cast of *The Tempest* was about two-thirds Capitol Rep regulars. Those from elsewhere, in addition to a few of the minor parts, were our Miranda, Ferdinand, Caliban, and Ariel, most of them, it turned out, quite good. I was excited by the read-through and the first few days of blocking. The steady professionalism provided by us old-timers mixed in with the energy and enthusiasm of the newcomers was creating a powerful chemistry that boded well for the production.

Capitol Rep's founder and guiding light, Zena Fitzmorris, had been directing many of the Shakespeare plays herself and wasn't about to pass up the opportunity to do this one. Those of us who knew and respected her were delighted. Her *Tempest* would be a traditional one, which, to my mind, would get its message across far better than another of those updated versions with geometric sets, trapezes, and characters dressed in lab coats and wet suits.

Miranda and Ferdinand were equally matched in beauty— she pale and lovely in a Pre-Raphaelite kind of way and he a tall Adonis with broad shoulders and vivid blue eyes—but, we quickly realized, unequal in ability. She was a better actor than he, by a good bit. He was such a pleasure to look at, however, that I for one didn't much care. He was certainly good enough, and, though I was certain he was gay from the moment I saw him, their portrayal of young love at first meeting was entirely convincing.

The stocky, thirtyish Brazilian actor brought in from California to play Caliban was riveting from his first entrance. His exotic face with its thick black eyebrows, which he could crease together into a straight line, and his hunched-over, fitful way of moving created, without a hint of costume or makeup, a compelling monster who projected exactly the right combination of menace and innocence.

It was Ariel, though, who was the real revelation. A slender young man with a smooth, just-past-boyish face—too pretty to really be called handsome, too handsome to be no more than pretty—he moved with the grace and assurance of a gymnast combined with the easy, fluid carriage of a dancer. The first time he sang "Come unto these yellow sands and then take hands," followed by "Full fathom five thy father lies," that room full of hardened pros who'd seen it all sat entranced, no one moving. His voice was clear and pure like a boy soprano, but with a rumble of baritone in it that gave it substance and authority.

I was moved, and shaken, by the songs, and at the next break, I went over to tell him so. That I was moved, not that I was shaken.

He looked a little startled as I walked up to him.

"That was amazing," I said. "Both your singing and the way you held our attention. A tough audience like us. You've done this part before?"

He smiled and shrugged. "No. But I've been working hard ever since they offered it to me."

"It shows. You're to be commended."

"Thanks," he said.

"Your name is James, I believe?"

"Well . . . yes. Formally. But call me Jimmy."

There was a hint of the South in his voice.

"Hi, Jimmy. Call me Ian."

"Thanks," he said. "I will."

He held out his hand. I gave it a squeeze.

"You know," he said, "I have to tell you this is really exciting for me. You're a hero of mine."

"What are you talking about?"

"I've come down twice from New York to see you. King Lear last spring and Macbeth the year before."

"Why would you do that?"

He shrugged, smiled that shy smile again. "Word gets around. They said if I love Shakespeare, which I do, you were somebody I ought to see. And they were right."

" 'They'? "

He laughed. "Yeah. 'They.' People who've moved on from Capitol Rep. Phyllis Griffin and Angelo DeMarco mostly. Both of them said tell you hello when I got a chance."

"I appreciate that. And your kind words. But . . ." I was feeling nervous, awkward almost, and wasn't exactly sure why. "I'd better go find some coffee before it's time to start in again. Nice to have met you, Jimmy. I look forward to working with you."

"Me, too."

I turned to go.

"Could we . . . ?" he said.

I turned back.

"Could we have dinner some night? I'll treat. I don't want to be this close and miss the chance to get to know you."

I was still feeling nervous, but decided I was being foolish. He was only a kid. A nice-looking, talented kid.

"I think I'd like that," I said.

"When?"

I laughed. "I don't know . . . Tomorrow?"

"Great! Tomorrow it is."

2

The wine came. Jimmy tasted it, nodded his approval, and watched as the waiter poured it.

He picked up his glass, held it out toward me, and said, "To friendship."

I smiled, clinked his glass with mine, and said, "To friendship."

We looked at the menus, chatted about possibilities, and ordered—salmon for him, chicken for me (the least expensive thing they had, since he was paying). We talked about theater, Shakespeare, my years at Capitol Rep. Warm-up stuff.

About halfway through our entrées, he said, "I understand you live alone. Is that right?"

"Yes."

"Do you . . . ?" He grinned. "I can't stand it. I sound just like my mother. 'Do you have a girlfriend?' "

"No. No, I don't. I don't have a boyfriend either."

"Ahhhh. And if you were to have one or the other, would it be a boyfriend?"

"Yes."

He smiled and nodded. "Good."

"Why good?"

"Just . . . good. Did you ever? Have a boyfriend?"

"I did. A wonderful one. For almost eight years."

"And . . . what happened?"

"He died."

"Oh, god. I'm sorry. Of AIDS?"

"Yes."

"And you were . . . ?"

"Spared. Untouched. Isn't it ironic?"

"It's sad, is what it is. I'm so sorry." He was close to tears. "That damn disease. I *hate* it. When did he die?"

"Nineteen eighty-seven."

"Twelve years ago?"

"Yes."

"And you've been alone ever since?"

"Yes."

"Oh, my god. So . . . you weren't spared, or untouched, after all."

I looked up at him quickly. "You're very perceptive."

"For somebody so young." He nodded. "I know."

I smiled. "I didn't mean to . . ."

"It's all right. I'm used to it. Then . . . you've . . . ? I mean, all this time, you haven't been with *anybody*?"

"Oh, no. I've 'been with' plenty of people. Plenty of men. But briefly. Always briefly."

"To protect yourself."

I stared at him again. "You read minds?"

He smiled. "I'm Ariel, don't forget. A creature of air and fire. Of course I read minds."

"What else do you read in mine?"

He tilted his head and looked at me intently for a second or two.

"That you're lonely. That in a way you want to be. That . . ." He narrowed his eyes, then widened them. "That your suffering has been a blessing as well as a curse, because the wonderfulness of your acting these days is rooted in your sorrow."

"Dear lord," I said. "How old *are* you?"

"Twenty-five."

"Going on fifty."

"In some ways, I wish I *were* fifty."

"Why on earth is that?"

"Because then you'd take me seriously."

"Oh, I *do* take you seriously. You'd be astounded how seriously I take you."

"No. I don't mean what I'm *saying*. How perceptive you think I am. I mean . . ." He leaned toward me, his breath making the flame of the candle dance. "What I really mean is, a brief affair is not what I would hope for, but I would take it and be glad, if it meant I could be close to you—for a while."

I felt my emotions going into reverse, stampeding for the exit. I leaned back in my chair.

"That's not going to happen." I took a sip of my wine. "Not even briefly."

"No?"

"No."

"Because you're afraid."

"Of what, Ariel mind reader?"

"Afraid you'll end up caring too much."

"Aren't you being a little arrogant?"

"No." He shrugged. "Just reading your mind."

"Well . . . It's not going to happen."

"I'll fight you."

"You'll lose."

"I'm younger and stronger."

"I'm more experienced."

"I'll outlast you."

"I'll wall you off, so you'll never get through."

"But I will. I've read your mind, remember?"

3

Rehearsing a play is a fascinating process for me. Still, even after all these years. Parts of it are simple and straightforward—when and where I will enter, where I will stand, in what direction and how quickly I will move. Memorizing the words I'm to say is easy. Figuring out why I say them, however, and what it is they mean, is far more complicated. Hardest of all are the questions of who my character is, beneath the words, why he does what he does, how and by what subtle degrees he changes from the beginning of the play to the end.

Prospero is a role full of depths and contradictions. He is able, through his magic and with Ariel's assistance, to control the winds and the waves. He is powerful enough to cause men to sleep or wake or stand transfixed, but is incapable of altering what's in their hearts. He has no trouble seeing the evil in Caliban, but is seemingly oblivious to the history of oppression and neglect that are at its root—and to the half-buried dignity and yearning that live alongside it.

Zena and I worked hard to come to grips with how I would play this intriguing and enigmatic man. We came to see him as wise but still learning. Vigorous and energetic rather than serenely, austerely above it all. A part of the action, not merely pulling strings from on high. Glad to have his occult powers, but a bit frightened by them as well. Impatient to achieve his goals, but also aware of the inability of man—even a man with such potent magic at his command—to rush the unfolding of human destiny.

Since the play is all about power, who has it and who doesn't, Zena and I also explored the political implications of Prospero's actions. The way the high moral ground of his plan to win back his native Milan is undermined by his harsh subjugation of Caliban, whose island he has seized control of for his own purposes. And the philosophical ones: If knowledge is power, is lack of knowledge necessarily a sin? Is that lack to be pitied or condemned?

Joao's interpretation of his role fit in perfectly with this view of Prospero and of the play. His Caliban was as much man as monster, seething with desire for all the things he cannot have, from Miranda to simply not being ugly and misshapen anymore. Joao's soft, beguiling accent and growly voice, his wide eyes and furrowed brow, his menacing presence offset by edgy uncertainty, aroused fear and sympathy, at the same time and in pretty much equal measure.

And our Ariel. Flighty. Evanescent. Mercurial. Lithe, graceful body. Impassive face. Silver-toned, ethereal voice. Dangerously enchanting. And, for me, ever present. He and Prospero have so many scenes together that I spent quite a bit of time, those next few weeks, working with Jimmy. He was so good—so damn good—I enjoyed every second of it.

We chatted at breaks, about our roles, mostly, and the play, and quite often he would walk with me to my car on his way to the Metro. But each time he asked if we could have dinner together, or a drink somewhere, I'd say no. Sometimes, after a solitary glass of wine at home, when my guard was down, I'd find myself wondering why. What made me so adamant. Memories of what I'd gone through with Trevor? That was such a long time ago. Fear? Of the unknown? This seemed closer but somehow not the whole story. Relief at not having another person's needs to contend with? Maybe. Or maybe it was something as simple as habit. Settling into a rut that seemed comfortable because it was familiar. I didn't like these questions, though, the uncertainty they made me feel, so I started avoiding them as well.

One afternoon, as we headed for the parking lot, Jimmy asked, "Are you going straight home?"

"No," I said. "I need to pick some things up at Eastern Market."

"Can I ride along?"

"Sure."

It was a gray day, again. Spring was having a hard time taking hold. We drove a couple of blocks in silence.

"You're going to think I'm a presumptuous kid," he said at last, "but I don't care. I have to tell you . . . I'm worried about you."

"Why is that?"

"Because you work so hard at being unhappy."

I laughed, careful not to look at him.

"I've gotten good at it over the years," I said. "It doesn't take much work anymore."

"I wish you'd let me change that."

"But I won't."

"Why not?"

"Surely I don't have to explain it to you."

"Try. It's not all that clear to *me*."

"Well . . . Just look at all the differences between us. I'm old enough to be your father, for one thing."

He sighed, and I couldn't help smiling. We're also very much alike, I thought. Dramatic to the core. I've used that exact sigh myself, many times—to make sure my exasperation was being noted.

"You can be so tiresome sometimes," he said. "And *so* predictable. Thousands of men are old enough to be my father. *Millions*. But only one is, and it's not you. All right?"

He sighed again. "You keep coming up with these lame excuses. Talking about things that don't really matter. I notice you don't say you find me unattractive, or boring, or that you can't imagine spending time with me."

This time I did glance over at him, and quickly back at the car in front of me.

"I find you unattractive," I said, "and boring, and I can't imagine spending time with you."

He laughed. A lilting laugh that made me shiver. "I don't believe a word of that."

I circled past Eastern Market and found a parking place in the next block.

As I turned off the motor, he put his hand on my arm. I liked the feel of it, so I moved my arm away.

"You can't keep hiding like this," he said. "It's no good. You're too young to close yourself off for the rest of your life. You need to come on back to the real world."

"No, I don't," I said. "I'm safer right where I am."

"But you're *not*. You just think you are. I may be young and inexperienced in a lot of ways, but I *do* know this: that life has a way of catching up to you wherever you are. The only question is whether you're going to enjoy yourself, let yourself be a part of the good things, like being close to other people, before that happens. Now, while you still can."

I watched an old black man walk hesitantly across the street.

"Close to *you,* is what you mean," I said.

"I hope so, yes."

"But *why*?" I looked over at him and wished I hadn't. "Why are you so persistent? I really don't understand. What is it you're looking for?"

"I . . ." He took a deep breath. Then another. "What am I looking for? Meaning why am I attracted to you? I've thought about that a lot since I met you, and I think . . . Well . . . It's part hero worship, I'm sure. Respect and admiration for who you are and what you do. And why not? But it's more than that. It's . . . I'm tired of insubstantial people. I grew up with too many of them, and I'm tired of it. Do you understand that at all? Probably not. I just . . . I want to be with somebody . . . solid. Real. Somebody who's been around the block a couple of times and has some idea what life's all about."

"And you think *you* know that? What life is about?"

He laughed. "A little, maybe. Some. I'd say I've been about halfway round the block. But I'll tell you one thing: I'd walk the rest of the way with you. In a second."

Put your arm around him, you idiot, said a part of my brain. No way, said the rest of it. Too dangerous.

"What makes you so certain of that?" I asked.

He laughed.

"*Certain?*" he said, still laughing. "Of course I'm not certain. Who ever is? If you're looking for 'certain,' you better stay by yourself. That way you're at least *certain* to be lonesome."

He reached for the door handle, stopped, put his hand back in his lap.

"Look," he said. "It sounds like I'm preaching, I know that, and I don't mean to. But . . . For whatever reason, it matters to me what happens to you. So I . . ."

He rubbed the back of his neck and wrinkled his forehead. He looked so earnest, so open and uncomplicated, I wanted to lean over and kiss him. Right there on that busy street, people all over the sidewalks. But I held myself back. Let the moment pass.

"It seems to me," he said, "that you . . . I don't know. You try to take charge of what's going on around you. Stage-manage it, in a way. But you can't do that. Not forever. You're an actor on the stage. Be an actor in life as well. You've got to get back out there so that, even if things disappoint you or bring you pain, at least you've been a part of them. Not just standing in the wings watching it all happen."

Pain? What did this kid know about pain? I didn't want to hear any more. I was feeling closed in. Claustrophobic. I opened the car door.

"Thanks for the lecture," I said. "I appreciate your concern, I really do, but . . . I'd better get started with my shopping."

He sighed that sigh again as he was getting out of the car, and I smiled, in spite of myself. He saw it and smiled back.

"You're a formidable adversary," he said.

I nodded. "Oh, yes. 'I have bedimmed / The noontide sun, called forth the mutinous winds, / And 'twixt the green sea and the azured vault / Set roaring war.' "

He laughed again. That wonderful, silvery laugh.

"So you have," he said. "With my help, of course. But now . . ." He wrinkled his forehead. "Now it's time to ease off, just a bit. Let the winds die down and the waves be calm. Rest a little . . . with me. You'll be glad you did."

I smiled. "You're pretty formidable yourself. But . . . I've still got those groceries to buy."

4

Dress rehearsal was a disaster—missed entrances, flubbed lines, lights that came and went at bizarre times—which gave us hope that opening night would be fine. It was. As soon as the curtain went up, an atmosphere of hushed expectation began to build in the audience. We actors quickly hit a good rhythm, feeding off the energy coming our way, intensifying it, and sending it back out again.

Everything was going splendidly, but I was a wreck. Being onstage with Ariel was testing all the reserves of focus and concentration I'd built up over the years. For most of his scenes, when he wasn't disguised as a harpy or a nymph, Jimmy wore the filmy little sarong of pinks and lavenders the costumer had made for him. Nothing else. Nothing . . . else. He looked wonderful. His thighs and calves were shapely. His chest was slender but pleasingly muscled. It was his skin, though, so much of which was on display, that kept doing me in. Smooth, silky-looking, unblemished, almost radiant. I had a hard time taking my eyes off it. The night before, at dress rehearsal, I'd been distracted by so many other concerns, what was going well and what wasn't. This night was a very different story. Whenever Jimmy was around, he was all I could see.

My surroundings added to my sense that things were tilted somehow, vaguely out of balance. Each time I stepped onstage, I felt myself moving through an insubstantial world. Fragile. Illusory. With gauze and netting and papier-mâché, the designer of our set had created an enchanted tropical island at once familiar and oddly dreamlike. Spanish moss that dangled from the flies, swaying each time we stirred the air. Shadowy recesses in which shapes seemed to lurk just out of sight. Rocks that might be rocks. Trees that might be trees. A place where spirits surely dwelled.

By force of will, I made it through Act I, and was then, thankfully, offstage for all of Act II, where I had a chance to recover my composure. I sipped at a cup of stale coffee and went outside, briefly, to breathe the fresh night air. The next act, with its technical complications of the disappearing banquet, was touch and go but, from the audience's point of view, went along smoothly enough.

Then came Act IV. In front of the cell where Prospero lives and studies. A not-so-shadowy recess toward the rear at center stage. As the scene begins, Prospero happily gives his daughter to Ferdinand, who through his uncomplaining toils has proved himself worthy of her. Prospero turns to Ferdinand and says, "All thy vexations / Were but my trials of thy love, and thou / Hast strangely stood the test."

Wait a minute, I thought. Jimmy? Wait. I . . . Things are blurring here. 'My trials of thy love'? I shook my head and continued with my speech: "Here, afore heaven / I ratify this my rich gift."

Ferdinand answered, though I barely heard him. I called for Ariel, and Jimmy came rushing in, bare skin gleaming.

"What would my potent master?" he said. "Here I am."

"Go bring the rabble, / O'er whom I give thee power, here to this place," I said.

"Each one, tripping on his toe," he answered, in that voice full of honey, "Will be here with mop and mow. / Do you love me, master? No?"

"Dearly, my delicate Ariel. Do not approach / Till thou dost hear me call."

Instead of exiting, as he was supposed to do, he knelt before me and reached for my hand. I hadn't called. Had I?

Startled, I looked down at him. His beautiful, smooth chest was heaving. His dark eyes were alive and shining. He looked more appealing than a man has any right to.

"Say what I see in your face," he whispered. "Say you love me."

I squeezed his hand.

"You imp," I whispered. "Of course I love you."

He laughed, stood up, winked at me, laughed again, and ran offstage.

I turned immediately to Ferdinand. "Look thou be true," I said to him. "Do not give dalliance / Too much the rein; the strongest oaths are straw / To th' fire i' th' blood."

Dear god, I thought. Strong oaths? *My* oaths? Yielding to fire in the blood? What is this? What's happening here?

The goddess-spirits descended for the wedding masque, and I was quickly caught up in its complex unfolding. I felt my agitation giving an edge to my performance that was all to the good.

At the end of Act V, after he has forgiven all his enemies, Prospero reluctantly gives Ariel permission to go. The Fates are busy in my life, I thought. Prospero frees Ariel, Jimmy bewitches me. But I was going willingly now. So very willingly.

The applause after my Epilogue was immediate and prolonged. The audience rose and cheered—for Ariel, for Caliban, for me.

As soon as we were backstage after the final curtain call, Jimmy ran over, put his arms around me, and held me tight. I moved back just a bit, put my hand under his chin, tilted his face up toward me, and kissed his mouth. He held me tighter. I moved my head so I could see his eyes. He winked at me. The imp.

"You had a lot of nerve," I said, "courting disaster like that, when things were going so well."

He laughed. "What disaster? The scene was between you and me. No way were we going to let it be a disaster."

I shook my head and kissed him again.

"You were still taking an awful chance," I said.

He shrugged. "I had to risk a lot to gain a lot. Right now, I'd say the trade-off was just fine."

I looked around. People were grinning at us, and Joao patted me on the back. Zena pushed her way through.

"So *this* is what all that reckless ad-libbing was about?" Her eyes were narrow, and her mouth a thin line.

"Yes," said Jimmy, his arm around me. "Isn't it terrific?"

She stared a second or two, then smiled. "In fact it is. Finally beating some sense into this stubborn man's thick skull. But don't you *ever* . . ." She put her fist against Jimmy's cheek. "Don't you ever do such a thing to me, ever again."

Jimmy smiled and shrugged. "No need to," he said. "Not now."

Later, at my house, on my big king-size bed, Jimmy lay sleeping in my arms, his breathing light and even, his hand resting on my chest. I tightened my arms, and he nestled in closer beside me.

Yes, I thought. Oh my, yes.

5

That weekend, Jimmy moved into my town house, into my bedroom, and into my life. I drove him up to his furnished apartment north of Dupont Circle just after lunch on Saturday to get his things. One trip was enough. He didn't have much to bring—some pictures, two boxes of books, his favorite pillow, and a stack of CDs—but he settled comfortably into the house as if he belonged there.

As far as I was concerned, he did.

Those next weeks were an exciting and satisfying time in my life, and in his, too, I think. A smash hit of a play. Ecstatic reviews that singled out Jimmy, Joao, and me for special praise. An extended run by popular demand. And Jimmy himself—sweet, funny, affectionate—filling the places I'd left empty for so long.

From the beginning, time rushed past us in a whirl of activity. Arriving at the theater, side by side, late more often than not, holding hands sometimes, when we felt especially irreverent. Both talking a mile a minute. Laughing, always laughing. Putting on our makeup, getting into costume, pacing in the hallway, building a sense of momentum inside us and working to maintain it till time to go on. Giving each performance everything we knew how to give. Feeling currents of electricity crackle between us when we were onstage together. Winking at each other every time we arrived at that moment in Act IV when Jimmy gambled, and we both won.

Afterward, grabbing something to eat and then finding ourselves, more often than not, far too exhilarated to sleep. Never waking up, therefore, till well into the morning of the next day. Lingering over a late breakfast or an early lunch, whichever appealed to us, each trying to probe the other for details of his life. Toward evening, except for Mondays, heading back to the theater to get ready for another performance.

In between, most afternoons, we'd run errands. Quite suddenly and unexpectedly, we had a life together that was domestic enough to include errands. Grocery shopping. Putting gas in the car. Mailing a birthday present to his cousin. Picking up shirts at the laundry. Buying the things we needed to make the house Jimmy's home as well.

There were three rooms, besides the bath, upstairs—a big master bedroom at the back overlooking the garden; a smaller room I'd made into my study/library, complete with rolltop desk and floor-to-ceiling bookshelves; and a guest room up at the front of the house. On one of our 'errand' afternoons, we bought a futon and another desk. My plan was to have Goodwill come haul away the twin beds that had been in the guest room and turn it into a study for Jimmy, to give him a piece of the house that was all his own. I wanted to pay for these things, had every intention of doing so, but Jimmy insisted. Not to be deterred, I insisted back.

Well into the argument, right there on the second floor of the furniture store, Jimmy frowned, sighed that sigh of his, and said, "Look, Ian. *Every*thing in the world isn't about you. Trust me."

Of course he was right. Of course he wanted to feel that he was doing his part, contributing to what we were building together. It wasn't easy, but somehow I found the wisdom, and the grace, for once in my life, to just back off and shut my mouth.

I loved him. This was the central truth of everything that was happening—I loved him. The fact that he'd known all along that I would took away none of the pleasure I was now feeling. I loved being with him. I loved talking with him, delighting in his intelligence and quick wit. I loved his laugh. And, with a fervor I would have thought was behind me, I loved making love to him.

The question of safety occurred early to both of us, and we went dutifully off for our tests. When they came back negative, we congratulated ourselves on our good fortune and put all thoughts of danger aside.

From then on, the wide expanse of our bed became part playground, part altar, candles burning on both bedside tables so I could see every inch of his lovely body—and, I suppose, so he could see mine. His skin was as unbelievably smooth and sensual as I had imagined it would be. I loved touching it, and he loved being touched, my fingers brushing lightly from his shoulders to his stomach to his legs and back up. We came to enjoy, above all, a position Jimmy discovered, me lying on my back, him on his knees above me, facing me as he settled down onto my erection, me holding firmly onto his, him controlling, with mounting passion, the pace of our orgasms, moving his hips up and around, slowly, then faster and faster. We learned, by paying attention to each other, to come together, almost every time, me exploding up inside him, him spurting, with the vigor of youth, far out onto my chest, all the while looking down at me, laughing. Silvery, joyful laugh. Wonderful, magical boy.

Was it all, then, tranquillity and bliss? It was not. I was older—so much older—set in my ways, used to being in charge, impatient and irritable when I wasn't, when my routines were interrupted, my obviously good advice was ignored. Capable of speaking sharply, woundingly, when things didn't go my way. Willing, even eager, to carry a grudge—for days, if necessary—to make it clear that I was seriously aggrieved.

And Jimmy, no way of getting around it, was . . . young. Impulsive. Thoughtless at times. Inexperienced with this kind of daily intimacy. Absolutely addicted to procrastination. He left wet towels on the floor of the bathroom, dirty dishes in the sink, crumbs and bits of jelly on the kitchen counter, sections of newspaper strewn across the living room floor. He 'forgot' to put the lid back on the milk bottle, the top back on the toothpaste, and CDs back into their cases. He played music too loud, stayed in the shower too long, never phoned when he said he would, and refused even to consider making the bed.

"You do it," he would say, "if it matters so much to you."

Not easily intimidated, this kid.

But I loved him. And I began to realize, when I got over being huffy long enough to give the matter some rational thought, that it was, in part, these daily irritations—the very ordinariness of them—that made me love him so much. He was forcing me, single-handedly dragging me, out of myself. Out of a sterile, hermetic world in which order and tidiness counted for more than the warmth and laughter of an extraordinary, though forgetful and messy, young man.

6

Jimmy came into my study where I was reading, some Chopin ballades low on the CD player. I glanced up as he sat in the other wing-back chair. He was frowning.

I smiled at him.

"What's up?" I asked. "You look glum."

"We're about to have a visitation."

"Oh?"

"My parents are coming up from Texas. I sent them some reviews of *The Tempest,* and they're dead-set on seeing it. That was them on the phone. They've got plane reservations for week after next."

"You sound . . . what? Less than enthusiastic."

"Yeah. I guess I do."

"But they *should* see you. You're wonderful. You started out magnificent, and you just keep getting better and better. They'd be crazy not to come see it. No?"

He grinned. "I love hearing you say that. Maybe we

should start this conversation over, so I can hear it again."

"No need. I'll just remember to tell you more often. Which'll be very easy, since it's the absolute truth."

"Thanks, Ian." He got up, came over, and kissed the top of my head, then went back and sat down. "But . . ."

"But you're still uneasy about them coming. Right?"

"Right."

"Because of me?"

"Partly."

"Face-to-face with your ancient lover."

He laughed. "Not *ancient,* surely."

"But . . . older than they are, no doubt."

He shrugged.

"Oh, god," I said. "I *am* older, aren't I?"

He nodded.

"How much?"

"A few years. Not so much."

"And they don't know that yet?"

"Not . . . exactly. That I've moved in with you, yes. And why. They're adjusting to that, they say. But not . . ."

"Not my age."

"No. I didn't see any need to . . . just yet. Them down there, and us up here. Just one more complication."

"So, you think they'll mind."

"Yes. I do."

"I see. Then . . . What does that mean?"

"For us? Nothing. For them, I don't know. They'll have to deal with it the best they can."

"It doesn't matter to you?"

"Which? Their minding, or your being older?"

"Either. Both."

"I love you, Ian. Surely you know that by now. More than

I could ever have imagined. You are who you are, and that's who I love. Maybe it'll be a problem later . . ."

"Yeah. When you're forty and I'm *seventy*, for god's sake."

"Maybe. But not now. Do you understand me? It's not a problem now, for me. And we need to be careful not to make it one."

I smiled. "You're right. Of course you're right."

"Good," he said. "Which brings us back to my parents. This isn't going to be an easy visit, believe me, and we've got to be prepared for that. Protect ourselves."

"Meaning?"

"Well, for one thing, they'll be staying at a hotel."

I went immediately into 'gracious host' mode.

"But that's silly. They could stay here. It's a big house."

"Not big *enough*. Can you see them huddled together on the futon in my study? I can't. Or them in our bed and *us* on the futon? Even worse. They'd spend all their time trying to picture what goes on in that bed when *we're* in it. No, thanks. And . . . god! All four of us bumping into each other on the way to and from the bathroom? I don't think so. A hotel is best."

"Did they suggest that, or did you?"

"They did, thank goodness. No, it's definitely best."

"Then . . . when *will* I see them?"

"Well, let's decide. They're arriving on that Saturday, planning to see the play Sunday night. Going home on Tuesday. Can't stay long, they say. My father's got business to tend to. Always. But . . . We could have them over here for lunch on Monday, couldn't we? No performance that night."

"Sounds good to me. Meet them on my home turf. And . . . you'd be spending time with them before that, I guess? On Sunday? Showing them around?"

"If you don't mind."

"Of course I don't mind."

Was that true? The thought nagged at me, briefly. I did mind, a bit, maybe more than a bit, being left out. But not enough to make an issue of it. Better this way. Let them do things with Jimmy first. Get comfortable. Then come here and . . . see what happens.

"Have they been to Washington before?" I asked.

"No. First time."

"Well, then. You'll have lots of places to take them. It'll all work out just fine."

"I hope so," he said.

Those next two weeks, Jimmy was restless, edgy. I asked him about it a couple of times, but he kept saying he was fine, just hoping for the best. I let it drop.

When that Saturday arrived, he took my car to pick them up at the airport and came back smiling, saying they were in good spirits, glad to see him, pleased with the hotel. It had a nice restaurant they thought would be fine for dinner that night. They'd watch a little TV afterwards and go to bed early. Get some rest. See Jimmy in the morning for a tour.

I laughed. "Morning? You're getting up to show them around in the *morning*? This I've got to see."

He made a face. "I know. Don't think I don't. It's going to be grim. Maybe I can take a nap at the Smithsonian. While they're wandering around."

That night's performance was okay. Not one of the best. Part of the normal ups and downs of a long run. We came directly home, had a sandwich, and went right to sleep. The alarm the next morning had no effect on Jimmy. He slept on as if he hadn't heard a thing. Probably he hadn't. I pushed him. Pulled him. Yelled at him. Nothing. Dead asleep.

Finally I managed to get him sitting up on the edge of the bed, his head nodding. I eased him onto his feet somehow and walked him, naked, down the hall to the bathroom. I left him there and went back to bed. After ten minutes or so, I realized I wasn't hearing any noises. I went down the hall again and found him asleep on the toilet, leaning against the sink. I got him up, struggled to pull some clothes on him, combed his hair, and sat him down beside the phone in the bedroom, where he called the hotel to let his parents know he'd be a little late.

I'd planned on going back to sleep once he'd left, but after all that, it was impossible. I gave up, had some breakfast, and started fretting around the house. Our cleaning woman, Milagros, a Guatemalan refugee, had come on Friday, so everything was sparkling, but I found myself fluffing and tidying and vacuuming here and there anyway. I finished making the soup for tomorrow's lunch, read a while, took a nap, and was smiling and composed when Jimmy got home about four.

It had been a good day, he said. Sunny. Warm for April. He'd driven them around town first—Tidal Basin, Lincoln Memorial, Capitol. Lunch at a little Greek restaurant on Pennsylvania Avenue and afternoon visits to the National Gallery, both buildings, and Air and Space. They'd be taking a cab to the theater that night and to our house for lunch the next day. All very tidy.

"And did you have a chance to talk with them," I asked, "about me?"

"I did. Over coffee at the National Gallery cafeteria."

"And?"

"What I expected. Mom said, 'Well, now, isn't that interesting,' and Dad said, 'Whatever makes you happy, son.' "

"So . . . it's okay, then."

"Far from it. You obviously don't understand Texasspeak."

I laughed. "Obviously."

"No," he said. " 'Interesting' means 'what on earth has gotten into this loony boy's head?' Mixed in with a bit of '*where* do you suppose I went wrong?' And 'whatever makes you happy' means 'you're gonna have a tough time convincing *me* this is a good idea.' "

I laughed again. "That bad, huh?"

He nodded. "I'd say so, yep."

"Well, let's get on over to the theater and knock their socks off tonight. That'll fix 'em."

He hugged me tight.

"It's a deal."

7

If their socks stayed on during *that* performance, I thought as it was ending, they'd've had to be in a coma. We were terrific. All the technical glitches had been worked out by then, and everything hummed along smoothly. Ferdinand and Miranda overflowed with youthful love. Caliban was menacing and heartbreaking. And Ariel. Splendid. Jimmy surpassed himself in every way. After the seventh and final curtain call, we all hugged each other with delight. Jimmy threw on a robe and ran out to see his parents. He came back slowly, solemnly.

"What?" I said. "Surely they were impressed."

"Hardly," he said.

"*No?*"

"No. Mom said 'very nice' a couple of times, and Dad said, 'Guess we better start looking for a cab.' "

"Which, in Texas-speak, means what?"

"That they hated it."

We slept fitfully and were up the next morning by ten. Lunch was at one. We were both nervous, unsure of what to expect. I finished getting the food ready, and Jimmy made a final swing by the flowerbeds in the garden out back, pulling the last of the weeds and nipping off dead blossoms. By quarter of one, we were sitting in the living room, fidgeting. Jimmy heard the cab stop out front and had the door open as they came up the steps.

"Beautiful day," said his mother. "Just look at that sky."

"Mom, Dad," said Jimmy. "This is Ian McBride. My parents, Mary Beth and Henry Davidson."

"Hello, Ian," said Mary Beth, smiling. "I recognize you even without your makeup."

"Good," I said. "Nice to meet you."

"Ian," said Henry, holding out his hand.

I shook it.

"Nice to meet you," I said.

They were a well-dressed, handsome, prosperous-looking couple. She slender (consciously and carefully so, I was willing to bet), he strong and athletic. A golfer for sure. Probably a tennis player as well.

And they both looked so young. Fresh, unlined, tanned faces. Attractive and very young. God.

"Well," said Mary Beth brightly. "Here we are."

"Yes," said Jimmy. "Here you are."

"Good of you to let Jimmy use your car," said Henry. "To pick us up and then haul us all over town. We appreciate it."

"You're very welcome," I said. "My pleasure."

"Classy car, too, by the way."

"Thank you."

Henry looked around.

"Been here awhile?" he said. "This house? Looks like it."

"Yes, it has," I said.

"When was it built?"

"Nineteen oh two."

He whistled. "That long ago. Is it solid? Built well?"

"I suppose so. I've no reason to believe it isn't."

"But you don't *know*?"

"Not personally, no, I don't. Construction's not something I'm very familiar with. But . . . An inspector went over it before I bought it, and he seemed to think it was all right."

"Mmmmm," said Henry.

"I just love the way you've done it up," said Mary Beth. "The antiques and the beautiful rugs and all. Especially the rugs. They're . . . ?"

She looked at me questioningly, her hands making little circles in the air.

"The real thing?" I said. "Yes, they are."

"Ah-*hah*," she said. "Very pretty."

We walked down the hall, past the dining room, through the kitchen, and out into the garden.

Couldn't be a better time for this visit, I thought. The spring bulbs were in bloom, and the perfume of the hyacinths, faint but unmistakable, filled the air. Many of the daffodils and jonquils were still left. Tulips of every color. Tiny, pale-pink flowers all over the cherry trees. The quiet murmuring of the little fountain in the far corner added just the right touch.

"Isn't this amazing!" said Mary Beth. "*So* beautiful. Do you help keep it up, Jimmy? At least a little bit?"

"I do, Mom. I love it out here."

"Well, no wonder."

"I see you've got bars on the door and all the windows," said Henry. "This neighborhood all right?"

"Not too bad," I said. "We have to be careful, but . . ."

"I wouldn't want to live that way, I can tell you," he said. "Too much like bein' in jail."

I nodded and smiled and said nothing.

As we went back down the hallway past the stairs to the second floor, neither of them asked to see the upstairs rooms, and Jimmy didn't suggest it. I got the three of them settled in the living room and went to bring us all champagne, in my best crystal glasses, and hors d'oeuvres. We had white wine with lunch—vichyssoise, crab salad, and asparagus. Mary Beth said complimentary things about each dish and asked for recipes. Henry ate in silence.

"So," said Jimmy, after he'd served the chocolate mousse and coffee, "since we're being so careful not to talk about it, I'll ask. What did you think of the performance last night?"

"Well . . . ," said Mary Beth, glancing at her husband. "I . . ."

"We don't know *what* to think," said Henry, "quite frankly. I mean, what was it about? I've never been so confused in all my life. I mean, Shakespeare, sure. *Romeo and Juliet. Macbeth.* Those I can get. But what on earth was *that* thing about?"

" 'Thing'? " said Jimmy. "That 'thing,' Dad, was one of the greatest plays ever written."

"Well, you'd never prove it by me. Magic spells. Pagan goddesses flyin' in out of nowhere. And fairies, for pity's sake. We couldn't make head nor tail of it from start to finish. Could we, Mary Beth?"

"No, we couldn't. But what I . . . Well . . . I just don't understand why you couldn't've had more *on,* James Arthur. Everybody else did. But you . . . in that tiny little scarf contraption. So flimsy it left *nothin'* to the imagination."

I'd been watching Jimmy's face through all of this. I'd seen it go from amusement to disbelief to outright anger.

"You're wrong there, Mom," he said. "*Every*thing is left to the imagination. Everything. That's the whole point. Ariel *is* imagination. That's a lot of what this 'thing' is about."

"Him? Imagination?" said Henry. "I never heard such twaddle. Where'd you get *that* idea? He's a fairy. He runs around on tippy-toe singin' songs that make no sense and doin' . . . fairy things. What's that got to do with imagination, for cryin' out loud? Imaginary things are what you can't see. I could see *you* all right, flittin' around practically naked. Whatever possessed you, son, to get up there like that, with no clothes on in front of hundreds of strangers? Runnin' around swoopin' and carryin' on. I couldn't believe it. You'd never catch your brother—*or* sister—doin' such a cockeyed thing as that, I can tell you."

"No," said Jimmy. "I'm sure you wouldn't."

He was struggling to hold on to his composure.

"Tell me," I said. "Did you enjoy your afternoon at the Smithsonian yesterday?"

Mary Beth turned to me with a smile of relief.

"Yes, we did," she said. "Very much. Such pretty paintings for me and all those planes for Henry. We both enjoyed it so much. We're goin' back, matter of fact, as soon as we leave here. I can't wait to see the First Ladies' dresses."

Henry opened the door of the cab Jimmy had called. We waved from the porch. They waved back. They got in, and the cab pulled away. As soon as we were inside the house and the door was closed, I put my arms around Jimmy and held him as close as I could.

"Are you all right?" I asked.

"No."

"Will you *be* all right?"

"Probably. If you keep holding me."

"No fear. I'm not going anywhere."

"Good," he said. "Me neither."

I'd been rubbing one hand up and down his back. He leaned his head against my shoulder.

"If I were a cat," he said, "I'd be purring."

"So purr."

He laughed.

"We have one thing to be grateful for," I said. "At least."

"What's that?"

"The subject of my ancientness didn't come up."

He laughed again and squeezed me tight.

"I'll say it didn't. Preempted by all that clucking over my naked body."

"Without question the most beautiful thing I've ever seen," I said.

He stepped back, holding on to both my hands.

" 'Thing'? " he said, frowning. " 'Thing'? "

I laughed.

"You know what I mean."

He winked.

"Of course I do. Want to see it? Right now?"

"You bet your sweet life."

8

The run of *The Tempest* finally ended. Our season was officially over (the two plays we'd preempted postponed till the following year), and summer was not far away. Zena decided she couldn't extend it any longer, even though crowds were still showing up. It was all right. We'd had a good long run—thirteen weeks. We were satisfied.

Jimmy and I soon found, however, that we had time on our hands.

"Let's go somewhere," I said one night as we were cooking supper. "Someplace you've never been but always wanted to go."

He stopped chopping onions and looked over at me, wide-eyed.

"*Could* we?" he said. "I mean . . . could we?"

"Of course. Why not?"

"But . . . Just *go*? Pick someplace wonderful and . . . go?"

"Yes, my dear. Anyplace in the world."

"The *world*! Oh, my lord."

"What were you thinking of? Cleveland?"

He laughed. "Well . . . San Francisco maybe."

"If that's what you want, sure."

"But wait . . . The *world*? Europe, you mean?"

He looked so excited I wanted to hug him. I was skinning chicken, though, and my hands were a mess. I'd hug him later.

"Of course," I said. "Europe. South America. Australia. You name it."

"Gosh, I . . . I've never been outside the country. Except for a couple of trips to Juárez."

"Then pick a place. One you've dreamed of seeing. Rome? Paris? London? Madrid?"

"Spain," he said. "That's it. Spain. I've always loved . . ."

"No explanations. Spain it is. I've never been. You've never been. Let's go."

After four busy days in Madrid, full of museums and art and the National Palace, we arrived by bus in Granada on a Tuesday afternoon. The hotel we'd located in a guidebook back home was nestled at the base of the steep hill crowned by the Alhambra, that magnificent palace built by the Moors. We'd made a good choice. It was a small hotel, more like an inn, three inner stories overlooking a central courtyard. We unpacked, walked around town till after dark, stopped for couscous at a Moroccan restaurant, and went right to bed.

We slept late the next morning and headed up the hill toward the Alhambra a little before eleven. We gave the guard the tickets we'd bought at our hotel and walked inside. I stopped dead still, unable to move or even speak. It was the most exquisite structure I'd ever seen. Arches of what I knew must be carved stone but looked like clouds of meringue rippled around the courtyard. Nothing here pressed heavily toward the ground, the way gravity forces other buildings to do. These arches floated, tethered to the columns that, rather than holding them up, were there to keep them from drifting away.

"I've never seen such a place," Jimmy whispered. "Couldn't ever have imagined it."

"Oh, but you have," I said quietly. "You built it, my darling Ariel. I know you did. There's no other explanation. You took wind and running water . . . and one of your songs . . . Turned them into stone and made . . . this."

He squeezed my arm.

Purely by chance, we'd arrived in Granada just in time for one of their many festivals. Cruz de Mayo, they called this one, and the whole city would be taking part. Preparations began on Wednesday for that weekend's three-day celebration. We were booked through till Monday, so we'd see it all.

Groups were hard at work in every park, every plaza, every courtyard, every little neighborhood bar. Soon each of these places had its own cross covered with fresh flowers mounted on an altar. Surrounding the altar were those things the creators valued most: gorgeously embroidered shawls, silver candelabra, shiny copper pots, paintings of saints or the Virgin Mary. The display in the courtyard of our hotel was the most beautiful of all.

By luck again, we were staying near the heart of the festivities. From midmorning on Friday through all of Sunday night, the streets outside the hotel were jammed with children, students, middle-aged couples, old people, all laughing, singing, dancing. Many of the women and girls had gotten out their extravagantly ruffled gypsy dresses and were wearing them proudly, fresh flowers stuck in their upswept hair. Men dressed in tight suits of black and gray rode through the streets, the horses as handsome and elegant as the riders. Those of us walking ahead of them moved aside, smiling and waving as they passed.

The crowds were so dense we had no choice but to go in the direction they were heading. That was fine with us. They knew better than we did where we all wanted to be. The first time we went out on those crowded streets, I worried briefly about pickpockets and the wad of pesetas in my billfold, but those thoughts quickly left my head. Just as well. At the end of the weekend, all that was gone was what I had spent.

On each venture out, Jimmy and I laughed and sang as we went, losing sight of each other from time to time but coming together again eventually. Sometimes we walked along arm in arm, the way many other pairs of men were doing. Whether they were lovers or friends or strangers who'd just met, we neither knew nor cared. On every block, it seemed, there were little stalls selling beer, wine, sherry, and all kinds of food, the cooking smells an irresistible temptation. We drank, sherry for me, beer for Jimmy, ate cheese and ham and olives and potatoes, baked and fried. When our hands weren't full, we clapped in time to whatever music was closest to us.

Late on Saturday, about nine o'clock, as the sun was beginning to fade, we came to a lovely little square, maybe halfway up the hill of the Albaicín, the old Arab quarter of Granada. On one side of the square, a platform had been erected, and recorded music blared at us from speakers on the ground. Up on the stage, serious-faced boys and girls, little pictures of grace and enthusiasm, were stomping out the soul-stirring rhythms of flamenco.

"I *love* this," Jimmy said, his eyes shining. "Isn't it fabulous? It's what I was *hoping* to see."

He moved as close to the platform as he could get. I followed and watched him as he watched the dancers—intently, nodding every now and then. He swayed in time to the throbbing of the music, clapping the same syncopated patterns as the boys and girls. A different group took the stage, then another. Each time, the dancers were older, more skillful and secure. I could see that Jimmy was following it all carefully—the intricate footwork, the sharp but fluid movements of hands and arms, the haughty upward thrust of their heads. He nodded, clapped, swayed.

The last group, young men and women in their twenties, was of course the best. Strong and sure of themselves, they shook the stage with their rhythmic stomping. After they finished their second number, one of the men walked to the edge of the platform, shouted something, and spread his arms. Several children and a couple of teenagers climbed the stairs on the far side. The music began again, trained dancers pairing up with the neophytes.

Jimmy skipped the stairs entirely and simply leapt from the ground onto the platform. He moved to the back of the stage and began to dance. I edged through the crowd until I could get a clear view of him. He stood erect, his head held high, his feet hammering the floor. I was astounded. He wasn't just good, he was superb. A slender boy from Texas with gypsy fire in his blood.

The other dancers began to move away from him, to give him room and, it seemed to me, to let the audience see him better. The most accomplished of the young women moved to his side, and the two of them, now the only ones dancing, stomped and posed and whirled. I could almost hear the crackle of the electricity with which they were filling the air around them. As soon as the music stopped, the crowd shouted for more.

"Americano," they yelled. "Bravo."

Jimmy turned to the young woman. She smiled and nodded. The other dancers moved to the rear of the platform. The music began again.

This song was the most passionate of all, the guitars a blur of rising and falling sound, the singer wailing some tragic story of lost love. Jimmy and the young woman were more than a match for the music. Only their sweat kept her dress and his shirt from bursting into flame. When the song ended, the crowd shouted and clapped and whistled its approval. I looked around. The little square, half-full when we'd arrived, was now packed. I looked up at Jimmy. He was smiling and bowing and blowing kisses at the audience. Maybe it was the highly charged eroticism of the music. Maybe it was a renewed awareness of the scope of his talents. For whatever reason, I loved him more at that moment than I ever had before.

He jumped to the ground. I started toward him. He was immediately surrounded by excited young men, all smiling, all talking at once, reaching out to touch his arm, his shoulder. I stopped and stared. What was he thinking, in the midst of this crowd of admirers? They were so . . . eager. So handsome. So young. He could go home with any one of them, gay *or* straight. They would adapt—for him. I could see that in the way they looked at him, leaned toward him. But . . . Would he? Did he want to? Should I fade away and let him savor this triumph?

He nodded at them and smiled, but began looking around. When he saw me, he waved and started in my direction. I pushed my way toward him. As I reached his side, he put his arms around me and held me close. He was breathing hard. His shirt was soaking wet.

He moved back and said, "Let's go find something to eat. What is it—midnight?"

"Just after ten-thirty."

"Lordy," he said. "I'm *starving*."

"Where on earth did you learn flamenco?" I asked as we walked down the hill, arm in arm.

"Miss Velma's School of the Dance. Kimberley, Texas. Surprised?"

"Speechless."

9

After we got back from Spain, Jimmy and I decided to rent a beach house for the summer. We drove over to the Delaware shore and found one we both liked, south of Rehoboth, off by itself at the edge of the water, just behind some low dunes. More rustic than most of its neighbors, it stood there serene and self-contained. And quite beautiful. Jimmy was worried about whether we could afford it. I assured him we could.

It was a big, rambling place, full of wicker furniture and sisal rugs and lots of rattan. Two stories, with porches on both floors that looked out toward the water. The wood shingles on the outside walls had weathered to a soft, almost velvety gray. We discovered that the builders had known exactly what they were doing. When we opened all the windows, cool air would begin to circulate throughout the house, even on the hottest, stillest days. From somewhere would come breezes that ruffled the sheer white curtains and moved gently across our faces.

One thing we had in abundance was extra beds. Friends came and went—mine from Washington, Jimmy's from New York, ours from Capitol Rep. They mixed, mingled, overlapped. I ended up doing most of the cooking and cleaning. Jimmy put himself in charge of entertainment. Many nights after dinner, he would sit in the front room at the tinny, out-of-tune upright piano and play while the rest of us sang. Show tunes. Old sing-along songs. Hymns. He knew them all. Well, *almost* all. The older guests would try hard to stump him, and sometimes they succeeded. He would laugh, shrug, and launch into a song he *did* know.

The nights we didn't sing, Jimmy would organize a game of Charades. With so many theatrical people in the house, the games were intense and flamboyant. Hard-fought. Often hilarious.

Most of my friends liked Jimmy. A few did not. A couple of them were certain he was just using me to advance his career; another assured me that Jimmy was shallow and immature, that the age difference was far too great, that all I was doing was making one last, pathetic grab at staying young.

One of my oldest friends, an economist at the World Bank named Barney, got me off for a walk along the beach, just the two of us. He leaned toward me and said earnestly, "I smell trouble, Ian."

"What kind of trouble?" I asked.

"That boy will break your heart."

I laughed.

"Laugh all you like," he said. "But it's true. He will."

"And on what, exactly, do you base this opinion?"

"Intuition. Mine's damn good, as you very well know. And this is a strong one."

I laughed again.

"Is it?" I said. "Well . . . My *experience* tells me different. So you can just go peddle your intuition someplace else."

Barney stiffened and narrowed his eyes.

"Fine," he said. "Suit yourself."

He walked on ahead down the beach and didn't look back.

Jimmy's friends, all actors, all young, ran the gamut from eager to know me to aloof. A few made time to sit and talk with me. Others I barely saw. But . . . the size of the house and the expanse of the beach, just out the back door, made who got along with whom immaterial, really. We sorted ourselves out, wandering off, alone or in groups, to swim or sunbathe or stroll along the shore. We'd come back to eat, read, take naps, play cards. We drifted, suspended in a world cut off from the one we'd left.

Jimmy and I brought one thing along from home, however. We argued. Not all the time, but often enough. Averaging maybe once a week. He'd go out, late, to one of the gay bars with a group of his friends and not get home till three—or even four.

"Where the hell have you been?" I'd ask, seething.

"Dancing. I told you."

"*Just* dancing?"

"No, Ian. I also talked and drank. And maybe even laughed."

"*And?*"

"For god's sake, Ian. *And* nothing."

Maybe Barney's right, I would think.

Jimmy would get furious at one of my patronizing friends.

"That asshole treats me like I don't know what I'm talking about," he'd say.

"Well . . . Sometimes you don't," I'd reply.

"I appreciate your support, Ian. I really do."

"Why should I support you when you're wrong?"

"Because you're *supposed* to love me."

I'd decide he wasn't helping out enough around the house.

"Here I am sweating my butt off in that kitchen three times a day," I'd say, "and you can't even do a little laundry now and then? Fold up a sheet or two?"

"All you have to do is ask," he'd say.

"I shouldn't have to *ask*," I'd say. "You should *know*. If you were paying any attention at all, you'd *know* what needs to be done."

That kind of thing.

Never anything of real importance. More like a honing of egos, with sparks shooting off whenever rough spots rubbed up against each other. In my more reasonable moments, I could see they were all part of the process of settling in together, adjustments we still needed to work out. Me, on one side, eager for him to just listen to me, since I knew better; him, on the other, determined not to end up under my thumb.

Foolishness, really. On my part certainly. And perverse. As if I were testing the limits of my good fortune.

But we got over them reasonably quickly. Jimmy did, at any rate. I was more likely to let things drag on for a day or two, so that people could see what I had to put up with. Then I'd be stricken with remorse and run around assuring everyone that Jimmy was, in fact, wonderful. A gem. No fool like an old fool.

Our upstairs bedroom opened onto a screened-in porch overlooking the ocean. It had a musty old daybed with a lumpy mattress, and sometimes, especially on those rare occasions when we had the house to ourselves, we'd sleep out there. Well . . . We'd get around to sleeping eventually. First, we'd make love, always more enjoyable when the rest of the house was empty and we didn't have to give any thought to being quiet. Then we'd talk late into the night. Which for us, of course, meant the early hours of the morning.

"It's lucky, isn't it?" Jimmy said, one night toward the end of August, as we lay out on that porch. "That we both enjoy staying up like this. And then sleeping as late as we can the next day. I always have. Slept late when I could. Ever since I was little. I liked school all right, but I *hated* getting up to go. Saturdays, forget it. And vacations. Never up till noon. How about you?"

"I wanted to sleep late, most every morning, seems to me. But my mother wouldn't let me. She thought it was immoral somehow. And lazy. Certainly lazy. She made sure I knew how disap*point*ed she was when I did."

"It's better to be the baby of the family. Although I guess you didn't have much choice about that. Even so, it's much better. By the time I came along, my parents had given up, pretty much. On the strict discipline stuff. I had to show up for supper on time, and not be late for school—or *church*, heaven forbid—but other than that, I was pretty much on my own."

"Sounds ideal."

"Maybe. In a way. I'm glad you've adjusted, though. Gone

back to what you wanted to do all along. I mean . . . Imagine if one of us was an early bird. Disaster."

I laughed. "It'd never work, that's for sure. But then . . . If we didn't like staying up late, we wouldn't be in the theater, would we? It's almost a prerequisite."

"Or . . . ," he said. "We'd have to go out to Hollywood. *They* get up at the crack of dawn, I hear."

I shuddered. "Wouldn't you know? There goes *my* movie career out the window."

"Doesn't bother me," he said. "I like theater better anyhow. For now at least."

"Why *is* that?" I asked. "I used to wonder about it a lot, but then I stopped. What is it that attracts us to that crazy life? With all its neuroses and damn hard work. It can't be just a desire to show off."

"Oh, *can't* it?" He laughed. "But . . . you're right. It *is* more than that. For me, anyhow."

"So . . . Why, then?"

"Why?" he repeated. "Mmmmm. Maybe it's . . ."

He was quiet for a minute or two. I could tell he was thinking. I let him think. The sound of the waves was soothing, hypnotic. I turned toward it. Through the screen I could see a dark sky full of stars. A slight breeze brought the smell of salty water and seaweed—and old crab?

"I had a hard time, growing up," he said at last. I turned back toward him. "A really hard time. Nobody in my little Texas town had the slightest idea what to make of me. My grandmother, some, later on, but she was the only one. My poor parents didn't have a clue. Not a clue. Well, why would they? I wasn't like anybody they'd ever seen, not *anybody* in our whole spread-out extended family. From the time I popped out, I was this weird little kid. I . . . Just weird. I often wondered if they thought maybe things got mixed up at the hospital. That they brought home the wrong baby."

He laughed. I could feel him shrug.

"The wrong baby. Yes, indeed."

He was quiet again for a bit. I watched the stars. He sighed, and I rubbed my hand up and down along his arm. His skin was so smooth. We'd made love not half an hour earlier, but touching that satiny skin made me ready to go again.

"What confused me the most," he said, "was that my brother and sister were just . . . relentlessly normal. Drove me crazy. He was like our father—loved sports, all of them. They'd sit in front of the TV together, hollering and whooping. About a touchdown or a . . . I don't know. A home run. A *car* race, for god's sake. She was like our mother—Little Miss Homemaker. Loved to dress up. Started shopping, probably, when she was five. Collected dolls and jewelry and boyfriends. Smiled *all* the time. Bright little cheerleader smile.

"They're both older than me. Not by much, but . . . it seems like more. Believe me. They're . . . reliable. Predictable. Never caused Mom and Dad a moment's worry, to hear my parents tell it. I, however . . . I was this . . . oddball. Not one thing or the other. Not like anybody. Because of the way I felt, I thought maybe I was supposed to've been a girl, you know? I liked pretty things. I cried when I was unhappy. Also when I was happy. And I was . . . soft. Not hard and tough like my brother. But I wasn't like my sister either. Not at all. I wasn't interested in her kind of dressing up—ruffles and high heels. Too ordinary. I preferred capes and feathers and tights. Her whole way of seeing things was hidden away where I couldn't get at it. Everything was a mystery to me.

"Till sixth grade, when I was in my first play. The teacher picked me to be Aladdin. Out of nowhere. *Me*. It's hard to explain what that meant to me. It was the most exciting thing that had ever happened. Like the world suddenly turned upside-down. Or . . . rightside-up, more like. Never mind it was a very ordinary grade-school production, with cardboard sets and thrown-together costumes. For me it was magic. A way out of the confusion, the . . . bewilderment that had always surrounded me.

"When I was up on that stage, that dinky platform at the far end of the cafeteria, I knew, for the first time in my life, who I was and what I was supposed to be doing. I wasn't Jimmy Davidson, that skinny little sissy who'd eaten lunch alone, many a day, in that very cafeteria. I was Aladdin! I was the one who rescued the princess and carried her off on a fiery stallion. Pretend, of course, but *I* could see him. I could hear his snorts and whinnies and feel his strong muscles between my legs. I *was* Aladdin. Jeweled vest. Gold turban. Cape flying out behind me. I was a prince! Do you understand what I mean?"

"Oh, yes," I said.

"It changed everything for me. I didn't *need* to be a girl if I could be a *prince*! Well . . .

"We only gave two performances. All that work for just two performances. But when they were over, nothing was ever the same. Ever. I was different. The way people saw me was different. Because I was *good*. Nobody could deny that. They might not know what it meant, and it might not really matter all that much to them. But they couldn't deny it.

"I joined the drama club in junior high—couldn't *wait* to get there—and it became my home, in a way. No. Not 'in a way.' My home. I belonged there. For the first time ever, I really belonged. I made friends, like I'd never had before. Because we cared about the same thing. Oh, I cared about it more than the others. More than the teachers even. For them it was something to do. For me it was . . . my love. It gave me a place to act out the things that were missing in my life. And somehow, acting them out actually *put* them there. Made them part of me in *fact*. Does that make any sense at all?"

I hugged him tight. The stars were so bright I felt them reaching down to touch us. I turned his face to mine and kissed him.

10

Jimmy and I went back to Washington right after Labor Day. It seemed strange to be there, that first night, away from the sound and the smell of the ocean, but we both agreed we were glad to be home.

I went over to Capitol Rep the next afternoon to see Zena Fitzmorris. She'd spent the week of the Fourth of July with us at Rehoboth Beach and had come back to sort out the next season's schedule.

"What have you decided?" I asked. "Still starting off with that Mamet play we didn't get to last season?"

"Yes," she said. "It's all cast and ready to go. Well, two substitutions, but basically intact. We'll start rehearsals the end of the month."

"And follow up with *Art* after that?"

She shook her head. "I don't think so. You remember telling me you'd like to do some more O'Neill?"

"Absolutely."

"I'm wanting to capitalize on the success of *The Tempest*, get you out there again as soon as I can. So I thought . . . *Long Day's Journey into Night.*"

"James Tyrone," I said. "Incredible role. Thanks, Zena."

"And what do you think of Jimmy for Edmund? Could he handle it?"

"I haven't a doubt in the world."

"He'll have to audition."

"Of course. Just to be sure. *And* to be fair."

I found Jimmy outside in the garden, tidying up the perennials we'd left untended all summer. When I told him, he was thrilled.

"Wouldn't that be te*rrif*ic," he said. "Us onstage together again. I'd love it. And in *that* play. Like a dream come true."

As soon as he and I started working on his scenes for the audition, I knew the part would be his. His Edmund was intense, wary, vulnerable. As much *of* this world as his Ariel was not. There were depths to this boy I had not begun to see.

Jimmy went off to his audition, called to say he was waiting to hear, called again to say he'd done it. He would play Edmund.

"Why am I not surprised?" I said.

We went out for dinner to celebrate. A new French restaurant everyone was raving about. Jimmy looked handsome, quite elegant, in the suit he'd just bought.

"The best thing of all," he said after we'd ordered and were sipping our wine, "is I get to stay here with you—for a while, at least. Not have to go back to New York looking for work. I was dreading that."

"Me, too," I said. "God. I've been wishing for something like this, but . . . I could hardly believe we'd be so lucky. You know . . . I'd decided if you *did* have to go back to New York, I'd . . . look for something there, too. And if I couldn't find anything right away, just hang out up there with you. Till I did."

He stared at me. "But you love it here. Your work. And . . . what you've built up."

"I do. But I love you more. I don't think I could bear being without you . . . even for a little while."

"Oh, my god, Ian," he said. He put his hand on top of mine and squeezed it. He swallowed hard.

The waiter brought our plates of escargot and set them in front of us.

"Just *smell* that garlic," I said. "Marvelous."

"No problem with 'garlic breath,' " Jimmy said, "if we've both got it."

I laughed.

The waiter took away our plates of empty shells and served our rack of lamb. We dug in.

"Are you as excited about *Long Day's Journey* as I am?" Jimmy asked.

"I . . . am," I said.

He looked up quickly and narrowed his eyes.

"But?"

"No 'but,' " I said. "I am."

"Don't dance around with me like this, Ian. It's no good. You say you love me, enough to make enormous sacrifices, and then you . . . avoid things that really matter."

"Like?"

"Like you *are* upset about the play."

"Why would I be upset, Ariel mind reader?"

"Because I'll be playing your *son*. And it'll just remind people how much younger I am."

"Bull's-eye. Again. How do you do that?"

He smiled. "It's not so hard. You've been fretting about this ever since we met. It's part of why you were so adamant about not giving me a chance. It drove you crazy when my parents were here, and made you cranky and irritable all summer, when I'd go out with my *young* friends. I don't have to be a mind reader to see that. Just somebody who loves you very much and wishes you wouldn't keep being your own worst enemy. You're determined to make it *be* something whether it really *is* or not. And you shouldn't. You honest to god shouldn't."

"I know you're right. At least, my head knows you're right. Sort of. It's my . . . what? My gut, down where the demons are, that isn't sure."

He smiled. " 'Sure' is what we never get to be. We don't have any guarantees. Nobody does. We should be glad for what we *do* have, you and I. Which is a lot. Can't we just let it *be* that . . . for a while?"

I put my fork down and reached over to take his hand. I held on to it. Who cared who might be looking?

"I wish these rotten thoughts didn't come around to haunt me," I said. "Do I ever! But I can't seem to keep them out. And the better I know you, the worse it gets. The more I see how talented and smart and . . . *desirable* you are, the more I think that *every*one, everyone younger and handsomer, must surely see it, too. And the more I love you, the more afraid I am of losing it. What we have."

He shook his head. "You see what I mean? Your own worst enemy. You let what *might* happen tomorrow take away from the pleasure of what *is* today. I used to do that . . . a lot. I'd wish for this and wish for that. And feel sorry for myself when my wishes didn't come true. And then it hit me—like a two-by-four. 'I'm spending all my time *wishing*,' I thought, 'and none of it *living*.' That's when I decided to leave Texas, go to New York. Just like that. No assurances. No guarantees. I just realized that if I was going to *do* what I wanted to do, I'd better go *do* it."

I rubbed my thumb along the side of his hand.

"That's one of the benefits of my growing up weird and . . . different," he said. "I've known for a long time that nobody was going to give me anything. Not anything I really wanted. I was going to have to go get it myself. And you know what? It's been a blessing for me. It made me work harder than I ever would have otherwise. I had to figure out where I wanted to go, and then work like hell to get there."

Our food was getting cold, but I couldn't have cared less.

"And where is that?" I asked.

"Here," he said quietly. "Living here. Loving you. Playing Edmund Tyrone. After that, who knows? But for now, I'm happier than I've ever been. You're older than I am, that's a fact. You're a pain in the butt when you don't get your way. You're neurotic and volatile and you've got a *huge* ego. But I love you.

"I don't wish you were younger. If I wanted somebody younger, I could go out and *get* him. Right now. Tonight. I *could*. I'm not blind. I see how people look at me—here, New York, Granada, for heaven's sake—and I know what it means. But I don't want that. I don't want somebody shallow who's never been anyplace. Or done anything. I want you. And I've *got* you. If you don't let your fears and . . . insecurities build a wall I can't get over.

"Don't do that, Ian. Relax. Just love me. You do that real good, when you want to. When you put that other stuff aside. So . . . quit worrying so much and just love me."

I smiled.

"I've got it all backwards, haven't I?" I said. "You're the one who's older. Aren't you, really? You're just disguised as this lovely young boy. You're really old and wise, and I'm the one struggling to catch up."

The next afternoon, we went to join a spa that had just opened over in Northwest. We planned to use the exercise machines and swim two or three times a week. Jimmy found a dance studio downtown, where he could settle into the routine of daily classes he enjoyed. I went back to my habit of reading whenever I didn't have to be doing something else. Now, though, I read for enjoyment, not to hide from my loneliness.

It was a comfortable time for both of us. Those weeks together seem to shimmer in my memory, unhurried, tranquil. Disconnected from what went before and what came after. Our talk at the restaurant had been a catharsis of a kind. With no other people around to spark disagreements or to be an audience for whom we could play out our little dramas, we drifted into a quiet, easy rhythm that moved serenely from day to day.

A phone call from Texas interrupted it, jarred it a little. "That was my mom," said Jimmy, who'd come down to the basement where I was moving clothes from the washer to the dryer. "It's her birthday on the 18th. Her fiftieth. I've been putting her off, but she says she wants us *all* there. No excuses. If we were already in rehearsals, maybe I could . . ." He shrugged. "But we're not. So I'll have to go."

"You might enjoy it," I said. "No? How long since you've seen your brother and sister?"

"Christmas before last. Martin and his wife have a new baby since then, so . . . Maybe it'll be all right."

We found him a cheap ticket, bought him a new roll-on suitcase, and made love every night that week before he left. His flight was at 8:45. *A.M.* I drove him to the airport, and we were both grumpy as we said good-bye.

11

Jimmy left on a Friday and called Saturday afternoon to say he was there and things were fine. Lots of relatives he hadn't seen for a while. Lots of food. He called again Monday night, late, to say the birthday party had been a great success. Out at the country club. Dinner and dancing. His mother was delighted with it all, so he was glad he'd gone. He'd be home on Saturday, as planned.

Thursday morning, the phone woke me out of a deep sleep. I rolled over and looked at the glowing green digits of the clock. Seven-nineteen. Jesus Christ. No one who knew me would ever call at such an ungodly hour. After four rings, the machine on the bedside table clicked on: "If you'd like to leave a message for Ian or Jimmy . . ." Good, I thought. I'll see who it is and call back later. When I'm awake.

"It's Zena, Ian. I know you're there. Still in bed. Pick up the phone and talk to me."

Zena? What on earth could *she* want? Rehearsals didn't start till a week from Tuesday.

"Pick up the phone, Ian. You know I wouldn't call this early if it weren't important. Ian?"

She's not going to give up. Not *her*. I reached for the receiver.

"Hello, Zena. Shall I pretend to be pleasant?"

"No jokes, Ian. Not now. Just listen to me very carefully. Jimmy's dead."

"No," I said. "No, he's not. What are you talking about? He's not..."

"He *is*, Ian. Listen to me. A reporter from the *Post* just called, wants to see me. They got the news last night and... there's an article on the front page of this morning's paper."

"No," I said. "No, you're wrong. He's in Texas. For his mother's birthday. He's called me from there, twice. You're wrong."

"No, Ian. I'm not wrong."

I wanted to scream. Shriek. Smash something. But I was too numb. Besides, none of this was happening. No need to scream. It wasn't happening.

"Ian? Talk to me. Don't go all silent like that. Say something."

"No. It isn't true. You're making this up. I don't know why, but you are. You've got it all wrong. Jimmy's in Texas."

"I know, Ian. That's where it happened."

" 'It'? What do you mean, 'it'?"

"He was beaten, badly, night before last. He died yesterday afternoon, in the hospital."

Oh, Jesus God. If this were true... But it couldn't be.

"Beaten? Robbed, you mean? What are you saying?"

"Just beaten. Some kind of 'hate crime,' the reporter said."

"*Hate?*" I wanted to laugh. "Now I know you're crazy. Who could hate Jimmy?"

"Two young hoodlums. Upset because he was gay, apparently. They've been arrested."

"Arrested? Then it's . . . ? If they're arrested, then he's . . . ?"

"Yes, Ian. Yes."

Oh, god. It *was* true. I'd have to cry. Again. The numbness would go away and I'd have to cry.

"Ian?"

"Oh, god," I said. "Oh, dear god."

"I'm coming over, Ian. You stay right there. Don't look at the paper, whatever you do. That's why I called as soon as I heard. So you wouldn't just . . . Ian?"

"I'm here."

"Don't move till I get there. Just stay where you are, and I'll be right over."

She hung up. So did I.

I stared at the ceiling. She needn't worry. I *couldn't* move. Too numb. I didn't have the strength. I could just lie there. Forever. Not move. I didn't have to move. I could just lie there. Forever.

But first, I had to know. Maybe she hadn't really called. Had she? I wasn't sure. Damn machine. Maybe that blink was someone else. Some other time. Maybe she hadn't called. Maybe it was a bad dream. I wasn't pushing the button to find out. But . . . If I looked at the paper and the story *wasn't* there, then I'd know. It *didn't* happen. She didn't call. Jimmy was all right. He was in Texas, where he was supposed to be.

I dragged myself out of bed. Everything was an effort. No energy was making its way to my legs and feet. It took all the will I could muster to force them to move. One. Then the other. Then the other. Toward the front door. The last place in the world I wanted to go. Down the stairs, one at a time. Agonizing. Moving in a fog, dreamlike. Walls wavering, in and out. My legs wavering. Feeling that I was going to pitch forward, fall to the bottom. Maybe I should. Fall and be done with it.

Moving, slowly. Nothing real. Nothing substantial. Only movement. Slow. Agonizing. Down the stairs. Across the hall. To the front door. Don't open it! Please God, don't let me open it. But I have to. I have to open it. To know he's all right.

Turn the knob. Pull the door. Slowly. Back. The paper is there. Lying there, still, quiet. Nothing bad. Not for me. Bad, yes. Bad things there. But not for me. Not today. That's all over. All in the past. Bad then, but not now. Please God, not now.

Pick up the paper. Close the door. Look at the front page. Force your eyes to focus. Force them. Look across. Bombing. Refugees. Election . . . campaign. Look down. Oh, dear god. No. No, dear god. It wasn't a dream. She did call.

Read it. Force yourself. Even though your brain is numb. Read it.

"CAPITOL REP ACTOR . . ."

Oh, my god. No. No, dear god.

Go on. Read the rest.

"SLAIN IN TEXAS."

Slain. Not hurt. Not beaten. Slain. Picture of Jimmy . . . smiling. Jimmy. Dead. Feel yourself breaking apart, inside. Everything breaking. Falling apart. She did call. She's coming. Here. No! I can't see her. Not her. Not anyone. I can't. I have to be alone. Starting now, I'll be . . . alone.

Up the stairs. Find some clothes. Car keys. Back down and out the door. Hard to keep moving. Hard to focus. Force yourself. Get in the car. Feel the tears. Feel the ache ... in your chest. Hold it back. Not yet. Drive. Onto the freeway. Out to the country. Keep driving. Hold it in. You've had experience, controlling emotion. Hold it now. Just a little longer. Into the picnic area. Park by the grassy hill. Lie face-down. The grass smells nice.

Let it go now. Let it go. Cry. Yell. Shriek. Hit the ground. Beat on it. The ground doesn't care. Can't feel it. Hit it. Don't hold back. Get it out. Cry so hard. For Jimmy. For all of it. For loving. For believing. For losing. For all of it. Keep crying, till it's gone. For now.

Some semblance of reason began to return. He was gone. He was dead. I loved him, so much, and he was gone. Slain? It made no sense. None. I'd have to read it ... so I would know. But the paper was at home. For now I'd have to let it make no sense.

Jimmy. Sweet, funny, lovely Jimmy. My Ariel. Gone to be fire and air once more.

Prospero

We are such stuff
As dreams are made on; and our little life
Is rounded with a sleep.

I

I made it through the rest of that day on a kind of autopilot, drifting with the erratic flow of my emotions. What saved me, I believe now, helped keep me sane, is that I simply went where my grief took me, not trying to fight it, not trying to, god forbid, understand anything about it. Just letting the sorrow come.

Unable to move—or unwilling to make the effort it would have required—I stayed at the picnic area for quite a while, sobbing, staring into space, sobbing again. No one came by to disturb me. Finally, feeling drained and a little chilly, I headed home. A note from Zena was stuck in the door:

You must have gone off to be by yourself. I certainly understand. But are you OK? I'm worried. Call me the instant *you get back. My office. I'll sit by the phone. The reporter from the* Post *is coming by at nine-thirty. I'm not looking forward to that.* Call me!

I put her note on the coffee table and picked up the paper.

I winced. No reprieve. The headline still said the same thing. The picture of Jimmy still smiled at me. An almost solemn smile, with a hint of mischief in it. Alert, knowing eyes. A formal portrait—college graduation, I guessed. His poor parents. They'd had to get it out from wherever they kept it and hand it over to the reporters.

It was a wonderful photo. Looked exactly like him. So much so it sent a jolt of pain shooting through me. I sat down to read.

"James Arthur Davidson left his native Texas to pursue a career in acting, first in New York, most recently in Washington. That promising career, and his life, came to an end yesterday afternoon in the place where he grew up—the small town of Kimberley in central Texas."

The numbness I'd felt earlier came to my rescue again, and I was able to read the whole thing straight through, then a second time. Not many details in this early story. He'd been beaten, left unconscious beside the road, found by a passing motorist, taken to the local hospital. He'd fought valiantly for his life, a hospital spokesman said, but, in the end, had lost. Two young men, Leroy Curtis and Carey Plummer, residents of Kimberley, had been arrested in connection with his death. Curtis had bragged about the beating to friends, leading to the arrest of both. The possibility that Davidson had been killed because he was openly gay was being pursued by the police.

Then came some history. He had attended Kimberley High School and was a drama and music major at the University of North Texas in Denton. Graduated with honors. Next, a rundown of his performances in New York. Impressive. Quotations from reviews of *The Tempest*. The end.

As I read, I could feel myself moving from sorrow to anger

to a cold, implacable hatred. Curtis and Plummer. Those bastards. I wanted them dead. They would be tried in Texas, famous for its enthusiasm for the death penalty. Good. Let them die. An eye for an eye. Violence begets violence. So be it.

These thoughts, I realized, were just what I needed right then. They were hardening my heart, putting the steel of vengeance into the formless lump of grief and loss deep inside me. So much the better. If that was what it was going to take to get through this, fine with me. They were evil and despicable. To Hell with them.

I put down the paper and went to the phone to call Zena.

"Ian!" she said. "I've been so worried. Where have you been?"

"Out to Virginia. To . . . lie on the grass and try to pull myself together."

"And?"

"I'm much better now, thank you. I'm . . . fine. Really. Considering."

A lie, but I didn't want her coming over again.

"I'm sorry I went off like that, this morning," I said. "I just felt like I had to . . ."

"It's all right," she said. "Of course it is. But you'll let me know if there's *anything* I can do."

"Yes. I will. I'm . . . better at doing these things myself. Did that reporter come by to see you?"

"He did. Didn't have anything new to tell me, though. Sorry. Wanted information about Jimmy's connection with Capitol Rep. Got quotes from everyone who was around. I gather there'll be quite a big story tomorrow. It's getting nationwide attention, he said, because of the gay angle. I believe it, because just as *he* was leaving, the TV people started showing up, swarming all over the place, interviewing, filming. An absolute madhouse, but . . . Not much I could do about it."

"Did you tell them . . . about me? Jimmy and me?"

"I didn't. And I'm pretty sure no one else here did either. I hope that was the right thing to do. We were afraid they'd just descend on you. Camp out on your doorstep. It'll come out eventually, I'm sure. No way to stop it—and I can't imagine you'd want to. But we were hoping to buy you a little time. Is that okay?"

"Perfect. What about the funeral? Did anyone say?"

"Day after tomorrow. Saturday morning. Some Presbyterian church in Kimberley."

"Good. That'll give me time to get there. If I can *find* the place. I'll call you as soon as I get back."

"Please. We can talk then. About . . . things."

"All right."

"You're *sure* you're okay? I could . . ."

"I'm sure. I appreciate your concern, but . . . I'm sure."

"Well . . . Don't forget . . . You'll be representing all of us down there. Taking with you the love—and admiration—we all had for him."

"Thanks, Zena. I . . . Thanks."

I called the travel agent Capitol Rep always used. He'd never heard of Kimberley, Texas, either, but he managed to find it on some kind of map on the Internet.

"The closest I can get you is Dallas/Fort Worth," he said. "You'll have to rent a car and drive from there. About an hour and a half, looks like. Maybe two."

"Fine," I said. "You arrange it."

"*Tomorrow* you need to be there? No way you're going to get a cheap fare."

"I don't want a cheap fare. Book me in first class. I'm in no mood to be jammed up against anyone."

He found me a flight leaving at quarter of ten. Big relief. I wouldn't have to get up at the crack of dawn. I could pick up my ticket at the airport, he said. He took my credit card number. I thanked him and hung up.

I looked over at the grandfather clock. Not quite four-thirty. I was starving. I'd had nothing to eat all day. I went to the kitchen and nibbled on some leftover chicken. A little cottage cheese. I couldn't bear to go upstairs. See our bedroom, our bed. Jimmy's endearingly messy study. I couldn't bear it. Nor did I want to go anywhere near the answering machine. I'd had the presence of mind to unplug the downstairs phone after I'd finished talking with the travel agent. Every so often, though, I could hear the faint sounds of the phone up in the bedroom ringing and the machine clicking on. Four rings, then click. Ring. Click. I'd have to deal with all that some other time.

I turned on the CD player in the living room, put on the Fauré *Requiem,* and cried my way through it. The high, clear voices of the "In Paradisum" were a knife straight to my heart. When it was over, I wiped my eyes, put on some Bach cantatas, got a bottle of very old Scotch out of the liquor cabinet, and drank till I passed out on the couch. Maybe not the best anesthetic there is, but it certainly did the job.

The next morning, I woke up a little past six-thirty. Amazing. I could have taken an early flight after all. Jesus. No, I couldn't! I still had to pack! But that meant going upstairs. Could I do it? I'd have to. No choice. I sat up. My head pounded. Breakfast first? My queasy stomach heaved a bit at the thought. Just a little juice, then I'd wait for the plane. I was going first-class, after all.

At the top of the stairs, I went directly into our bedroom, didn't look around toward Jimmy's study at all. The numbness was back—helped a good bit by my hangover, no doubt. I glanced at the answering machine, then stopped to count. Fourteen messages? No way. I couldn't handle that. Not now. With any luck, I'd be out of the house before people started calling again.

I got out my suitcase, started packing, dark blue suit, white shirt, dark blue tie, black shoes, gold cuff links, numb through it all. I laid out clothes for the plane trip, threw what I'd been wearing—grass-stained slacks, smelly shirt, underwear and socks—into the hamper in the closet, and headed down the hall to the bathroom, eyes on the floor all the way. It worked. I showered, shaved, gathered up the things I needed to take with me, and went back to the bedroom to dress. Thank god for routine. I was moving along in a daze, not really thinking about anything. A great blessing.

I took my suitcase downstairs, plugged the living room phone back in, called a cab, and watched from the front window till it came. On my way out, I picked up the morning paper. In the backseat of the cab on the way to the airport, I looked at the front page. Bigger headline than yesterday. Bigger story. Different picture of Jimmy. This one as Ariel. Head and a hint of bare shoulders. Lovely. They'd gotten it from Zena, no doubt. I couldn't read the story, though. Couldn't even begin it. Later I would, but not now. I needed the numbness to stay with me a while longer. I folded up the paper and stared out the window.

At the airport early, a first for me, I got my ticket, checked my suitcase, stopped by a water fountain to swallow a Dram-amine, and walked toward my gate. On a rack outside one of the newsstands, I saw a copy of the *Times*. Story about Jimmy in the upper left-hand corner. The graduation photo. Zena was right. It was becoming big news. Was that hopeful? Did it mean people cared? Hard to tell, this soon. Maybe reading the stories would help me decide. I bought a *Times* and tucked it under my arm with the *Post*.

My pocketful of change set off the security alarm. I had to put it all in a plastic dish, go back through, and retrieve the change. All of this, I see now, was helping to keep me going. Things to do. Things to think about. Attend to. The little rituals of modern life. Mindless, familiar. Just what I needed.

At the gate, a TV hung from the ceiling, tuned to an all-news channel. Would Jimmy pop up there, too? Break this welcome spell of hazy inattention? Sure enough, he did. First the graduation picture. Then an earnest, sober-faced female reporter. Footage in Texas. Henry and Mary Beth, looking stricken, trying to avoid the cameras. Footage at Capitol Rep. The Ariel picture. Suddenly Zena was there, talking about *The Tempest*. I got up and went to look for a cup of coffee.

2

The first-class compartment was a sanctuary for me—quiet, spacious, comfortable. One of the best decisions I'd ever made. I was over by the window in the last row, and the man in the aisle seat beside me was intent on his laptop computer. Rows of figures and some pie charts were all I could see. Good. Let him concentrate on making money and not on me.

The soft leather seats were wide and well-padded. Plenty of room for legs and knees and elbows. Unlike those cramped rows back behind us. Everyone up here spoke quietly, politely. No screaming kids. No chattering females. No salesmen telling loud, off-color jokes.

By the time breakfast came, my stomach was behaving itself and was more than ready for some food. An excellent omelet, fresh-fruit plate, a croissant, and surprisingly good coffee. A $1,200 breakfast, but who cared? Certainly not me.

After the flight attendant—a tall, sleek young woman—

had taken away my tray, I sat with another cup of coffee gazing out the window. It looked as though one continuous cloud was covering the eastern half of the United States. Up where we were, the sun was shining. Underneath, it was not.

The faint, monotonous hum of the engines—the unbroken expanse of white down below—some piece of all this repetitiveness was eating away at my defenses, bringing the active part of my brain back to life. I didn't want to be, but I was thinking about it again. And once I started I couldn't stop. Thoughts poured in, gaining momentum as they came. All in a jumble. Pain. Loss. Incomprehension. Guilt.

Hardest of all was the guilt. All the time Jimmy was being beaten, lying unconscious, fighting for his life, I'd had no idea. Had gone blissfully on with my own life, as though nothing so unspeakable could be happening in the world. My world.

I'd had no premonitions. No apprehension. No sudden waking in the night, full of dread. If he'd called out to me across the miles, heart to heart, I'd taken no notice. Hadn't heard. Too caught up in myself and my own concerns for it to get through. I began to punish myself by reconstructing, in great detail, what I'd been doing during all those long hours.

Tuesday night? Out to dinner at John and Phoebe's. Both actors at Capitol Rep who'd been there as long as I had. Old friends. Good friends. We'd laughed a lot. Laughed while those fiends were beating Jimmy. Laughed as he lay unconscious, bleeding. Laughed and laughed. How could I have heard him calling to me for all the laughter?

Later on at home, reading awhile and then drifting off to sleep, sleeping soundly the way I always do, I hadn't heard him then, either. Hadn't known I ought to be listening.

I should have known. I should have. All that next day, as he lay in the hospital, that beautiful body broken, his tough, gallant spirit slipping away, unable to hang on, I should have known. I should have had *some* inkling that all was not well, that Death was stalking him, hovering above him, waiting to take him. Some small *hint.*

But no. Wednesday? I'd slept till noon. *Slept!* I was good at that. Had gotten up. Puttered around. Paddled happily away in the pool at the spa. Gone to a movie, for Christ sake, in the afternoon. A movie! *Notting Hill.* Love and romance. More laughter. God.

He died in the afternoon. While I was at a movie. Laughing.

Tears were running down my face, but at least I wasn't sobbing, gasping like before. At least they were quiet tears, so no one else had to know. I turned as far as I could toward the window, where no one could see.

"More coffee?" said the flight attendant. "Sir. More coffee?"

I shook my head and waved my hand. She must have gone away. She didn't ask again.

He'd died in the afternoon. While I was at a movie. Laughing.

Did he regain consciousness? 'Fought valiantly,' they'd said. What did that mean? That he'd come out of his coma for a while, and then...? Had he asked for me? Did he know why I wasn't there? That I would have been if there'd been *any* way at all?

I wished I really *was* Prospero. Then I'd've known. That my Ariel was dying. Weak as he was, he could've transported me there. He had the power. I had the book and the staff, but he had the power. To get me there in time. In the blink of an eye, I could have been beside him. Gone with him when he left. To where the bee sucks and the bats fly and the owls do cry. Under the blossom that hangs on the bough. Merrily, merrily we could have . . .

3

I'd never seen such a place as the Dallas/Fort Worth airport. It was huge, chaotic. Flying first-class, I realized, being among the first few off the plane, just means you have that much longer to wait for your luggage. Wait and wait, while hundreds of other passengers mill around. I finally got my suitcase, got my car, got out my map from AAA.

Everything was freeways. Four lanes of cars on both sides, five sometimes, going in every direction—over each other, under each other, up and around. The world was nothing but cars, all on the move. No one was at home, surely. Everyone was out, in a car, driving. And driving *fast*. The speed limits, already high, were no more than suggested minimums for these race-car jockeys. We all rocketed along at seventy, eighty. And we weren't even out in the country. Malls. Gas stations. High-rise buildings. Solid suburbia as far as the eye could see.

No hope of going slower. All I could do was try to keep

up, stay in the right-hand lane, and pray I didn't miss my exit. That I remembered it correctly, since I didn't dare let my attention waver long enough to glance at the map again. Loop around Fort Worth, then off the freeway. I did remember. Southwest toward Kimberley. Quieter now on this smaller road. Two lanes with little traffic. Everyone else zooming along on the super-roads. No time for this kind of tranquillity.

The countryside was more agreeable than I'd expected it to be. Rolling hills, covered with dry grass and rocky patches. Gnarled, scrubby-looking trees with dark green leaves. Cattle grazing here and there. My god. Not herds of cows. Cattle. I was in Texas for sure. Still overcast, but warm. Seventy-five. Maybe eighty. Warm for late October. Well, probably not for here. The air through the open window felt good.

Little towns every few miles—the highway still going right through them—some more interesting than others. Most of them like movie sets. For *The Last Picture Show* or *Hud*. Out of another time entirely. An exception was Bainbridge, about an hour and a half from Fort Worth. A county seat, apparently, judging by the courthouse sitting in the middle of a rundown square. Surrounding it, though, were housing developments, a couple of them quite new, and at the outskirts of town a mall. Not Dallas-sized, by any means, but a mall nonetheless. Cineplex offering six movies, grocery store, McDonald's, Pizza Hut, Wal-Mart. Anywhere, America. Just looking at it made me very sad.

Ten miles or so farther on was Kimberley, the prettiest town I'd seen. Pretty main street. Quite a few places, miraculously, still in business—a florist, a fabric store, gift shop, feed and seed, café. I drove around looking. Beautiful old Victorian homes, well cared for. A park with a bandstand

and a public swimming pool. Smaller houses, neat, tidy. Big front yards, porches, trees. And churches. A good many churches. All of it very pretty.

So far as I could see, there was only one motel in town—a U-shaped row of single-story rooms, maybe thirty in all. Called the Prairie Schooner. Old-fashioned, but clean and comfortable-looking. Shaded by large trees. It had been there a while.

I hit the little bell on the counter in the office, and a middle-aged man with a leathery face and a toothpick sticking out of his mouth came slowly around the corner from a room back behind.

"Howdy," he said.

"Hello. I'd like a single room, please."

"How long?"

"Two nights."

"Thirty-eight dollars a night, plus tax. In advance."

"That's fine. Do you have nonsmoking?"

"We got what we got. Fill out this card, if you would."

I did.

"From Washington," he said. "Dee Cee." I heard the hint of a sneer in his voice. "What brings you all the way down here?"

"A funeral."

"That Davidson boy," he said, nodding.

"Yes."

"Frienda yours? Or . . . ?"

"Yes. A friend. Cash or credit card?"

"Cash is better. Costs me less. We knew he'd gone off up there. Doin' that actin' stuff. That how you met him?"

"Yes."

He looked me up and down and nodded.

"Figures," he said. "Course you coulda been a reporter. Or TV. They're flockin' in from all over. Most of 'em stayin' in Bainbridge, though, so I hear. Days Inn. TraveLodge. All a that. But we got our share. Texas papers mostly. Others too highfalutin for a down-home place like this. Still . . . You're lucky we had any rooms *left*. Day before the funeral an' all."

I handed him a hundred-dollar bill. He added everything up on his calculator and gave me the change.

"May I have my key, please?" I asked.

He shook his head and clicked his tongue.

"It's a real shame, the whole thing, is all I got to say. I feel mighty bad for those two young fellas been arrested. Lot of us do. Good boys, both of 'em."

I stared at him. "I beg your pardon?"

"They just got a little . . . rambunctious, you know how kids do, an' now look. Off over there at the jailhouse in Bainbridge. Locked up. Real shame."

I felt myself starting to shake. I closed my eyes. Am I dreaming? I thought. This has got to be a nightmare—some kind of hallucination. People don't talk like this. I opened my eyes. He was still there, chewing on his toothpick. Still looking at me calmly, as if we were discussing the weather. Or a football game.

"Please," I said. "I'm very tired. May I have my key?"

He reached beneath the counter and slapped a key on top of it.

"One oh six," he said. "Out the door to the left."

He cocked his head and narrowed his eyes.

"Thank you," I said, and walked out.

Sadness and anger. That familiar mixture. It's what my life was made up of now—sadness and anger. In *his* case, the anger was way out ahead. I could have leapt over that counter and throttled him. Gladly. Why hadn't I? I might yet.

The room was fine. Small and unimaginative, but spotless. With a strong smell of Clorox and air freshener. It was fine.

I *was* tired, but I was also hungry. I hadn't eaten anything since breakfast on the plane. I remembered the little café down on Main Street. I hung up my suit and dress shirt, washed my face, ran a comb through my hair, and went out to the car. Keep going, I told myself. That's the way to get through this. Just keep going.

At six-fifteen, the café was crowded. I had to wait a few minutes for a table, and service was slow. Finally, a stout woman with glasses, wearing a pink apron, brought me water and a menu.

"Well," she said brightly. "You're not from around here, either. Reporter?"

"Friend. Of Jimmy's."

Her smile went away. She nodded solemnly.

"My condolences. Dreadful thing. Just dreadful."

"Yes, it was," I said.

"We're not used to that kinda thing, a course. Not used to it a'tall. Peaceful place. Nobody ever locks their houses. Not like your bigger places. Not like *Bain*bridge. You wouldn't wanta live over there. But *here* . . . This kinda thing just never happens."

She looked around the crowded room.

"Still . . . ," she said. "Terrible thing to say, I know, but it's been awfully good for business. You decided yet?"

Thick pork chops. Real mashed potatoes, just right. Green beans that had been cooking for days, but had a nice taste of smoked ham. Iced tea. No complaints . . . about the food.

I stopped at a gas station to ask directions to the Davidsons'. It was a large house, fairly new. Out at the edge of town on a curving street. Cars parked all along the curb. A good many television vans as well. Under the streetlights, I could see groups of men and women standing around.

I parked on down the street and walked back. As I approached the driveway, the people gathered there stopped talking and rushed toward me. Bright lights came on, almost blinding me. I blinked. Microphones appeared, from all sides, aimed at me like rifle barrels. Beyond them were faces, the women's more frightening than the men's. Mouths rimmed in red, snapping at me. I tried to move backward, but I was surrounded.

"Are you a friend of the family? A relative?"

"Friend," I said.

They all began shouting at once, words piling on top of each other.

". . . tell us how his parents are . . . ?" ". . . is there to be a . . . ?" ". . . can you confirm when the . . . ?" ". . . if the lawyers for the accused . . . ?" ". . . any more word from the coroner about . . . ?"

"I'm sorry," I said. "I can't . . ."

They continued to shout.

"Please," I said. "I just got here and . . . I know a great deal less than you do. I just want to pay my . . ."

"But when are they going to release . . . ?"

"How long have you known . . . ?"

"I'm sorry," I said as I pushed my way through. "I can't help you."

They hung back at the far end of the driveway. That much decency, at least. Or maybe a court order.

I rang the doorbell. Waited. Someone peeked through the

curtains on a window to my right. I rang again. A young woman pulled the door open a few inches.

"May I help you?" she asked.

"My name is Ian McBride. Are Henry and Mary Beth at home?"

"And you are . . . ?"

"A friend of Jimmy's. I met his parents in Washington. In the spring."

"A friend," she said. "Just a minute."

She shut the door. I waited. She opened it again.

"They're not available right now, but I'll say you stopped by."

"Are you a relative of Jimmy's?"

"I'll say you stopped by."

"But . . . Should I call them later? I'm staying at the . . ."

"I wouldn't."

She shut the door.

Since my failure had been so obvious, the reporters ignored me as I walked back toward my car.

At the motel, I took a shower and stretched out on the bed with the *Post* and the *Times*. It was all unbearably sad. The pictures. The stories. The sense they gave of the magnitude of Jimmy's talent. What he was and what he could have become.

And Kimberley. Being here, in this alien place. Feeling so alone. Henry and Mary Beth. Unbearably sad. I turned off the lights and waited, in vain, for sleep to come rescue me.

4

I was up early on Saturday. Again? Was this going to become a habit? I pulled back the heavy green drapes to look out, and the sun poured in. Thank god.

The funeral was at ten, and the church was only five blocks away. Seven-thirty now. I didn't want to go back to that café, but there didn't seem to be anyplace else in town. I decided to get dressed, drive over to Bainbridge for breakfast, and back in time for the funeral.

I found a hash house near the Bainbridge Mall that served so-so scrambled eggs, indifferent coffee, but outstanding home fries and the best bacon I'd had in years. Just goes to show. Something.

Back in Kimberley, I found I couldn't get near the church. Cars parked everywhere. Rows and rows of television vans. And some kind of demonstration going on. It was warm again, and I could hear shouts through my half-open window. What on earth could it be? I parked on a side street and started walking toward the church.

The street out front had been closed off. On the far side, behind a police barricade, a group of men and women—about a dozen, it looked like, young to middle-aged—were waving placards that said:

"No fags in Heaven"

"No tears for queers"

"Free Curtis and Plummer—They're heroes!"

As they waved the signs, they chanted:

"Faggots go to Hell, not to Heaven."

"Faggots go to Hell, not to Heaven."

I was stunned. More angry than I'd ever been in my life. So angry I was trembling. My chest felt constricted. A well-dressed woman was standing beside me, looking irate.

"What is this?" I asked. "Who *are* these people?"

"A church group, so I'm told," she said. "Bused in from Kansas, of all places."

"To do *this*? They've come all that way to do *this*?"

"Unbelievable, isn't it?"

"Far worse than that."

It took a lot of hatred for them to go to all this trouble, organized so quickly. Well. I hated them right back.

The people filing into the church looked shocked, uncomfortable, unsure of what to do. A few shouted at the demonstrators, who shouted back. Television cameras outside the church were filming it all.

"You oughta be ashamed of yourselves," yelled a man in front of me. "Think how this makes his parents feel."

"*They* should be ashamed," a woman with a placard yelled back. "They raised the little sinner."

"And *you* should be ashamed," yelled a man standing beside her. "All of you. Going into a church for the funeral of a heathen. A fornicator."

I could have killed them both. The rage inside me was so great I could have taken out a machine gun and blasted the whole lot of them. But then I thought, no. That's no good. This day is for love and remembrance. Not hate and reprisal. Just let me get inside. Away from them and their venom.

Nine twenty-five. The church was already three-quarters full. I found a seat on the center aisle near the back. No television cameras inside that I could see. Thank god. People were murmuring. The organ was playing. Lovely old hymns. The kind Jimmy played so often, those nights at Rehoboth. Had he played here? Sung here? I was sure he had. The sounds inside drowned out most of the shouting. I was grateful.

I looked around. The church was simple. Old and very beautiful. Tall stained-glass windows down both sides gleamed with a softly colored light. Arrangements of flowers, some small, some elaborate, covered the front of the church—from wall to wall and all over the space around the altar.

The pews filled up, and latecomers had to stand across the back and down the side aisles. Though the church was large, it was beginning to feel stuffy, with so many people crowded in together. Women were fanning themselves with little cardboard fans. I saw one stuck in the hymnal rack in front of me. I took it out. On it was a picture of Jesus, kind face, long hair, white robe. Below the picture was an ad for a funeral home. I put the fan back in the rack.

Jimmy's casket—dark lustrous mahogany, closed—was at the front near the altar. Covered with red roses. Beautiful red roses. I wanted to cry, and I wanted not to cry. Which would win? For as long as I could, I would *not* cry. Not here.

At five of ten, Jimmy's family began entering through a door near the front of the church, led by Henry and Mary Beth. She looked weak and drawn. He was holding her up, trying to be strong. My heart went out to them. I hoped they'd been spared the brunt of the demonstration. That they'd arrived from a different direction. I hoped. Quite a large family. They filled the first four pews on both sides. I saw the young woman who'd answered the door the night before.

The service started. A prayer. Readings from the Bible— three Psalms, one, of course, the 23rd. We all sang "Abide with Me." I choked up and couldn't continue. Another prayer. Another reading—the one from Corinthians about love. I choked again. A young woman with a sweet voice sang "The Lord's Prayer" from the choir loft in the balcony up behind us. The minister gave the eulogy. Bland. All-purpose. Very little of Jimmy in it. Mostly about the tragedy of a life taken from us too soon, but . . . we are not to question the workings of God's will. After another hymn, "Nearer My God to Thee," the minister asked if there were any in the congregation who wanted to share their memories of Jimmy. If so, the family asked that they come forward at this time.

Jimmy's brother, Martin, went first. He talked, simply and movingly, about their childhood. About the little brother he had never understood but had loved very much. Several teachers spoke. A drama coach. Some friends, from Kimberley and from college. About his talent. The pleasure he gave to others. His generosity. Surface things mostly. Loving, but nowhere close to what Jimmy was *really* about.

There was a pause.

"Any others?" the minister asked.

I stood and walked toward the altar. Up behind the lectern as the others had done. The smell of the flowers was overpowering. I felt a stirring of uncertainty throughout the congregation. Wondering who I was? Or because some of them already knew? Mary Beth was looking straight at me. Henry was looking at his lap. What would I say? I had no idea. I began anyway.

"My name is Ian McBride, and I'm a stranger here in many ways. I'm a Yankee, I make my living acting on the stage, and . . . I am gay. A homosexual. It may surprise you to learn that I'm proud of *all* those things. But what I'm *most* proud of, the best thing I ever did in my life, was to love Jimmy Davidson."

I saw startled looks, people turning to whisper to each other, eyebrows raised. I didn't care. This wasn't for them. Not really. It was for Jimmy.

"I tried not to love him," I said. "I lost another lover to AIDS twelve years ago, and I was afraid. But Jimmy told me that was foolishness, that love is all we've got, and without it, life is barren and ultimately meaningless. And he was right. I had thought I could hide from love, but Jimmy wouldn't let me. For that, and for what I learned from him about caring and giving, I will be forever grateful.

"Yes, as you can see, I was the age of his parents, but parental love isn't the only kind there is. Yes, we were both men, but . . . love between a man and a woman isn't the only kind either. There are many kinds of love, and I can assure you, however skeptical you may be, that the kind Jimmy and I had was right up there with the best. Warm. Gentle. Passionate."

I was trembling inside, from the intensity of the emotion

I was feeling. But on the outside I was calm and unruffled. Training. Experience. Coming to help me when I needed them most.

"I don't know where he's gone now—I'm not as tuned to certainty as those people there outside the church—but I hope it's to a better place than this. The world he was born into didn't deserve him. He was a spirit of fire and air, in many ways beyond its comprehension. He was grace, in both senses of the word: his movements were effortless and pleasing to the eye, and he was a gift beyond what we could ever earn by merit.

"Too many people—those outside there most of all—can't stand to be in the presence of that kind of grace. Can't stand for any of us to be different from what they're comfortable with. If we are, they do their best to mold us to their own pattern. Subdue us. Clip our wings. But Jimmy knew better. He soared above all that, laughing, spreading love and joy to those with the wisdom—and the courage—to see.

"I don't know much about your God. His representatives here on Earth work hard at telling me there's no place for people like me within the circle of His love. But if He is who you say He is, and if compassion is at the core of His being, then Jimmy—my love, my Ariel—is there beside Him, making Him smile, showing Him what love is all about."

I walked down and stood beside the casket. I heard the rustle of shifting bodies and the hiss of whispers.

"Part of him is inside here," I said, "sleeping now. But another part, the best part, is still with us, still soaring. He is certainly still with me. He will never be gone—not entirely—so long as I'm alive. And I will miss him every day for the rest of my life."

I put my hand on the casket. It felt warm, soothing to

my touch. The movement and the whispers had stopped. I could see Jimmy's face so clearly, dark eyes shining, mouth curved upward in a smile.

"Good night, sweet prince," I said. "And flights of angels sing thee to thy rest."

I walked back to my place and sat down.

5

The minister said a benediction, after which we all stood while Jimmy's family left through a door to the right of the altar. As I moved into the aisle and walked out of the church, everyone I encountered looked at me a little uncertainly. I saw a couple of hesitant smiles aimed in my direction. A few people nodded. But no one spoke. Well, I thought, what could they say?

The demonstrators were gone. I wanted to believe they were in jail, for disturbing the peace, but more likely they were on their way back to Kansas. Their damage done. They'd be home in time to pray in their own church, to their own vengeful God, on Sunday morning.

I was near the end of a long line of cars that moved slowly from the church to the cemetery. I parked and walked toward the green pavilion-like structure that had been erected over Jimmy's grave. It was a beautiful day. Painfully beautiful. Bright blue sky, a gentle breeze. Birds singing in the trees, for heaven's sake. Definitely a Southern autumn.

A group of young people, off to the side of the walkway, seemed to be waiting for someone. As I approached, one of the young men said, "Mr. McBride? Could we walk along with you . . . for a minute?"

"Of course," I said. We all headed in the direction of the gravesite, the young man walking beside me, the others right behind.

"It's just . . . ," he said. "We wanted to thank you, all of us, for what you said back there. We're . . . We belong to the gay and lesbian group, up at North Texas? Susan and Carrie and Daniel and me. My name's Josh. And we . . . We decided to drive on down, soon as we heard, to be here today, because of . . . who Jimmy was and what he meant to us. I mean, we didn't know him so well, most of us. He was so much older and all. A senior already when I got there. But he . . . well . . . We admired him a lot. His openness about being gay, wherever he was. And how nice he was to everybody. So we thought we ought to . . ."

He hesitated.

"It was good of you to come," I said. I looked back at the others. "All of you. He'd've appreciated it."

"Thanks," said Josh. "We were . . . I mean . . . We wanted to say something, when the minister asked. So folks'd know we were there. But we were . . . kind of reluctant. You know? With those awful people outside, making such a ruckus. So when you . . . When you did, we were really glad."

I nodded. "I'm very grateful to you for telling me. I wasn't sure either, but I . . . felt like I needed to. For Jimmy."

We were nearing the gravesite. We stopped, and I smiled at the others. They smiled back.

"Well, we won't keep you," said Josh. "We just . . . Thanks. For everything."

"Thank *you*," I said. "You don't know how much this means to me. I've been feeling . . . alone and terribly out of place. Now I don't. So, thank *you*."

We shook hands all around, and they went off to join what looked like more students. I stayed toward the back of the crowd, watching, listening. This part of the service was simple. The minister spoke briefly, said a prayer, recited the words about "ashes to ashes," and it was over. People began lining up to greet the family. I turned to go.

"Ian? Mr. McBride!"

I turned back. Walking toward me was a short, round woman with the most beautiful white hair I'd ever seen. She held out her hand. I shook it.

"I'm Olivia Davidson, Ian. Henry's mother. Everybody calls me Livie, inside the family *and* out."

I smiled. "Hello, Livie."

"Hello, yourself. I just wanted to . . . I don't know . . . apologize, I guess, for the rest of the family. We're all of us mighty torn up, of course. Henry and Mary Beth are beside themselves. And they're takin' some of it out on you, I'm sorry to say. To relieve their *own* pressure, if you see what I mean. Doesn't really matter if that's fair or not, time like this, does it?"

"No," I said. "I guess it doesn't."

"I was over at their house last night. When you stopped by. I'm so sorry about that. I thought it was rude of them, and unfeelin', not to see you. At least say hello. I mean, it's got to be every bit as painful for *you*, for heaven's sake. But . . . They're not thinkin' straight. That's all I can say. Just completely . . . devastated. Well, aren't we all? Problem is, they're makin' it even harder on themselves than it already is. Aside from their grief, they just don't . . . How can I say it? They don't . . ."

"Approve of me."

"No, they don't. So much older than Jimmy. They feel like you should have had more sense. That you led him astray somehow. That he might have . . . reconsidered, if it hadn't been for you. And then maybe this wouldn't . . ."

She shook her head.

"And what do you think?" I asked.

"No 'think' about it. I *know* how things were. Jimmy and I had us some long talks when he first got down here. We're sort of buddies in that way. Confidants, I guess you'd call it."

I smiled.

"And he started tellin' me about you right off. How much he admired you. And loved you."

It was all I could do to keep from breaking down.

"And I told *them* that," she said. "Henry and Mary Beth. But . . . They don't want to listen. They're more interested right now in blamin', somehow, than in understandin'. Like today. What you said at the church? So beautiful it lifted up my heart and broke it at the same time. So full of love. Well, they don't want to see it that way. Thought you were eloquent, of course. Made them cry. But . . . They were hopin' to get through the service without havin' 'that stuff,' as Mary Beth put it, brought up at all. Especially not in church, in front of the whole town."

"I see. Pretend the funeral was for someone else entirely."

A flicker of a smile played around her mouth. "Somethin'

like that," she said. "And, too . . . They got the idea you might be puttin' them down. That maybe *they* were the ones you thought didn't deserve him."

"Well . . ." I hesitated.

"You do think that," she said, "don't you? Just a little."

"Just a little."

"And you're right—just a little. Jimmy told me about the performance they went off up there to see."

"Ah, yes. That."

"I wish *I'd* gone instead."

She looked directly at me, and there was humor and understanding in her eyes.

"I hope," I said, "I didn't upset you, too."

"Oh, no. Not at all. I'm very glad you spoke. And I'm glad you said what you did. Brought me closer to the Jimmy *I* knew than all the rest of it."

I leaned down and kissed her cheek. She patted me on the arm.

"I better be gettin' on back," she said. "They'll be expectin' me to do my part of the greetin' of everybody, but . . . You hang on, now. You hear me?"

"I will . . . Livie. You, too."

"Just be happy you knew him, for a while. And had a chance to love him as much as you did."

She smiled at me, patted my arm again, turned, and walked back toward the family gathered beside his grave.

6

I turned into the motel parking lot and saw, to my horror, three television vans and a large group of people gathered outside the door to my room. I had assumed at least a few reporters would be allowed into the funeral service, to take notes on what was said. Here was the proof that they had. A new angle to pursue. Jimmy's lover, a much older man, in town for the service and talking about their love. Irresistible.

Could I handle this? I'd have to sometime, no way out of it, short of suicide, but not today. I wanted the reports to be about Jimmy and his funeral, not about me. I parked over on the opposite side, away from my room. As soon as I got out of the car, though, the crowd started running toward me.

"Mr. McBride . . ."

"Mr. McBride . . ."

"Can I get a statement from you about . . . ?"

"When did you first meet . . . ?"

I pushed my way through, my room key in my hand.

"Please," I said. "I'm sorry. Not today."

Reporters continued to shout. Flashbulbs popped in my face. Cameramen continued to film. They weren't listening.

I made it to my door, got inside, and slammed the door behind me. I yanked the drapes shut. I could hear shouted questions from outside. Someone kept knocking on the door. The phone was ringing. I let it ring.

No need to stay, I thought. No need at all. I got out my suitcase, changed clothes, and packed. I peed, washed my face, took a couple of deep breaths, and went back through the mob. They shouted. I ignored them.

I went into the office and rang the bell. The man came out of the back room, just as slowly. No toothpick.

"I've decided to leave today rather than tomorrow," I said.

"No refund," he said. "You're past your checkout time."

"I don't care about that." I laid the key on the counter. "Thank you anyway."

He nodded.

Out through the horde of reporters to my car, saying nothing. Hoping I had the strength to get through this without exploding. I made it. Into the car, onto the street, through town to the highway. I half expected them to follow, a few at least, run me off the road, force me to talk with them. But they didn't. Back to the Davidsons', I guessed, to harass people there.

I was glad to be on my way out of this place. I'd find a hotel near the airport, where no one had the least idea who I was.

7

The thoroughness with which television can invade people's lives took me by surprise. It shouldn't have. I'd watched it so often from the quiet and safety of my home. Plane crashes. Murders. Hurricanes. Scandals. I'd sat through them all and seen the victims struggling, with little success, to retain some degree of dignity as they tried to get on with those lives that would never be the same. I had watched, detached, disapproving but fascinated, like everyone else. I'd just never expected to be on the receiving end.

That next morning, on my way to the gate for my noontime flight, I saw startled recognition in some of the faces passing by, whispers, glances. Oh, god, I thought.

I stopped at a newsstand to buy a Dallas paper. There it was. Large front-page story, with a picture of Henry and Mary Beth at the graveside. Below and to the left, a smaller story:

WASHINGTON ACTOR,
DAVIDSON'S LOVER,
SPEAKS AT FUNERAL

A photo of me leaving the church. Oh, dear god.

The next TV monitor I saw, I went over to look. Funeral coverage. The demonstrators. Graveside. Me fighting my way through the reporters to my motel room. Then me in Washington, receiving an award. Which one? Best actor for *Macbeth*, it looked like, year before last. Feeding the thirst for celebrity, even on a minor scale.

When I got to the ticket counter at my gate, a young man looked up at me. A double take. He recognized me, too. I handed him my ticket.

"Is there some kind of first-class lounge," I asked, "where I can wait for my flight?"

He looked at the ticket and back up at me.

"Of course, Mr. McBride. Please come this way."

The lounge was hushed, private, sealed off from the danger lurking outside. A long table just inside the door was covered with coffee, pastries, juices, sodas, wine. I took a glass of white wine and a bagel and went to an armchair off in the farthest corner. I read what I could of the newspaper I'd bought. At quarter of twelve, I walked out the door, to my gate, and directly onto the plane. A window seat again, which meant I could turn and look out, my unrecognizable back to everyone else coming on board.

I don't remember much about the flight. Lunch was quite good. Filet mignon. More wine. Afterward, I tried to read, some magazines the flight attendant brought me, but I couldn't concentrate. I leaned back, closed my eyes, and was soon asleep.

As the cab came around the corner onto my street, my heart sank. There were the vans I was beginning to hate. People milling on the sidewalk in front of my house.

"Just keep going," I told the driver, and gave him Zena's address. She was so efficient—and so logical. She'd know what to do.

She opened the door, looked startled only briefly, and reached out to hug me.

"Come on in," she said. "It's wonderful to see you. I've been watching . . ."

She shook her head.

"Was it awful?" she asked.

"Yes. There *and* here. They've staked out my house, so I thought . . ."

"You'll stay with me, of course. I keep the guest room ready. You're very welcome to it, for as long as you need it. I'll be delighted to have you. Come on out to the kitchen. I'll make us some coffee."

She fixed pasta for our supper, and we sat at the table drinking wine and talking for hours. About the trip, the funeral, Jimmy, his family. She was concerned and sympathetic. Asked questions. Told me again how much she'd admired Jimmy. How sorry she was.

I watched her as we talked. She was small, wiry, intense. Her nerves, under precarious control at the best of times, had been very much on edge, quivery, during the year and a half since her divorce. As if the connections were fraying and she was holding them together by force of will. But, even so, I felt comfortable with her, especially now. She was my friend. She understood about rough times.

We sat in silence for a while, lost in our own thoughts. She'd been tapping her fingers on the tabletop ever since we'd finished eating. Finally, she went ahead and lit a cigarette. She knew I hated them, but it was her house, after all, and she wasn't about to go all evening without one.

"Thanks, Zena," I said. "For giving me a place to hide."

She smiled. "What're friends for?"

She poured us another glass of wine.

"Let me know," she said, "if it's too soon to ask . . ."

"What?"

"*Long Day's Journey.* I'm wondering what to do about it. Cancel, you think?"

I smiled at her.

"It's not too soon to ask. Of course not. I know you need a decision. Whether to start rehearsals week after next. But . . . I . . . I've been mulling it over, off and on, and I think . . . I think we should do it. It's a great play, and everyone else is set. Except for . . . But . . . not right away. Could we postpone it maybe? Till the spring?"

"Absolutely. I've been *hoping* . . . I'd've canceled entirely, of course, if you'd thought it was going to be too much. But I'm very glad you still want to do it."

"What about . . . Edmund? Any ideas?"

"Well . . . Two of the others who auditioned when . . . When Jimmy did. And another possibility that's occurred to me."

"You think everyone'll still be available . . . if we postpone?"

"I know they will. I've done a little . . . checking. Just in case."

"So . . ." I felt like crying, but didn't. "Life goes on."

"Yes, Ian. It does. It *does*. What are your plans . . . till spring?"

"Travel, I think. Europe, probably. Far away. See Joel and Sid in London, for a start. They've been wanting me to come ever since they moved there. And then . . . I don't know. Somewhere else. I just don't want to be *here* right now. Sitting around. Avoiding the press."

"You can't avoid them forever. They'll just keep hounding you."

"I know. Any suggestions?"

"Let me set up some interviews for you. Over at Capitol Rep. My office. The Green Room. We'll find a place. That'll divert them from your house, anyway. And . . . may be enough. If we're lucky."

I stayed with Zena for almost a week. Sneaked back to my house that first night, well after midnight, to get the clothes I'd need and to water the plants. No one waiting for me at that hour. I decided to leave my car there, just in case they were keeping an eye on it. I hoped I could trust the cabdriver.

Zena arranged for me to see reporters from the *Post*, the *Times*, CNN, the networks, of course, *Time* and *Newsweek*, the *Advocate*, and a couple of smaller gay-oriented publications. I felt a particular loyalty to them. I talked about Jimmy. His talent. My career and his. *The Tempest*. Granada. Our life together. The funeral. It was enormously painful for me, but they seemed to be satisfied.

Each of them asked what I thought about the death penalty.

"I'm *for* it," I said. "Absolutely."

Most of the colleagues I bumped into at Capitol Rep, before and after seeing the reporters, were sympathetic and supportive. One friend pulled me aside to tell me, earnestly and emphatically, that I was crazy to keep saying no to the TV talk shows. "Think what it could do for your career," he said. "Audiences in the *millions*. You'll never have a chance like this again." I turned and walked away.

The interviews I *did* give—and the passing of time—eased the pressure on me. We'd gone beyond the brief attention span for most stories, even those involving sex and murder. I was able to go back home, not open the door unless I knew who was there, and let the answering machine screen all my calls.

First, though, that afternoon I got there, I had to sit through the calls already waiting, to clear the machine. The tape had reached its limit at twenty-seven and would accept no more. I'd've erased them all without listening, I think, if I hadn't been curious about one thing: Had there been a call from Texas, during those early days before I got down there? While Jimmy was in the hospital, or right after he died? Had Henry or Mary Beth, in the midst of their own grief, thought to call me? Or ask someone else to do it? They had not.

Call number one, of course, was from Zena. That awful morning when my long nightmare began. Next came calls from friends. Mine. Jimmy's. Distraught. Frantic for news. Worried about me. I was glad I'd decided to listen. Their own pain, sincere and loving, and their generous-hearted concern comforted me.

They were followed, though, by a string of reporters. Abrupt. Insistent. Calling again and again till the tape ran out. With great satisfaction, I watched the machine erase them. As if they'd never been.

Then I did the hardest thing I've ever done in my life. I

went down the hall and into Jimmy's study. The chaos that had irritated me at first now seemed somehow sweet. It made me smile, and that must be why I was able to stay. I had the feeling of opening a time capsule. Seeing everything just as it was. Touching things he had touched. Breathing the air he'd left behind. The first archeologist into King Tut's tomb. Treasures all around.

I ignored the pain, like a knot in my chest, and started picking things up—clothes, photos, CDs, books, magazines. Even a shriveled-up old orange rind. His script for *Long Day's Journey*. Marked with underlines and comments in the margins as he'd studied it. Oh, dear lord. I sorted, put things in piles. To keep. To throw out. To give away. To send home to Texas.

Everything about acting I kept. Scripts and books. Scrapbooks full of photos and clippings. The little pink and lavender sarong he'd worn in *The Tempest,* which I found on the floor under the futon. I also kept a stuffed giraffe I knew he'd loved and all of his CDs. Clothes, from here and the bedroom, I laid aside to take to one of the AIDS groups. Old magazines and newspapers—and the orange rind—I tossed into a garbage bag. Some family photos, some college yearbooks, some letters and birthday cards he'd saved I put in a box to send down to his parents.

That first night back in our bed, I felt so completely alone I thought I'd never sleep. I cried harder than I had since the day I heard about it, tossed awhile, cried some more. I went to the bathroom to get a sleeping pill, thought about taking the whole bottle, but ended up rejecting that notion. I did take two, and they worked. Eventually.

I left town as soon as I could get all the calls and letters, the ones from friends, answered and my trip arranged. A young actor at Capitol Rep, who lived in an efficiency way out in Virginia, moved in to house-sit, water the plants, and pay the bills with checks I left him. I stayed with my friends in London from late November till early January. On New Year's Eve, we welcomed the new millennium at a posh party—well-dressed, articulate gay men oozing self-confidence and savoir faire—that I tried to enjoy but didn't.

I went off to tour the hill country of Tuscany. Celebrated my birthday there, alone. Spent three weeks in Greece, two in Morocco. Trying hard to have a purpose, to be conscientious about seeing the sights, but basically wandering aimlessly, without much enthusiasm. Wherever I was, I would end up thinking, too often, how much Jimmy would have loved being there.

Most painful of all was the eighth of February, which I spent sitting on the terrace of an inn high on the crest of Santorini, staring at the impossibly blue Aegean far below, the anniversary of the day I first saw Jimmy, one year before, when he walked into a rehearsal room, and sang "Come unto these yellow sands," pure and clear and haunting, and I began, though I was foolishly unaware of it at the time, to fall in love.

8

I was back in Washington by early March, in time to begin rehearsals for *Long Day's Journey*. I was looking forward to it, and dreading it at the same time. I was eager to get back to work, tackle another of those roles I'd always hoped would come my way. Get out of myself and into another life. That's what I was born to do—play other people. I knew that as well as Jimmy had. But I also knew, deep inside me, how difficult this production was going to be. Constant reminders of 'what if . . .'

Stephen, a nice enough young man, had kept my house in excellent shape, with the help of Milagros's weekly visits, of course. The houseplants had clearly loved his attentions and were bursting out of their pots. He was disappointed, I think, when I didn't ask him to stay on. In Jimmy's study on the futon at the very least, or—was I reading the signals correctly here?—in the big king-size bed with me.

On his way out, he said he'd be happy to come back

anytime. He'd enjoyed the house. Living in the city, not stuck out in the burbs. The convenience of being so much closer to everything. I thanked him for his help, told him good-bye, said I'd see him around Capitol Rep.

Jimmy's presence still filled the house. As the days passed, I'd catch myself looking for him in his favorite chair, listening for his footsteps on the stairs, wondering how soon he'd be home. Outside, too. From the kitchen window, I could see the first of the crocuses, purple and yellow and white, sticking their heads up in the garden he had loved. I loved it, too, but couldn't bring myself to go out there. He was gone, but not gone. With me, but . . . out of reach. The sadness I now felt was beyond tears. It settled around me like a familiar old bathrobe and was always, always there.

I worried about that first day of rehearsals. Working with Jimmy's replacement. But it was all right. An easy, comfortable day. Brian was a nice-looking, pleasant young man who'd been with the company for three years. Zena believed he was ready for a challenge of this magnitude, and every passing day proved her right. He was good, determined to prove himself, getting better all the time. I was glad for him. We all were.

He didn't have the depth Jimmy would have brought to the role, but few actors their age did. He was fine, though, and toward the end of the first week of rehearsals, I realized I'd begun to see him as himself, an actor interpreting a role, not a usurper merely filling in for Jimmy. My admiration for him was entirely professional, but I was still delighted, relieved in an odd way, when he brought his girlfriend by to meet the cast and told us they'd just gotten engaged.

As long as I was at the theater rehearsing, I was okay. Caught up in all the activity, the feeling of accomplishment, the pleasure of being around people who know what you do and why you do it. It was later, alone in that huge bed, every night without exception, that I would miss Jimmy. So much that the pain was a physical presence there in the bed with me.

I started talking to him. Sort of in my head, but not entirely. I'd tell him about the day's rehearsal. What went well. What didn't. Thoughts I'd had about my performance. Or someone else's. He was listening. I was certain of that. Smiling. Nodding. I could almost hear him laugh. Almost. I'd feel comforted. Less alone. And then I could sleep.

We were a solid cast—Brian, our Edmund, two Capitol Rep regulars as Jamie and Mary, and I. We worked well together, but many of the rehearsals felt long and heavy, as the weight of destiny pressing down on that unfortunate, unyielding family affected us all. We found ourselves laughing and joking at every break, far more than we normally would have. Just to get away, for a bit, from all that claustrophobic intensity.

I liked our director. Craig Mattingly. Big. Blustery. Formidably intelligent. A man I'd never met but had heard a great deal about. Almost fifty now, he'd made a name for himself in Atlanta and then Chicago, long after I'd left the Goodman Theatre there to come to Washington. O'Neill was a specialty of his, and he'd directed many of the plays, all of the later ones. This was his third go at *Long Day's Journey*, and he brought with him an assurance and an understanding of the play that excited me.

One of the satisfactions, I'd discovered long ago, of spending time with a really great play, searching for its heart, is the lessons it can teach about the complexity of life. Hope trying to outrun despair. The joy we want desperately to hold on to being crowded out by sorrow. The way we keep look-ing, often frantically, for something we can't find because we're not at all sure what it is.

Long Day's Journey into Night is a graduate seminar in grief and loss. Those daily losses that accumulate over time to become more than we can bear. I loved being swept up in all that emotional turmoil—the sheer drama of it—day after day, but when we got to the end of the play, I found myself feeling . . . restless, unsettled. Round and round the Tyrones went, trapped in their past, never moving forward. Never able to understand well enough to forgive.

On opening night, Zena and Craig agreed to let me speak to the audience before the curtain went up.

"The play you will see tonight," I said, "is about memory. Eugene O'Neill's visit to his own past to see what sense he could make of it. We here at Capitol Rep would like to ded-icate our performances of this play to the memory of a col-league, an extraordinary young actor, James Davidson, who is no longer with us. He was killed last fall, in one of those random acts of violence that mock our desire to feel safe and secure in our well-ordered lives.

"His death came only a few months after his stunning success here as Ariel in *The Tempest*. He was already a fine actor and showed promise of becoming one of the best. But that, now, will never be.

"What O'Neill found as he wrote this play is that 'sense' is not something we're always allowed to discover. All these months later, Jimmy's death still makes no sense, and maybe it never will. But he loved acting, performing, creating lives—however flawed or triumphant—on the stage. So by continuing to act, continuing to search through our heritage of marvelous plays for some inklings of truth about why we're here and what our lives are all about, exploring together the fickleness—and the beauty—of our existence, we honor Jimmy. His life *and* his death."

Caliban

>   *... and then, in dreaming,*
> *The clouds methought would open, and show riches*
> *Ready to drop upon me, that when I waked,*
> *I cried to dream again.*

I

Long Day's Journey was good. One of the better productions we'd done at Capitol Rep. The audiences were attentive and visibly moved. The critics were respectful. But, for me at any rate, in spite of the passion in much of O'Neill's prose, the performances remained earthbound. They never soared. There was no magic about them. I wondered, night after night, especially during that final, agonizing scene between Brian and me, what things might have been like if Jimmy had been playing my younger son. *He* would've soared. He didn't know how not to.

Jimmy was back in the news by then. Leroy Curtis, one of the young men who'd struck the fatal blows, had pleaded guilty. He'd been sentenced to life imprisonment, with no possibility of parole. Some kind of bargain with the state, I was sure. Too bad. He'd be alive—while Jimmy was not.

The other young man, Carey Plummer, however, would be standing trial. Speculation was that he would plead 'mitigating circumstances.' Ridiculous. What could possibly 'mitigate' such an outrageous act? With any luck, he'd be found guilty, and a properly bloodthirsty jury would sentence *him* to die. One, at least, would be better than nothing.

The run of *Long Day's Journey* ended late in April. Plummer's trial was scheduled for early June. I intended to be there for the whole thing. Two days or two weeks or two years, it didn't matter. I wasn't about to miss one second of it.

Stephen agreed to come house-sit again. I got a ticket—coach this time, no need to be foolish—and flew back down to Texas. The trial was to begin on a Tuesday. I arrived in Kimberley the Saturday before, to give myself time to get settled. I'd thought about staying in Bainbridge instead. The trial would be there, in the county courthouse, and I was still irritated by the callousness of the man at the Prairie Schooner. But, I decided, I'd be punishing myself needlessly. Substituting the commercial nothingness of Bainbridge for the very real charm of Kimberley. Besides, I could just ignore Mr. Toothpick.

He was there to check me in, but was curiously subdued. Not so chatty as before.

"Here for the trial, I reckon," he said.

"Yes," I said. "I am."

He pursed his lips but didn't comment.

I drove over to Bainbridge for dinner—Mexican food, quite good—and a movie. An insipid comedy full of teenage vulgarity that did nothing but take up time. I drove back to the motel and went right to bed.

Sunday afternoon I called Livie.

"Bless your heart," she said. "Where are you?"

"Here in Kimberley. At the Prairie Schooner."

"I was wonderin' if you might be comin' down."

"Nothing could have kept me away."

"No? Well, it's wonderful to hear your voice. I've thought about you a lot."

"And I you. How've you been?"

"Oh, so-so. Good days and bad. You?"

"The same."

"This trial's got me all upset, of course. I don't want to miss it—nor do I want to go. Really. Hear things I'm not a'tall eager to hear. Terrible dilemma."

"Not for me. I'll be right there for every bit of it."

"Will you? Well . . . The good thing is we'll be able to spend some time together while you're here, you and I. Get to know each other."

"I'd love that."

"Shall we start tonight? Go out for supper someplace?"

"Great idea. Where do you suggest?"

"There's always the Chat-'n'-Chew, down on Main Street."

"I've been there."

She laughed. "I detect a lack of enthusiasm."

"Indeed you do."

"The food, or Myrna's mouth?"

It was my turn to laugh.

"Plump? Bleached blond hair? Glasses?"

" 'Plump' is bein' kind, I'd say, but yes. That's Myrna."

"Then the answer is Myrna's mouth. The food was fine."

"No problem. We'll just go to the Hook, Line, and Sinker, out west of town. Best fish in Central Texas."

"Who names these places?" I asked.

She laughed again. "Bit of Yankee snobbery here? Lookin' down on our quaint little ways?"

"Point well taken. I'll try to be more careful."

"You *better*. If you plan on bein' here awhile. I'll pick you up at five-thirty. That all right?"

"Perfect."

The fish place was crowded. "Sunday's a real popular time for eatin' out," Livie told me. Everyone there knew her, no surprise. A few eyebrows flew up when she introduced me, but Southern manners took over, and people were cordial enough. They said hello, smiled, and were pleasant, but included Livie, not me, in their conversations.

I looked around. It was a comfortable place, not too big, homey. Knotty-pine walls. Picnic tables with red-and-white-checked tablecloths. The head of a longhorn steer on the far wall. Stuffed fish with gaping mouths on the side walls. How many times had Jimmy been here? I wondered. Too many to count.

Wonderful smells were coming from the kitchen. Fried smells. Bread smells. Country-western music filled the room, but people were just talking louder than it instead of listening to it. A woman with a catch in her voice sang mournfully about lost love. I ought to write one of those songs, I thought.

After a wait of maybe fifteen minutes, we were shown to a booth in the back corner. Ideal for talking, away from prying ears.

"Get the special," Livie said. "Fried in a ton of grease, but you won't be sorry."

She was right—about the grease *and* about not being sorry. Everything was delicious. We talked about my travels, *Long Day's Journey,* her sad Christmas, the mood in town.

"Lots of division," she said. "Bein' aggravated, I'm afraid, by so much publicity. So many gay rights people pokin' around, turnin' it into a *cause*. Editorials and columns everyplace you look about hate and small towns and Texas and intolerance. All jumbled in together, so it's impossible to separate one from the other. Texas *means* intolerance, way it sounds. People're gettin' their backs up. Feelin' attacked and misunderstood."

"Well, of *course* they're misunderstood. Who on earth could understand feeling sympathy for two killers? Especially *these* two?"

She shook her head. "You're tryin' to make it simple. Good and evil. Black and white. And it won't work. It's *not* simple. Nothin' that involves people's deepest emotions ever is. Jimmy left, you see. Chose to remove himself. Go way off up there and not come back very often. Those boys, Carey and Leroy, are still part of the town. The community. Loyalty, and pride in this little place, are very important to people around here. Jimmy seemed not to care much about them."

"For very good reason."

"*I'll* grant you that. His leavin' made perfect sense to me. Look, I'm not tryin' to defend all this, goodness knows. I'm just tellin' you where the things you can't understand are comin' from. You want some coffee?"

"Love some."

"Sallie Mae? Yoo-hoo! Two cups of coffee, please, sweetheart."

"Milk or Cremora?" the young woman asked.

"Not for me," I said.

"Me neither," said Livie. "Just black. Thanks, honey."

She turned back to me.

"And then, of course, there's the rest of it," she said. "His bein' gay. And not *ashamed* of it. That's the worst by far. They could've accepted the *bein'* gay, most of 'em. If he'd just hung his head and been morose and . . . tragic about it all. No. It's his bein' secure and happy—even *proud*—of this affliction that sets people's teeth on edge. Takes it way beyond their comprehension."

"They don't *have* to 'comprehend' it. Jesus. I couldn't possibly care less about that. All they have to do is just leave us alone. Let us live our lives the best way we can. Is that asking so much?"

"For me, no. Certainly not. For most of the others, yes. It's askin' more than they can handle."

The waitress brought our coffee.

"Thanks, honey," said Livie. "Dessert, Ian? They got scrumptious pecan pie."

"Not for me. Coffee's fine."

"That's all for right now, Sallie Mae. Thank you, sweetheart."

She watched the young woman walk away.

"Nice girl," she said. "Not real bright, but . . . pretty."

My coffee was too hot to drink yet. I set it back down.

"You know . . . ," I said. "You've been explaining everyone else's reactions. Tell me how *you* feel. About all this."

"Oh . . . Torn apart inside, mostly. Even though I didn't see Jimmy much the past few years, I still miss him terribly. Can't believe he won't ever be comin' back. And I'm angry. At those boys. And their stupidity. And at everybody else who helped create the climate that made what they did possible. It wasn't just them. No, indeed. That's what I've been tryin' to explain to you. They were just the tip of the iceberg. The place where ignorance and bigotry bumped up against opportunity. That was the real difference for them. Opportunity."

I nodded.

We sat for a minute, drinking our coffee.

"I've thought about this so much," I said, "since Jimmy died. Especially while I was traveling, spending all that time alone. And what I . . . What I just can't work out, for the life of me, is *why*. Why it's so hard for people to just let us be. They have this compulsion to destroy what they don't feel comfortable with. They can't bear to just leave us alone. Let us just *be* what we are. Why is that?"

"Human nature."

"That's no excuse."

"People don't need an excuse when they're surrounded by so many others who believe exactly the way they do."

"Which is why we leave these places. People like Jimmy. Like me. To get away from all that. Find a place where we don't have to . . . *struggle* all the time. What 'loyalty' are we supposed to feel toward a place that makes us fight for our right to exist? Still . . . Maybe we ought to be grateful, in a way. Maybe they force a kind of courage on us we might otherwise not be able to muster. The courage to . . . what? Tackle the world. 'See what all we can become.' Jimmy said that to me, not so long ago. Nobody's going to give us anything, he said. Not *us*. We have to go out and get it."

She nodded. "He was a wise one, that boy. Wise beyond his years."

She glanced at her watch.

"Speakin' of courage, how do you feel about stoppin' by Henry and Mary Beth's on our way back? Give you a chance to say hello."

"I don't know. You think I should?"

"I'd say it's worth a try. If they're rude again, which I doubt, you'll at least've shown you're a bigger person than they are."

2

Mary Beth opened the door. I was shocked by the way she looked, thin and weary. I hoped my reaction didn't show in my face.

"Ian," she said, trying to smile. "Livie told us you were back in town. Come on in, both of you. Henry!" She yelled down a hall to the left. "Livie's brought Ian by. We'll be in the den."

We walked through the wide hallway directly ahead into an enormous room. Big fireplace in one corner. Television set, about the same size, in another. Overstuffed chairs and sofas. A large Navajo rug, red and brown and beige, on the floor. A tasteful, but somehow austere, room. I looked around. No books. Anywhere. It made me uneasy. I don't trust rooms with no books.

"Won't you sit down?" said Mary Beth.

I did. On one of the sofas. Livie sat beside me. Bless her.

"Somethin' to drink?" asked Mary Beth. "Iced tea? Coke? Ginger ale?"

"Ginger ale would be great," I said. "Thank you."

"You know me," said Livie. "Can't ever get enough iced tea."

Mary Beth nodded and left the room.

"So far so good," Livie whispered. "At least you're inside the front door."

I smiled at her.

"Here you are," said Henry.

I stood up and offered my hand. He shook it.

"Hello, Ian."

"Henry," I said.

He leaned over and kissed his mother.

"Hello, Livie. Sit, sit, sit," he said to me. He went over and sat in an armchair across from us. Grief had had its effect on him as well. Circles under his eyes. A crease across his forehead. I was sorry. Was there a way I could comfort him? I couldn't think what it might be.

"Mary Beth off gettin' us somethin' to drink?" he asked.

"She is," said Livie. "You all right, son? You're lookin' tired today."

"Not sleepin' well. Haven't, really, since . . . When'd you get here, Ian?"

"Yesterday afternoon. I wanted some time to settle in . . . before Tuesday."

"Ah, yes," said Henry. "Tuesday. You here for the duration?"

"Absolutely. As long as it takes."

He nodded. "Good. I'm . . . glad. It's gonna be rough . . . on all of us . . . I'm afraid."

"Afraid so," I said.

Mary Beth came in with a tray.

"Ginger ale for Ian. Here you are. Iced tea for the rest of us."

She put the empty tray on the coffee table and sat in another of the armchairs.

"I haven't had a chance yet, Ian," she said, "to thank you. For sendin' us the box of . . . Jimmy's things. I kept meanin' to write you a little note, but I . . . Somehow the time's just gotten away from me."

"It's all right," I said. "I understand."

"But we *should*'ve written," said Henry. "We've talked about it a number of times, haven't we, Mary Beth?"

She nodded.

"Written to thank you for sendin' us the box. That was very thoughtful. And to . . . apologize. We . . ." I could see him struggling. "We weren't very nice to you at the . . . When you were here before. And we're sorry."

Oh, my god, I thought. Please. Don't let me cry, not here. Not in front of them.

I cleared my throat.

"Thank you," I said. "That's very . . . Thank you."

"We've done a lot of thinkin' since . . . then," said Mary Beth. "Both of us. And we've . . . This is so hard." She took a deep breath. "*Every*thing is so hard." She looked away, then back at me. "But . . . We think . . . We don't understand about it, that's a fact. Didn't then and still don't. I mean, him lovin' you . . . like that." She stopped again, took another deep breath, and plunged ahead, hoping, it seemed, that momentum would somehow carry her through.

"I just can't help thinkin' . . . we both can't . . . that if he hadn't met you . . . What he'd always dreamed of bein' himself—a famous actor. Well-established. Successful. Beautiful home, and a nice car. We could see how all that would impress him so much that he . . . And I blamed you. After it happened. I was so angry . . . both of us . . . that we couldn't see you then. We just couldn't. But now . . . Well . . . We don't understand it any better, I have to say, and we still think maybe things would've been different if you . . . If somehow he hadn't . . . But we can see, now, that it wasn't your fault. That's the important thing. You didn't set out to . . . You just met—who knows why?—and he . . .

"So I'm sorry. We both are. And we're glad you stopped by . . . to give us a chance to tell you so. Aren't we, Henry?"

"Yes. We are. It's . . . Once we were able to live with our own grief, a little, we began to think how terrible it's been for *you*. So we . . ."

He looked over at his wife, pleading silently for help.

They were moving through uncharted territory, I could see that, and the effort was taking its toll. I needed to give them a rest.

"Thank you," I said. "I'm very grateful to you for this. And to Livie for bringing me by. We all loved him. In our own ways. And that's what matters. So . . . let's just forget all that and go on from here. All right?"

Mary Beth smiled.

"All right," she said.

"We've been out to the Hook, Line, and Sinker," said Livie. She winked at me as she said it. "Big crowd. The Rosses with their grandbabies. Sweet kids. Andrew and Lucille Cartwright. Oh, and Royce Daugherty and his new wife. Forget her name. He introduced us, but it's gone right out of my head."

"Did you have the special?" Mary Beth asked me.

"Oh, yes. I certainly did. It was wonderful."

"Could you finish it all?" asked Henry, chuckling.

I was happy to hear him laugh.

"Barely," I said. "No room for dessert, that's for sure."

"They do have big portions," said Mary Beth. "I have to order the child's plate. And sometimes even that's too much."

We chatted, amiably, about food, my trip down, the weather. This was going to be a *hot* summer, Henry said. He just hoped it wouldn't be too dry—they hadn't had nearly enough moisture the last year or so. About how fast Bainbridge was growing. Henry, a contractor, which Jimmy had told me but I'd forgotten, was making a lot of money over there. Shopping malls. Subdivisions. But even so . . . What was happening to that town was sad. A real shame.

There was a lull. I was rummaging around in my head for a topic that wasn't Jimmy or theater or sadness when Livie stood up. She clearly had terrific radar.

"We best be movin' along, Ian," she said. "I'll drop you by the motel and head on home."

At the door, Mary Beth pulled me down and kissed my cheek. Henry shook my hand and nodded at me.

"Thank you for comin'," said Mary Beth.

"I'm very glad I did."

"We'll have you over for supper one of these days, you and Livie."

"I'd like that."

In the car, on the way back into town, Livie said, "Well, sir. I have to say I'm mighty proud. Of all of you. Henry and Mary Beth doin' their level best to apologize—and you bein' so gracious in acceptin'. You always that forgivin'?"

"Not at all. In fact, I surprised my*self*. No, I'm much more likely to dig my heels in and hold a grudge. But . . . I know what that kind of hurting feels like. And I could see they've already got more than they can handle. So . . . If there's a way I can ease that burden, I'm happy to do it."

"Good man," said Livie.

As we drove down Main Street, I heard sirens behind us. A fire truck roared past, screaming, and turned into the parking lot of the Prairie Schooner.

"What on earth . . . ?" said Livie.

We turned in right behind. Directly ahead of us was a burning car, flames shooting high into the sky. A small red car, now mostly black. The one I'd rented in Dallas. Fear grabbed hold of me and wouldn't let go.

"Dear god!" I said. "What *is* this?"

Livie parked near the street, and we got out. I felt myself shaking. One of the firemen came toward us.

"Stay on back, please, Miz Davidson," he said. "You don't wanta be too close till it's out."

We stopped and stood watching as he went back to the others. We were maybe thirty feet away, but the heat was still intense. Flames leaping and dancing. Beautiful, in a horrifying way. The smell, though, was awful. It hit my nose head-on, but also seemed to be seeping in through my pores. Rubber. Metal. Plastic. Burning and melting. The worst possible odors all mixed in together. My stomach churned . . . with nausea from the smell. And from the fear that was growing stronger with every passing minute.

It's me, I thought. I'm the real target. They hate me this much. Would they be burning *me,* if they could?

The firemen began spraying water onto the car. Most of

the windows were broken, and water poured inside. The flames hissed and spit as they leapt around it, tried to hold on, but couldn't. They subsided, flickered, and went out. Smoke billowed up in a thick gray cloud. Then it, too, was gone. All that was left was a twisted, blackened shell. Bombed-out remains in the middle of a war zone. And the smell. Livie and I walked closer. On the wall of my room, just under the window, was a spray-painted message: YAN-KEE FAGGOT—GO HOME!

I wanted to cry, or smash something, or both. I did neither. I just stood there, trembling uncontrollably. I felt Livie patting my arm.

Groups of people were standing at the far end of the parking lot, in the doors of other rooms, out on the sidewalk near the street. Were the ones who did it still there, watching me?

Cars slowed down as drivers craned to get a look. Drivers behind them honked. The man from the office walked toward us, frowning. He was shaking his head.

"Would you just look at this mess," he said. "I never saw such a thing."

"Nor I," I said.

He looked from the car to the message on the wall to me.

" 'Fraid I'm gonna have to ask you to leave, Mr. McBride," he said. "I can't run the risk of havin' any more of this. It could ruin me."

Let's *hope,* I thought, but what I said was, "Fine. Suits me." I was trying hard to control my trembling and was succeeding fairly well. "I'll sort all this out with the car rental company and be gone tomorrow."

"Sooner would be better," he said. He chewed on his toothpick.

I stared at him. "What do you mean—*now*? Just leave? At night, without a car?"

"Lord help us all," Livie said to him. "What is this? A conspiracy to make me ashamed of my own hometown?"

She turned to me.

"You bet your sweet life *now*, Ian. You go on in there and pack up your suitcase. I'm takin' you home with me. Let's see if these cowards have the nerve to mess with *my* car and *my* house!"

"Thanks anyway," I said. "I appreciate your offer, but I don't want to impose on . . ."

"Hold it, hold it, hold it," she said. "We got some sortin' out to do here. Do I honestly *look* like a woman spends much time bein' imposed on? I been hardheaded and jut-jawed ever since I was a little girl, and it's just gotten worse the older I get to be. Which means I don't like bein' con-tradicted. Not a bit. Now, if you don't *want* to come stay with me, that's a different story. Just say so. But if you think you're bein' polite somehow, or that you oughta spare me some bother, you can forget it. If I hadn't'a wanted you to come, I wouldn't'a brought it up in the first place."

She narrowed her eyes, just like Jimmy used to do, and looked up at me.

"So which is it?"

"I'd love to stay with you," I said.

She rolled her eyes.

"Then what in the Sam Hill are we standin' around out here jabberin' about? Go pack your bag."

She turned away.

"As for you, Frank Perkins. I've never been so riled up in all my born days. You are the most . . ."

I went inside and started packing.

3

When I came out of the motel room carrying my suitcase, a car with SHERIFF written across the side was parked just behind the burned-out wreck. Livie was talking to a man in a khaki uniform. He had a badge pinned to his shirt pocket and a Stetson on his head. I looked at his feet. Boots, of course. I set down my suitcase and walked over.

"Ian," said Livie. "This is our sheriff, Ernie Wright. Ernie, my very good friend Ian McBride. I'm takin' him home with me, soon as you're through talkin'."

She tilted her head and stuck her chin out toward the sheriff, daring him not to be nice to me. He touched the brim of his Stetson, nodded, and said, "Mr. McBride."

"Hello, Sheriff."

He was tall, brawny, with a wide, deeply tanned face. Broad chest and big hands. No way did I want *him* to know how frightened I was. His eyes were a little distant, uncertain of what to expect, but not unfriendly. Would they have been more hostile if I'd met him without Livie? I couldn't tell.

"Sorry 'bout all this," he said. "Pretty inhospitable welcome."

"Yes," I said.

"I'll be needin' to ask you a few questions. If you don't mind."

"No, of course I don't mind. Where?"

"Come sit in my car here. Be easiest. An' most private."

"Will you want to talk with me, too, Ernie?" Livie asked. "I got plenty to say."

"Sure will, Livie. Course. But . . . How 'bout you come by my office in the mornin'. That be all right?"

"Absolutely."

"That way I won't need to keep you—or this gentleman—here all night."

"Thanks, Ernie. I'll go wait for you in the car, Ian."

I nodded.

The firemen were gathering up their equipment.

"I've already talked to them," the sheriff told me. "An' to Frank Perkins, who phoned it in. After you an' I chat awhile, I'll see what the other guests here have to say. Mebbe somebody saw somethin' helpful. Livie tomorrow . . . an' then we'll see."

I went to the passenger side of his car and got in. He got in, too, and turned on the overhead light. Must be an extratall car, I thought. He didn't have to take off his hat.

He was polite, efficient. Asking, writing, nodding. About when I'd gotten to Kimberley. Everything I'd done since I'd arrived. Where I'd gone. Whom I'd talked with. Chronologically first, then randomly, filling in anything I'd forgotten the first time through.

"Aside from the . . . obvious," he said, "anybody here got a reason to be upset with you?"

"By 'the obvious,' I assume you mean that everyone here knows I'm gay. And why I'm here. For Jimmy's trial."

"Yep," he said.

"That seems to be more than enough, doesn't it?"

"Mebbe. Mebbe not. We can't go leapin' to any conclusions. Can you think of anythin' else? Any other reason?"

"I can't. No. I've only been here once. For Jimmy's funeral. Other than that, I've never even been in the state."

"Know anybody here? B'sides Livie?"

"Henry and Mary Beth Davidson. That's it. Oh . . . And the man who runs the motel."

"Frank Perkins?"

"Yes. He checked me in—and out—when I stayed here last fall."

He nodded.

"That all?"

"All I can think of."

"Now about the car," he said. "You git me the papers, an' I'll report it to 'em for you. Make it more official-like. Explain the circumstances."

"I'd appreciate that, very much. I've been wondering how I was going to handle it. The papers are right here in my pocket. I got them out while I was packing."

He unfolded the papers, looked at them, refolded them, and put them into his notebook.

"Well, then, Mr. McBride. I'd say that's about it for now. Much obliged. You mind comin' by to see me agin in the mornin'? Livie's comin', as you heard, an' you could ride over with her."

"I'd be glad to. What time?"

"Less say, ten o'clock? Gimme a chance to do a few other things first."

"Fine. Ten o'clock it is."

"Downtown Bainbridge. Across from the courthouse. Well, Livie knows."

"Thank you, Sheriff. You've been very kind."

"Not a'tall." He touched his hat and nodded.

I got my suitcase and put it in the backseat of Livie's car. As she turned onto Main Street, a few gawkers still on the sidewalk waved to her. She waved back.

"I'm so sorry, Ian," she said. "I just can't begin to tell you how bad I feel. It's all such a nightmare. First Jimmy. Now this. It's like I don't know this place a'tall. Like I'm a stranger here, same as you. Almost eighty years I've lived in this little town. Never anyplace else. And I feel like a stranger."

She turned into a long driveway.

"Oh, my lord, Livie," I said. "Is this it? Is this your house?"

"Indeed it is. Since the day I got married."

"I love it."

A big, beautiful, two-story Victorian rose up beside us, gleaming in the moonlight. Wild with gingerbread trim, porches, turrets, gables, cupolas.

"It's like heaven," I said. "I *love* it."

"Guess you'll be happy enough here, then. I reckon."

She took me upstairs to one of the extra bedrooms at the front of the house.

"This was always Jimmy's favorite, when he stayed over," she said. "He got a kick outa sleepin' on this old sleigh bed. That okay?"

An overwhelming desire to break down and cry, so familiar now, came over me, but I held it in.

"Yes," I said. "Very much okay."

"Get yourself settled, then, and come on down to the kitchen. Back of the house. You'll find it. I feel like a nice cup of warm milk, to calm my frazzled nerves. How's that sound?"

"Perfect."

"Bathroom's there. Second door on the right. Towels in the linen closet."

I did find the kitchen. Livie was standing by the stove.

"I'll show you around the house tomorrow, when there's more light," she said. "Lots to see, but . . . not tonight. I'm kinda tired."

"Me, too."

We sat at the kitchen table drinking our milk.

"Honey in here?" I asked.

"And a little cinnamon. Soothing?"

"Very."

In this tranquil room, a summer breeze coming through the open window, crickets chirping outside, I could almost believe that dreadful thing had never happened. I took a couple of deep breaths and tried to steady my hand.

"Just how bad *is* it?" Livie asked.

My head jerked up.

"What?" I said.

"You're obviously scared out of your wits, and you got every right to be."

"Well . . . I am up*set*, I guess. A little."

"A little," she said. "Right. Wanta talk about it?"

"I'd rather just get some rest."

She nodded.

"You go on up, then. I'll wash these few dishes and be right along."

4

Alone in the dark in that strange bed, I was alert, wary, apprehensive. A wind had come up, and the old house creaked and groaned. I found myself jumping, insides twitching, with each unfamiliar sound. Was someone there? I held my breath, listened, let it out. Not this time. But . . . what about the next?

No one locks their doors here, that loudmouthed waitress at the café had told me. In Bainbridge yes, but not here. And, of course, everyone knows it. Common knowledge. By now, everyone also knows where I'm staying. *That* piece of news would travel fast. So anyone could come here, anyone. Walk right in, sneak up the stairs . . . Who was going to stop them, Livie? Certainly not me.

I was terrified. I *hadn't* wanted Livie to know—some re-sidual macho foolishness?—but I was. I was a grown man, for heaven's sake. Fifty-seven years old. Competent. Sure of myself. But I was terrified.

I crept to the front window, floor creaking with every step. The window was open about six inches to let in the cool night air. In the moonlight, the street looked quiet and peaceful. No movement. No sound but the wind in the trees. A pickup turned onto the street. Panic clawed at my chest. I moved to the side of the window. But it kept going. The street was still once more. I heard a dog bark, far away. Then nothing.

When I was satisfied the pickup wasn't coming back, I crept to the door of my room, and on into the hall. I stood for a minute, listening, trembling. Nothing. From the bathroom window I could see the driveway. Livie's car. Just sitting there. No flames. No shattered windows. Just a car, sitting there.

Out in the hall, I listened again. The only sounds I could hear were a creak now and then—and the faint rumble of snoring, regular and untroubled, from Livie's room at the other end of the hall. I went back to my room. Back to bed. Scratching! Over at the side window. I sat straight up. Only a tree branch moving in the wind. Wasn't it? It was. I lay back down.

The smell of lavender sachet and clean sheets surrounded me. If I was going to be wide-awake like this, I wanted to be thinking about Jimmy, about the nights he'd spent in this big, comfortable bed, about how much being here made me miss him, but I couldn't. Fear completely filled my mind, left no room for him.

I'd never expected to be this frightened. Like so many others in this fortunate country, I had believed I was safe. Things happened to other people, certainly—Trevor died, Jimmy was murdered, towns I'd never heard of were leveled by tornadoes—but my own life went on from day to day, comfortable, privileged, with me in control. I could take the normal precautions—eat properly, exercise, never drive when I'd been drinking—and I'd be fine.

But now, in the remembered glow of that burning car, I could see this wasn't so at all. I wasn't in control. I was weak, vulnerable, and very much afraid. I'd been pretending, all along, relying on the false sense of security we build around ourselves simply to get from one day to the next. And I couldn't do that anymore. The truth of how things really are—precarious, capricious—had come crashing in on me. Not just Trevor or Jimmy. It could happen to me.

The wind had died down, and the house wasn't creaking anymore. I heard a dog bark again, off in the distance. Sounded like the same one. Even farther away, a train whistle. Once. Twice. It seemed calm out there. Almost serene. But I knew now that calmness was deceptive. Hiding the unexpected. The unimaginable. I should just leave, I thought. What am I doing here? I'm not a crusader. All I want is to see that justice is done.

Justice! What a hokey, antiquated concept. Out-of-date, like this beautiful, creaky old house. Or maybe it was still in fashion, but only for those who 'deserved' it. Fair treatment for queers? Not in this place. Here they beat you up. Torch your car. Run you out of town. But I wasn't going to run. Even though I was scared to death—no hero, far from it— I knew I wasn't going to run away. I wanted that bastard to pay. And I wanted to be here to watch it happen.

Then I realized. I *did* fit in here, after all. They were in love with retribution, and so was I. They went at execution with gusto, I read about it all the time. Clearing out death row one inmate at a time. It was the same gusto with which they'd burned my car, sprayed that warning on the wall, wasn't it? Well, good. Maybe their Old Testament sense of just deserts would be my salvation. Maybe they *would* convict that killer. And then fry him the way they'd fried my car. I was so pleased with this thought I drifted off to sleep.

I woke up at quarter of eight. Shocking for me. Livie was in the kitchen. As I walked through the door, I smelled coffee brewing.

"I heard you rattlin' around up there," she said, "so I put the pot on. Scrambled eggs okay?"

"Sure."

"I'm not a great cook, as you'll discover to your sorrow, but I *can* manage scrambled eggs. Drink your orange juice."

I did.

"Henry called a little while ago," she said. "He and Mary Beth are shocked and awful sorry, he says. They hope you'll be all right."

"I will."

After breakfast, Livie took me on a tour of the house. Graceful, high-ceilinged rooms. Antiques from her family and her husband's. Real ones handed down, not somebody else's leftovers. Wonderful old pieces. Great rugs. Silver. Crystal. A Tiffany lamp, designed by Tiffany himself, I was sure. Bookshelves in almost every room, many of the books leatherbound and elegant.

In the parlor, where Livie said she spent most of her time, was a portrait of a man standing beside the marble mantelpiece I'd just seen in the formal living room.

"Who's that?" I asked.

"My husband. Elton."

"Handsome man. Very distinguished."

"He was. And intelligent and gentle and kind. Excellent provider, as you can see."

"Sounds like you had a good marriage."

"One of the best I know of."

"How long were you married?"

"Thirty-eight years. And seven months."

She looked at her watch.

"Don't mean to rush you, but . . . we better be gettin' on over to Bainbridge."

Livie parked on the north side of the courthouse square. The sidewalk was full of reporters. Of course. As I got out of the car, they shouted, pushed, shoved microphones in my face. I'd learned my lesson, though. Avoidance didn't work. Merely postponed the inevitable. This time I was calm, polite.

"Look," I said over the din. "We've got an appointment at ten. It shouldn't take long. After that, I'll be happy to answer your questions. All right?"

They kept shouting, but let us pass. I waited, flipping through magazines in a reception area, while the sheriff talked with Livie. Then she waited while he talked with me. We basically went over the same ground again. One new question was about a green Camaro. Had I seen it around the motel? I said I didn't remember it.

"Does this mean you have a lead?" I asked.

"Mebbe. We'll keep you posted. You plannin' on bein' around?"

"As long as the trial lasts."

He nodded. "The rental company'll be bringin' you a new car down from Dallas. Around two? I gave 'em Livie's address. They've had the other one hauled away. What was left of it."

I smiled. "Thanks, Sheriff. You've been a big help."

"What I'm here for. Partly, anyways. I'll be in touch."

"You know where to find me."

Outside, I talked with the reporters for what seemed like hours, but was really more like twenty minutes. Lots of interest in the burned-out car, the warning on the wall, my being here for the trial. Livie stood by me through it all, answering the questions that were directed at her, looking from me to the reporters the rest of the time. I found not running, not trying to hide from them, a relief. Let them ask. All I had to do was tell them what I was thinking, what I hoped for. Conviction—and the death penalty. I was emphatic about that. I even began to enjoy the attention, a little.

You incorrigible old ham, I thought.

Livie and I ate lunch at a Chinese restaurant in Bainbridge. Not great, but all right. We chatted some about our talks with the sheriff, the experience with the reporters.

She sat back in her chair and narrowed her eyes.

"Still not ready to talk to me about it?" she asked.

I was startled. "I thought I was."

"Did you? Well, you're not. You told a heckuva lot more to those reporters than you've been tellin' me."

"I'm not very good at ..."

She patted my hand.

"It's all right," she said. "Up to you. But ... I'm guessin' it's pretty lonesome inside there. Where you hide out."

I nodded. "It is."

When we got home, just after one-thirty, two cars were parked out front. The little blue one was for me. The other was to take both drivers back to Dallas. I signed the new papers, took the key, and gave the young men a $20 tip.

"I'm headed up to take me a nice long nap," said Livie. "I recommend you do the same."

5

Late in the afternoon, Livie found me on the screened-in side porch, in a wicker armchair, crying quietly. I closed the book that had been lying, unread, on my lap and set it on the table beside me.

"I'm sorry," I said, wiping my eyes with my handkerchief.

"Sorry, fiddlesticks," she said. "I do the same thing, twice a day, regular as clockwork. You just haven't caught me at it is all."

She sat in the rocking chair across from me. "I hope you know how glad I am you're here."

I smiled at her. "Thanks. I like being here."

She rocked back and forth, watching my face. "But . . . you're missin' our Jimmy particularly much, right about now."

"Yes. Particularly much. Being back here, where he . . . Makes me realize how much I've lost. He's gone now. And I'll never be that happy again."

"Oh, but you will. Jimmy was a wonderful boy, no question about it, and I'm sure you'll always cherish his memory. But you don't wanta get the idea happiness is all behind you. No, indeed. Thinkin' that too much'll just make it come true. You want to fight those kinds of thoughts. Push 'em away. Tell yourself you *will* be happy again, eventually. You did it before, with Jimmy."

"I did, but . . . Not this time."

"Well, yes! *Especially* this time. Because you loved Jimmy so much."

"How do you figure that?"

"Don't *have* to figure. It's true. People who've loved the most are the ones with the best reason for lovin' again. It's not like poor ole Romeo and Juliet, bless their hearts. Only one great passion per lifetime. If you find it, you're lucky, and when it's gone, that's it—you've used up your allotment. No, no. Just the opposite. The ones that've loved the most . . . They're the ones really know what it's about. Know how it makes the whole shootin' match worth all the bother." She narrowed her eyes and nodded, once. "Now, it's not gonna be right away. Course not. Takes time to get over that kind of sorrow. But sooner or later, when another chance at love comes their way, they grab it."

"You mean, just flit from one to the next? I could never do that."

"Don't be silly. You're not listenin' to me a'tall. Course that's not what I mean. I'm *sayin'*, love the one you care about as hard and as well as you can. Give it all you've got. But if you lose him, like you've done, don't close yourself off. Keep open the possibility of lovin' again. Not to forget the one that's gone, you'll never do that. But to honor him— and the love you had for each other."

"You believe that?"

"I do."

"But that's not what happened to you. You told me your marriage was one of the best. Right?"

"It was."

"And how long has he been dead?"

"Eighteen years."

"Well, where's his replacement? I haven't heard anything about your finding another love. To honor *him*."

She rocked back and forth, looking straight at me.

"That's right, you haven't. Heard about it. Nobody has. Not a soul. But . . . Maybe you should."

"Wait a minute. Are you saying there *was* someone else? After your husband?"

"Let me tell you a story. And then you decide." She settled back into the rocking chair. "This is gonna be a Texas-style story, with some meanders to it, so just be patient."

"Meander away. I'm not going anywhere."

"Well . . . ," she said. "Back in the days when Elton and I were settin' up housekeepin', folks that were as . . . comfortable . . . as us had people to help out. Somebody to cook and clean house, for sure. Ladies, like I was supposed to be, ladies of a certain *position,* didn't do menial things like that. We were meant to be more . . . decorative, and some other woman, some hardworkin' woman, usually colored, did the cookin', cleanin', washin' up, laundry, all of that.

"Now, if you were *really* comfortable—if you married a doctor like I did, an up-and-comin' doctor whose patients thought he was God Almighty come to walk on this Earth and just *threw* money at him—well then, you also got to have a sort of caretaker-handyman-gardener-chauffeur kind of person as well.

"We were really lucky, as it turned out, Elton and me. Elton was a good man, as well as a wealthy one—not a combination that happens all that often. Not around here, at any rate. And he'd go off, once a week, to the other side of the tracks, to the colored part of town, to see what needed to be done. Never made a big deal about it, never told anybody he was doin' it, so lotsa folks in town didn't have any idea. He wouldn't charge those people over there for what he did, just let 'em give whatever they could. Well, sir, we were always up to our eyeballs in eggs and chickens and collard greens. And catfish! We had the best catfish ever came out of a Texas river.

"One night, real late—we'll say it was rainin' for the sake of drama—a man come runnin' up from the colored shacks to say his wife was real bad. Her baby was on the way, and the midwife couldn't get the poor little thing out, turned around backwards like it was. There was so much blood all over the place the man was scared out of his wits. Right quick, Elton and I both threw our robes around us, knew we couldn't waste time foolin' with clothes, and got down there fast. I figured there'd be some way I could help out, even if it was just holdin' that terrified woman's hand.

"It was a frantic time, touch and go, but Elton managed to save the mother. Lost the baby, a little boy, but . . . saved the mother. Stitched her up the best he could. She was so torn up she couldn't ever have any more—this would've been her first. Their first. But she was alive. Sarah was her name. Buster was her husband. He must've had another name—I'm sure he did—but nobody ever called him anything but Buster.

"They were so grateful, both of 'em, Buster and Sarah, that they offered to come take care of us, from then on. Out of gratitude for Sarah's life. No pay. Just room and board. Well, we wouldn't hear of it. We'd be real happy to have 'em come work for us, more than happy, but we'd pay 'em. A good livin' wage, plus room and board. And that's just what happened. Elton had a man come make an apartment up in the loft of the garage. More of a barn, really. Well, you've seen it."

"Yes," I said.

"They moved in out there, and were with us from then on. They did so many things for us—cooked, cleaned, watched the kids, kept the place together, in *every* way. I did lots of volunteer stuff. At the school, the hospital, the library. Not the church so much, the way so many of the other women did. It was too . . . churchy for me. Know what I mean?"

I nodded. "I think I do."

"Where is it you're from?"

"Connecticut."

She rolled her eyes. "Lord help us. A Yankee for sure. I never in my *life* met anybody grew up in Con*nec*ticut. But I'm guessin' . . . your lives didn't revolve around the church the way they do here."

"You're right. They didn't."

"Well, I have to say . . . Now, this is either treason or blasphemy—or both—but there's a way you're lucky. Here, it's *all* church. And you have no idea how that can wear you down. There's just . . . no gettin' away from it. Not really. It's like Muzak, always there playin' in the background, even when you're not actually, specifically listenin' to it. Cause *every*body down here, 'cept the real rotters, of course, but everybody else goes to church—one kind or another—Baptist, Methodist, Presbyterian, Church of Christ. Not so many

Catholics, of course, and even fewer Jews. Count *them* on one hand, matter of fact, in this little town. No. When we say church, we mean Protestant. *Real* church.

"There's a hierarchy, though, you can be sure of that. Wherever people really *care* about somethin', there's *always* a hierarchy. Our church, First Presbyterian, is at the top of the heap socially. And, since a good bit of what goes on at church around here *is* social, that counts for a lot. Now, I wouldn't be a'tall surprised if folks of other denominations might dispute me on that—us bein' top of the heap, I mean—but they'd just be foolin' themselves. We got your doctors, your lawyers, your bankers. Even a airline pilot, lives here for the charm and commutes all the way over to Dallas.

"The Methodists have a few of these kind of prominent citizens, I'll grant you that. A few. So they're prob'ly next down the line. But the real workin' people are almost certain to be Baptist or Church of Christ. You see what's happenin' here? You see why I've had a hard time bein' too serious about it? We're talkin' about status, not love and compassion."

She shook her head.

"And right after status comes demeanor . . . how you conduct yourself. My goodness sakes, that's *all*-important. It gets to be like a . . . performance—somethin' *you* must know quite a bit about. It can't exist without an audience. The point is to be *seen* to be devout, and those to whom it matters the most enter into this kind of . . . conspiracy. You know what I'm sayin'? You acknowledge my piety, and I'll acknowledge yours."

She rocked for a minute, shaking her head.

"It's all a question of in-ness or out-ness, don't you see. Anybody knows how to carry all this off is automatically included. Anybody doesn't won't ever be. Belongin' means acceptance, warmth, safety. Not belongin' . . . Well, that's too frightenin' to even think about.

"So . . . I could feel uneasy about church all I wanted, but I didn't have much choice about *goin'*, every single Sunday of my life. Me bein' the wife of the town's leadin' doctor—to whom, you can be sure, I never breathed a word of all this. Daughter of the man that founded and ran the town's only department store. Gone now, of course. The store, I mean. Well, my father, too. But he was gone long before his store went under. Wal-Marted out of existence. My brother's the one got to watch it die.

"Now, how on earth did I get *here*? Oh. What it was I did back then to keep myself occupied. Not the church so much, is what I was sayin'. Mostly the hospital and the town library, with some tutorin' over at the high school thrown in. It may surprise you we've even *got* a hospital, dinky town like this. But we do, thanks to my husband. It's where they took Jimmy . . ."

She shut her eyes, clenched her fists. I saw her struggling to hold herself together. She succeeded. She opened her eyes, smiled at me, and shook her head.

"Here I am chatterin' on like a magpie without a lick of sense in order to keep *you* from feelin' sad, and then I . . ."

"It's all right," I said. "We've both got a lot more grieving to do before we're through."

"We do indeed." She shook her head again. "How'm I *ever* gonna get back to the point of my story? Assumin' it's got one."

"It does," I said. "The secret you've never told anyone else."

She smiled, almost shyly.

"Oh, yes." She nodded. "So . . . Sarah and Buster took care of *every*thing while the kids were growin' up. And after all four of 'em were married and gone, they kept right on takin' care of Elton and me. Sarah's breast cancer came on her fast. Before she knew anything about it—or so she said—it was all through her body. We sent her to every specialist we could locate, over in Dallas and down to Houston, but there was nothin' they could do, they said. Just ease the pain till it was over.

"After she died, the place seemed mighty empty. I started doin' most of the cookin' then, since it was just Elton and me. Nowhere near as good as Sarah, dear woman, but we didn't starve. Buster hung right in there, stalwart like always. He never let on about the sorrow I could see he was feelin'. He got his own meals, cleaned the house, did the laundry. Carried on with things.

"Then, a few years later, out of nowhere, Elton had his heart attack, right there in his office, between appointments. Gone, in a flash. Still young, seemed like to me, and vigorous. But just . . . gone. It was months before I could even believe it'd happened. I sleepwalked through the funeral, then moped around, stayed in bed a lot. Gained all this weight."

She slapped her hips.

"Buster fretted about me. Tried to get me to go out, take an interest in things again. But I wouldn't. Absolutely no desire to. All I wanted to do was just lie there, feelin' sorry for myself. So . . . no surprise . . . I caught a cold that turned into pneumonia. Doctor—new, *young* doctor—said I needed plenty of rest. Well, that was fine with me. I planned on just restin' up there till I *rotted*.

"All through it, Buster brought my meals up on a tray,

made sure I took my medicine, carried the dirty dishes back down to wash 'em. Emptied my bedpan. Day after day after day. He moved into the house—to that tiny little room back behind the kitchen. So he could be close by in case I needed him.

"For a while, I thought I was gettin' better, though I had no desire to be well enough to leave that bed entirely, but then, one afternoon, my fever went sky-high, and I couldn't stop coughin'. Buster called the doctor, who wasn't about to come by to see me—*those* days are gone—but he did prescribe a different medicine, that Buster went right down to the drugstore to get.

"Little by little, the coughin' eased up, and the fever went down, and I wanted a bath so bad I could taste it. I was so weak, though, I could hardly move. Buster had to hoist me up and walk me, with his arm around me, to the bathroom down the hall. He got me settled and drew my bath for me. All I had to do after he left was slip off my nightgown and step into the tub. Felt *so* good. Then into a clean nightgown when I got out. Buster waited outside the door and walked me back to the bedroom. When he'd hoisted me up onto the bed again and smoothed out the covers, he put his hand on my arm. I reached over and put my hand on his.

" 'Stay here by me awhile,' I said. 'Please.' He nodded. He pulled a chair over next to the bed and sat down. And we started in to talkin'. Both of us. First time. Can you imagine? Not just me rattlin' on like now, but real honest-to-goodness talkin'. About not much in the beginnin', but then, as the days went by, more and more about things that *did* matter. His life and Sarah's and how he felt about it. My life and what it was and wasn't. Funny, though, how different our perceptions had been. There wasn't much he *didn't* know about me or my life. And there was very little I *did* know about his. Oh, I *thought* I did, arrogant like we tend to be. I thought I knew all about him. He was so . . . familiar. After all, he'd been around for nearly forty years—way more than half my life. He was Buster. Good ole reliable Buster.

"Well, he wasn't. Not a bit of it. He was a whole lot more than that. More than I'd ever dreamed of. As his trust grew, and by some gift of grace outside of normal human understandin', he cut through the crap that'd built up over all those years and showed me who he *really* was. Intelligent. *Fiercely* intelligent. Aware of so many things. Good-hearted, but underneath that, angry. And resentful. Justifiably so. He knew very well what he could've been if . . . If things'd been different in the world. And he resented the hell out of the fact they weren't.

"Loved kids, and hated the waste of havin' spent his whole adult life lookin' after ours 'stead of his and Sarah's. Gave me a lot of respect for him, tellin' me that. Not pretendin' that mine and Elton's had been any kind of substitute for havin' his own. But it wasn't just disappointments and resentments. Not by a long shot. Good stuff, too. Things he'd loved. Ideas he'd had. Beauty he'd seen, and appreciated, all over. And I got to tell *him* things I'd never told another soul. Things I wished *I* could've done. Worthwhile things that had nothin' to do with hospitals or libraries. Things Elton, good as he was, would never've understood in a million years.

"Once Buster'd broken through his shell, taken off the mask he'd worn around us all his life, trusted enough to let me in close, he and I got to be real good friends. *Real* good. We started feelin' a need to touch each other. To verify, somehow, what that friendship meant. I'd reach out my hand"—she hesitated, then held hers out toward me—"and he'd take it in his. And right there would be the symbol of our lives. What they'd been. My hand—little, soft, white, useless for most things—lyin' there in his big, black, callused, capable hand."

She shrugged. Jimmy's shrug. Seeing it made me smile, though I also felt a twinge of pain. She only saw the smile, and smiled back.

"Before long, holdin' hands wasn't enough, and he came into my bed. I could never've imagined such a thing. Never in my life. But when it happened, it was the most natural thing in the world. And the warmest and most lovin'. It was such a miracle we just grinned at each other for days and days. Two old people like us, so different on the outside but now so close inside, findin' that whole world of pleasure and comfort in each other. Truly a miracle.

"But . . . Nothin's ever *all* good. That change, wonderful in every other way, took our friendship, which we already didn't want *any*body to know about, and moved it to that awful place of fear and anxiety, where we couldn't afford to let a single soul get even the tiniest whiff of what was goin' on. To protect him more than me, I thought back then. Well . . . Maybe. Maybe not.

"Anyhow, it meant pretendin' and denyin', most all the time. Durin' the day, when the kids or the grandkids were around, he'd have to shuffle along with his head down like he'd always done. Call me Miz Davidson. Never look me in the eye. I hated it. But we had no choice. Or at least we thought we didn't. Our histories were too strong.

"And then at night, after we'd lain there together feelin' close and comfortable, he'd have to go back down to that little room of his. We never locked the house—never *had*—so people just came and went, and we didn't dare run the risk of somebody comin' by real early and findin' him upstairs 'stead of down. There was always that fear at the back of our minds. Always. But at the front . . . Ah, well. That was all love. All love.

"And you know somethin' else? He brought me back to life in more ways than one. I got over that pneumonia in no time, got myself up and out of this house, and I've never been sick a day since."

She pursed her lips and nodded.

"So there you have it. That's my story. Long, but . . . worth it, I'd say."

"I'd say so, too." I was overcome with love, for both of them, myself.

"Did . . . Jimmy ever know any of this?"

She laughed. "Not a hint. He was one of the reasons we had to be so careful, since after he got to be seven or eight or so, he was over here all the time. I wished, every now and then, that I could tell him, when he was a little older, and so fond of Buster, but . . . Too dangerous. No tellin' what he might've said, or to whom. Poor lamb. Too dangerous."

"He'd've been glad, I think, if he'd known."

She nodded. "I hope so."

"Where . . . ?" I hesitated. "Where is Buster now?"

She looked straight at me. Her eyes went from bright and lively to dark and sad in an instant.

"Gone," she said.

"He died?"

"No. Just gone from me. He had a stroke . . . two years ago. Paralyzed his whole right side. One night after he left me and went down to his bed. I knew somethin' was wrong as soon as I woke up. No sounds downstairs of him movin' around. Startin' our breakfast. Sounds I'd heard every mornin' for all those years—and now they weren't there. All of a sudden, I was frantic. I ran down the stairs in my nightgown, callin' his name. And all the time, inside my head, I was sayin', 'No! Let him be all right. Just let him be all right.'

"But he wasn't. He was lyin' on his bed, unable to move. Lookin' at me with his big dark beautiful eyes. Lookin' but not able to say a word. Just little groans every time he tried. I threw my arms around him. I knew I had to call for the ambulance as soon as I could. Get help. But I needed to be close to him, that one more time.

"He . . . was in the hospital here awhile, and his kinfolks came over from East Texas. A sister and two of her sons and some cousins. I never saw him alone again. When he got well enough to travel, they decided to take him on home with them. He still wasn't able to talk, and neither hand would work good so he couldn't write me a note. All he had was his eyes, and he told me with them, plain as day, what I'd meant to him. I tried my best to send the same message with my own.

"I wrote him a couple of times, innocuous things, sure he'd understand, but no answer ever came back. I don't know a thing about how he is. He might be . . ."

She shrugged.

"But we had those years. Almost fifteen of 'em. Good, happy years. Nobody can take that away. And one thing's for sure . . . I know, and he knows, that both of us, wherever we may be, are everlastingly grateful. For what we let ourselves find in each other."

She bowed her head, then looked back up at me.

"You know . . . ," she said. "I'd be glad for a Heaven . . . if it meant I could see him again."

6

Tuesday morning I woke early, before seven, and couldn't go back to sleep no matter how hard I tried. Seems as if nothing stays the same, I thought. Not even the most entrenched of old habits. I got up and walked to the front window. The morning was bright and sunny, the sky cloudless. It needed to be gray, stormy. But it wasn't.

I showered and shaved, dressed, went down to the kitchen. The coffeemaker was bubbling, and Livie was stirring a pot on the stove.

"Oatmeal okay this mornin'?" she asked. "I got raisins and some cinnamon in it to spice things up a bit."

"Thanks," I said. "Oatmeal's fine."

She spooned it into bowls, I poured the coffee, and we both sat down.

"Gonna be a rough day," she said, "I'm afraid."

"Afraid so."

"Mind if we go over in both cars?" she asked. "I wanta

be sure I can get outa there when I've had enough, but I don't wanta make you leave if you're not ready. That sound all right with you?"

"Yes. Fine. I . . . I want to thank you, again. For telling me your story yesterday. It was . . ."

She put her hand on mine, squeezed it, and smiled.

We left a little after nine, and I followed her to Bainbridge. She drove so fast I had a hard time keeping up. I saw to my dismay that the square was jammed. We had to park several blocks away, in a residential area.

The TV vans were there in droves, as were the demonstrators. The "faggots go to Hell" contingent was back, in much greater numbers, but by now the pro-gay forces had had time to mobilize as well. There were maybe even more of them than the others. Police barricades separated the two sides, whose adherents shouted and waved placards at each other. I held Livie's elbow and steered her through the crowd toward the courthouse door. Henry was at the top of the steps, waiting for us.

"It's standin' room only," he said. "But they've reserved a section for the family. Mary Beth's inside already, with the kids. Got here last night." He hesitated. "We'd . . . like you to sit there with us, Ian. If that's all right."

Tears sprang into the corners of my eyes. I blinked hard, and they stayed inside.

"Thanks, Henry," I said. "That's very kind of you."

"Better late than never." He smiled and patted me on the shoulder.

Right here in front of everyone, I thought. Good for him. It wasn't an easy thing for him to do, I knew that, which made me admire him all the more.

He spoke to a guard at the door, who let us through. We

went down a long hall with a shiny marble floor, our footsteps echoing loudly as we went. Into a large room jammed with people, conversation buzzing around us. High ceilings. Marble columns. Very ornate. At the far end, a dark mahogany jury box and an even more impressive bench for the judge. Henry led us down the center aisle to a row of seats about halfway back.

"Mary Beth wanted us here," he said. " 'Stead of right up at the front. Thought some distance might make it a little less painful."

"Oh, yes," I said. "I agree."

"You go on in by Mary Beth," said Livie. "I'll sit here next to Ian."

Bless her, I thought. Mary Beth looked up, smiled at me, and waved. I could see that she was having a hard time holding on. I smiled and waved back.

Just beyond her was her son Martin, whom I recognized from the funeral. He was talking to an attractive, dark-haired woman next to him, who I thought must be his wife. Then the young woman who'd answered the door the night I tried to see Henry and Mary Beth. Blond. Expensively dressed. Carefully made up. Jimmy's sister, Rosalind? Probably so. She was rummaging around in a very large purse. On her left was a stout man with a mustache, talking into a tiny cell phone.

Once we were settled and Livie had stopped speaking to people in the rows in front of and behind us—many of them relatives, I gathered, from what she was saying—I asked her about the ones sitting on the other side of Mary Beth.

"That's Martin next to his mother, of course," she said. "You remember him." I nodded. "Then his wife, Jonelle. Rosalind. Her husband, Alfred. Likes to be called Cinco, lord only knows why. Well . . . better than *Alfred,* when you think about it." I smiled. "That's the bunch of us."

Jimmy's immediate family—and me. All in a row. A powerful statement to the world, no question about it.

Henry put his arm around Mary Beth. Livie reached over to pat Mary Beth's hand, said a few words to her, waved to her grandchildren, then sat back and leaned toward me.

"Glad everybody's here," she said quietly. "For Mary Beth's sake, most of all. We weren't sure they'd all be able to make it. Martin and Jonelle've lived in Houston for a good long while. He's with an oil company down there. Just keeps movin' right on up the line. Close to the top now, I reckon—in the administrative end of things. Two kids. Boy and a girl. Home with their *'nanny'.*"

Her emphasis on the word spoke volumes.

"Rosalind and Cinco live out in El Paso. No kids yet. He's a partner in a company puts electronic equipment together just across the border in Mexico. Maquiladoras, they call 'em. Spin-off of that NAFTA business. Doin' very well, so they tell me. But . . . he and I have to be real careful not to get into a conversation about workin' conditions and salaries and such. We had ourselves a real knockdown drag-out once the likes of which you've never seen, and he wouldn't talk to me for over a year. We got it sorted out, though, and now we just avoid the whole subject entirely. I still worry about it—to myself, of course. But . . . he may be right. That he's payin' 'em more than they could ever've imagined makin' in the old days. Maybe . . ."

"What do Rosalind and Jonelle do?"

"*Do?*"

"Don't they have jobs? Work somewhere?"

Livie snorted.

"Not likely."

There was a stirring up front. I looked at my watch. Ten o'clock on the dot. The jury started filing in through a door to the right. Seven women. Five men. All but one young woman middle-aged or beyond. Two black women. One black man.

A serious-faced man came in through a door to the left on the far wall.

"All rise," he said.

We did.

The judge, an older man, mostly bald with a silver-gray fringe of hair, entered. We all sat, and the trial began.

7

First came a series of motions, a couple of which were not entirely clear to me. One was. The defense attorney, a tall, brisk, efficient man who chopped the air with his hands to emphasize a point, wanted some evidence suppressed. In particular a group of photographs taken of Jimmy just after the attack. The attorney argued that while the photos might—*might*—indeed be relevant, they were also highly inflammatory, prejudicial to his client. The judge denied the motion. I felt encouraged.

The attorney was standing beside a large table to the left down front. The killer was sitting next to the attorney's empty chair. I could see the back of his head. A bit of his shoulders. I was filled with unreasoning hatred. Get him, I thought. Give him what he's got coming.

The judge called for the prosecutor's opening statement. A young woman, maybe midthirties, stood up. My god, I thought. *She's* the one? She was of medium height, medium build, brown hair, not too short or too long. She wore brown horn-rim glasses, not much makeup. Nothing about her was especially memorable.

Why her? I wondered. Did she ask for the case? It had such a high profile, was attracting so much nationwide attention, I'd have thought they'd bring out their big guns. This woman must be good.

She stood very still. The courtroom was absolutely silent. Not a sound anywhere.

"Your Honor," she said. Her voice was quiet but resonant. "Ladies and gentlemen of the jury. This is a sad day for Texas. One of our finest citizens, a young man of enormous promise, is no longer with us. His life was cut short, snuffed out before it had really begun. Why? Not for revenge. He had not wronged either of the men who killed him. Not to eliminate a threat. He was the least offensive of men. Not even for greed. He was not killed in the course of a robbery, which might make *some* kind of sense. No. He was killed simply because of who he was. A handsome, gentle, loving, immensely talented young—gay—man."

She walked slowly up and down in front of the jury box as she talked, looking each juror in the eye, one at a time. Her phrasing was impeccable, her rhythm flawless. Oh, yes, indeed. She *was* good. She could give lessons to aspiring young actors.

"Two other young men saw him—at a movie theater— and were offended by his mere presence there. By the fact that he was different from them, and proud of that difference, not ashamed. They followed him, accosted him on a dark road, bludgeoned him without mercy, and left him there, mortally wounded, his life slipping away. He was found some time later by a passing motorist and taken to the Kimberley hospital, where he died the next afternoon, without regaining consciousness."

Thank god, I thought. A small blessing, but a blessing nonetheless. He *didn't* wake up. To suffer—and to know I wasn't with him as he died.

"There is no question about what happened," she continued. "The second man involved has confessed and will testify here before you. Testify that this man"—she whirled and pointed straight at Carey Plummer—"was there with him, was a willing accomplice, and is equally responsible for the death of James Arthur Davidson."

I heard a small sob down the row to my left. Mary Beth, I thought.

As the prosecutor sat down, the defense attorney got up. He too went over and stood directly in front of the jury box.

"The decision you will make in this case," he said, "is probably the most important decision you will ever be called upon to make. You will decide the course of the rest of this young man's life. Even whether he will *have* a life."

The man was talking more slowly than before, moving more slowly. He hadn't chopped the air once. Smart man, I thought. He can't let her be the more sympathetic figure.

"You will be sitting in judgment of him, and in order to judge well, you must try—you *must* try—to understand. If retribution is part of judgment, so is compassion. If a desire for justice is part, so is an obligation to be fair.

"My respected colleague, the prosecutor, has told you that this case is a simple one. That my client participated in the killing of a man because he thought this man was 'different' and that difference offended him. End of story. I assure you, ladies and gentlemen, that this case is *not* simple. Few things in life are. Certainly not the strongest—and deepest—of our emotions.

"All of us have histories that guide our destinies. I will lead you through some of this young man's history, and then leave it to you to decide—with fairness and with compassion—what is to be done."

Well matched, I thought, this man and this woman. No way to predict, on the basis of what we'd seen so far, which would be the one to tip the balance.

The prosecutor began to build her case by calling Sheriff Wright. He established who Jimmy was, where he had lived, in Kimberley and in Washington, his movements during the afternoon and early evening of the day of the attack. To the Kimberley library in the afternoon, home for supper, to a movie at the group of theaters in the Bainbridge Mall, alone. The defense attorney agreed to the accuracy of these statements and had no questions for the witness.

Next came the man who found Jimmy, a bartender who lived in Kimberley and was on his way to the club in Bainbridge where he worked. He was short, thin, middle-aged. Nervous. Unused to being in front of so many people, I thought.

"Which road did you take to work that night?" the prosecutor asked.

"Don't have a name, exactly," the man said. "Everbody calls it 'the shortcut.' Runs acrost from Oak Street, edge of Kimberley, over to the back entrance of the Bainbridge Mall."

"Please describe this road."

"Pretty dark, most of the way. Not many folks livin' out there yet."

"Any streetlights?"

"Lord, no. Whut for?"

"And what did you see as you were driving to Bainbridge?"

" 'Bout halfway acrost, I seen a car pulled off the road—other side, headed towards Kimberley. Clean off on the shoulder. Dark. Nobuddy round so far's I could see. I drove on by, then thought to myself, 'Now whut's that car doin', off by itself like that, nobuddy there?' So I turned round an' went on back, thinkin' mebbe somebuddy might be needin' some help."

"And then?"

"I pulled off an' parked behind the car, left my lights on so's I could see, an' got out. I called a couple times—'Hullo,' 'Anybuddy here?'—like that. But wadn't no answer. I walked round to the other side of the car, side away from the road, an' it was then I seen 'im."

"What did you see?"

"A boy, young man, lyin' there. Not movin'. I called to 'im. 'You hurt bad?' I said. Kinda foolish question, but it's whut I said. No answer. I run back to my car to git my flashlight, an' then I could see the blood. All over his face. Had on a light blue shirt. Blood all over that. Dark. Gettin' darker, seemed like to me. Could see he was breathin', though, just a little. So I knew he wasn't dead."

Oh, my god, I thought. That's Jimmy. My darling. Lying there in the dirt. Can I actually sit here and listen to this?

"What did you do next?" the prosecutor asked.

"Saw I needed to git help quick as I could. I stopped a second to think, though, tryin' to figger which'd be the closest phone. Then I thoughta the Atkinsons, just up the road a piece on towards Bainbridge. I turned round agin an' tore off up there. Run in the house without knockin'. 'Pologized, a course, but said I needed to use their phone. Told 'em why, real quick."

"What time was that?"

"Little b'fore ten, by my watch."

"How do you know that?"

"I looked to see the time, just as I was makin' the first call. Wonderin' how late I was gonna be for work. S'pose to be there by ten, but a course wadn't any way I was gonna make it. Called the amb'lance first. Then the sheriff. Then my boss. Said I might be a while, but I'd git there when I could."

"What did you do next?"

"Drove on back to the car to wait for the others. Wadn't but a few minutes, but I spent 'em talkin' to the boy. Didn't know who it was then, face was too bloody. Didn't know either if he could hear me or not. But I had the idea he'd at least have a sense somebuddy was there, lookin' after 'im. 'Hang on, son,' I said. 'Help's on the way. You keep hangin' on, an' you'll be all right.' "

His voice choked, and he put his thumb and forefinger to the bridge of his nose. The prosecutor waited.

"I didn't know then that I was wrong. That he wadn't gonna be all right a'tall. But it's whut I hoped for. Whut I wanted *him* to b'lieve."

Tears were sliding down my face. God love you, I thought. You're a good man, whoever you are.

"What happened next?"

" 'Fore too long, couldn't'a been more'n five minutes, the amb'lance pulled up an' then the deputy. Deputy sheriff, Petie Norris. Heard 'em both way off, a course, 'fore I could see 'em. The three from the amb'lance run right over to where the boy was lyin'. Petie run over, too, to have a look at the boy, how things was, an' I followed. 'Everthin' just the way you found it?' Petie asked me. 'Yes,' I said. 'Scared to touch the boy. 'Fraid of makin' things worse. An' I knew better'n to touch anythin' else.'

"Petie took a couple flash pictures, quick as he could, then let the amb'lance crew start tendin' to the boy. While they was doin' that, Petie had me tell 'im everthin' I knew. All whut I've said here today. Wrote it down on a pad of paper. Few minutes later, heard another siren, an' the sheriff come pullin' up. Sheriff Wright. The boy was already on a stretcher, goin' into the amb'lance. Sheriff took a quick look an' sent 'em on their way. Read over Petie's notes an' double-checked a couple things with me."

"What did you do then?"

"I said to the sheriff was that all, 'cause I was late for work an' gettin' later all the time. An' Ernie, that's the sheriff, said, yeah, I could go on in. Thanked me for my help an' said would I come by his office next mornin'. I said seein' as how I work all night, I don't usually get up b'fore lunch, so would afternoon be all right? He said it would, an' I drove on off to work. Though I have to say I wadn't in much of a mood to be . . ."

"Thank you, Mr. Barnes," the prosecutor said kindly. "I have no more questions at this time."

The defense attorney chose not to cross-examine. Smart man, I thought again. Better to leave the power of *that* testimony alone.

"It's after twelve, I see," said the judge. "We'll adjourn till two o'clock. Promptly."

"All rise," the clerk said, and we did.

8

I stood there wondering if I was going to be able to move. Livie, Henry, and Mary Beth seemed to be as dazed as I was. I didn't know what to think, or how to think about it. Henry recovered first. He turned to Livie and me.

"No hope of goin' out for lunch," he said. "Every place in town'll be jammed with that mob out there. *And* in here. So Clayton—he's my partner, Ian, in the contractin' business, lives here in town—he and his wife've asked us all over for a little somethin' to eat. They'd like you both to join us, if you would."

"I appreciate that," I said.

"Leave it to Alice to think of somethin' that practical," said Livie. "Come on, Ian. I'll drive you over. Be easier to meet the ones you don't know over there."

Livie was silent the whole way, a first for her in my experience. I was grateful and said nothing myself. She parked in front of an enormous house. Three cars were already there by the curb. We walked up a long sidewalk past the greenest lawn I'd ever seen. I couldn't conceive of the amount of water it must take to keep it looking that way.

A tall, slender woman with sleeked-back hair and bright red fingernails answered the door. She leaned over and kissed Livie's cheek.

"Wonderful to see you, my dear," she said. "And you're Ian, of course."

She held out her hand. I shook it.

"I'm Alice Granville. So good to meet you, at last. How are the accommodations at Chez Livie?"

I smiled. "Splendid."

"Come on in. We're out on the patio by the pool. Such a lovely day. Well . . . The weather anyhow. Not much else."

Livie and I followed her through several huge rooms past sliding glass doors onto a patio, shaded by a white awning. I was glad to be outside again. The air inside had been frigid. To our left was a long rattan bar. A red-faced man with a large nose was pouring wine into glasses lined up on a tray.

"Clayton," said Alice. "Ian's been good enough to join us."

The man shook my hand.

"Glad you could come," he said.

"Thank you for including me."

"Hello, Livie. Always a pleasure. White or red?"

"Red, I think."

"Same for me," I said.

He handed us each a glass, then walked with the tray toward the others, who were standing in the sunshine out by the pool. Livie took me over. I kissed Mary Beth, shook Henry's hand, met the rest—Rosalind, Cinco, Martin, Jonelle. Two other couples, clearly old family friends. The Lewises and the Applegates.

They nodded, smiled, and resumed their conversations. As I watched, I was struck most forcefully by the contrast between Livie and her granddaughter. Rosalind was thin, probably anorexic, and so tightly wound her movements seemed mechanical. Her beige tailored suit was straight out of *Vogue*, her hair carefully styled and lacquered. The highest heels I'd seen in years. Behind its layer of makeup, her face was as rigid and unmoving as her hair. She didn't smile.

It was a relief to look back at Livie—shorter, rounder, much rounder, light-years more relaxed. Her simple blue silk dress set off the startling whiteness of her hair, which she obviously did herself. Washed it, fluffed it up with a dryer, and that was that. On to other things. The skin of her face was smooth for her age, a rosy pink lipstick the only makeup I could see. Sensible, flat-heeled shoes. The best quality, no question about that, Italian maybe, but still sensible. A person could actually walk in those shoes.

I tried to listen to what was being said closest to me, turned from Cinco to Mr. Applegate and back to Rosalind, but found I couldn't concentrate. It all seemed surreal to me. A stage set, with performers reciting their lines, not an actual gathering of real people. I'd just been sitting in a room with one of Jimmy's murderers. Had just listened to a description of how they had left him. Could still see him in my mind, lying there bleeding. And yet here I was in this comfortable, privileged place, sipping wine. Standing beside a pool surrounded by chatter about the weather. When was it ever going to rain? Every bit as dry out in El Paso. Thinking of restricting the days when you can water your lawn. I wanted to slap a few faces. Wake people up.

"So, Ian."

I looked over. Clayton Granville was coming toward me.

"You're from up North, they tell me."

"That's right."

"How do you like it down here in God's country?"

"It's . . . nice here."

"*Nice!* Heckuva lot more'n *that*. You happen to be standin' in the best damn town in the state. *And* one of the fastest-growin'."

"Are you from here?"

"You bet. Born and raised right here in Bainbridge. Went off to Texas A and M and then the Marine Corps, but came on back quick as I could."

"You've seen a lot of changes, then. In the town."

"Progress, what I like to call it. Seen it, and helped make it happen. Few of us were able to take a dinky little one-horse county seat and turn it into what you see here today."

He beamed at me.

"You must be very proud" was all I could think of to say.

"Am. For sure. Mighty proud of my part in it all."

I wanted to just leave. Put down my glass and walk away. But I couldn't.

"You're a . . . theater person, so I hear tell," he said.

"Yes, I am."

"Well . . ." He shook his head. "Never could quite understand why a grown man'd wanta spend his life playactin' like that. Seems kinda . . . frivolous to me."

I felt my chest constricting. Imagine the nerve. A man willing to pave over his own hometown wasn't one to talk about unnecessary occupations. My tongue was all ready with a few stinging retorts, but I held them in. Livie would have gone right ahead and delivered them, I knew that. Zinged them out, Devil take the hindmost. But I couldn't do it. Couldn't disrupt this day in that way. Jimmy's day.

I simply smiled and said, "It doesn't seem frivolous to me."

"Yoo-hoo."

I looked around. Alice was waving at us from under the awning.

"Y'all come on now," she yelled. "Lunch is ready, and we don't have that much time."

A yellow tablecloth had been laid over the bar. A young Mexican girl stood behind it, looking ill at ease. I could see what appeared to be chicken salad, guacamole, tomato aspic. We stood in line to serve ourselves. When I'd filled my plate, I saw that Livie was already seated between Rosalind and Mary Beth. I went to a group of chairs on the other side of the patio. Martin followed and sat beside me.

"I'm glad you came over this way," he said. "I can't . . ." He swallowed hard. "The chitchat over there was gettin' me down. I know they all mean well. Thinkin' murder's not a pleasant topic for lunchtime conversation. But . . . I don't really feel like bein' pleasant just now."

"Neither do I," I said.

He looked up and smiled sadly. He was handsome, too. Like Jimmy. Like their father. Like the whole family. Keep combining the right genes, and you get some very attractive people. His face was heavier than Jimmy's. More roughly hewn. They had the same eyes, though. Dark, but bright and alive. Did he have hidden depths, like Jimmy? Depths his life had not yet allowed him to explore? I hoped so.

"It's not that I want to talk about it, 'specially," he said. "I'm not sure I'd know what to say. But I can't see actin' like it's not even happenin'. The trial and all. It *is* happenin', and that's a fact."

"I know exactly what you mean," I said. "I don't really

want to keep torturing myself by thinking about it all the time. But I don't want to ignore it, either. There must be a middle ground somewhere."

"Mom's the one I feel the worst for. It's hit her so hard she can't . . . can't seem to find a way to deal with it. He was her baby, and she can't imagine that, all of a sudden, he could just be . . . Livie'll be fine. Oh, she loved him. Maybe more'n anybody else. But she'll be fine. She's tough. And she's too smart to let anything get her down for long. Dad'll be fine. I'll be fine. That's how we've been raised. I'm not sayin' it's gonna be easy, but . . . We'll find a way. And Rosalind. Well, she's got her own concerns. But *Mom* . . . She's started in blamin' herself. If she hadn't in*sis*ted he come on down for her birthday, he'd be alive right now. That kinda thing. Sad."

He'd been moving his food around on his plate as he talked. He lifted his fork to take a bite of chicken salad, but put it back down. He looked over at me.

"Here I am goin' on as if we were the only ones hurtin'," he said. "How 'bout you? You gonna be all right?"

"I'm not sure. Right now, I'd say no."

He nodded.

"I can understand that. If anything like this were to happen to Jonelle, I don't see how I could . . ." He sighed. "I don't know. Well . . . We'll have to be headin' back soon. Maybe we oughta at least try to get some food down."

"Yes," I said. "We should."

Everything was good, especially the guacamole, and I did manage to eat about half of what I'd taken. Livie came over to say she thought maybe we ought to get going. I thanked both the Granvilles and spoke to as many of the others as I could on our way out.

"You have a nice chat with Martin?" Livie asked as we drove toward the square.

"I did," I said. "I like him."

"He's a good boy. Or at least has the possibility of bein'. If he'd just stop tryin' so hard to please everybody. His father. His wife. His bosses. He spends every wakin' minute tryin' to please whoever he's with. I should think it'd be plumb ex*haus*tin'. Still . . . Better that than spendin' the same amount of energy tryin' to aggravate everybody, the way so many other folks do."

I laughed. She never ceased to amaze me.

We parked, even farther away this time, walked to the courthouse, and took our seats.

9

Back in the courtroom, the judge and jury in their places, the trial resumed. The prosecutor called for a Dr. Murray. A slightly overweight man, somewhere in his thirties, took the stand.

Oh, god, I thought. I know what's coming.

"Where do you practice, Doctor?" the prosecutor asked.

"Davidson Memorial Hospital, over in Kimberley."

"And what is your responsibility at this hospital?"

"I'm head of the emergency room there."

"And were you on duty, in that capacity, on the night of October 19th of last year?"

"I was."

"Where did you receive your medical training, Dr. Murray?"

"Baylor Medical School."

"With residencies elsewhere?"

"Yes. At Piedmont Hospital in Atlanta and D.C. General in Washington."

"Why did you choose those hospitals for your residencies?"

"I wanted to specialize in trauma care, emergency-room work. And I thought large hospitals in those cities would have . . . mmm . . . quite a bit of that kind of work."

"And were you right?"

"Oh, yes."

"Which means you have treated a great many patients with injuries brought about by violence of some sort?"

"Yes."

"Car accidents?"

"Yes."

"Gunshot wounds?"

"Yes."

"Beatings?"

"Yes."

"So you have seen a great deal more of this kind of . . . trauma than what one might expect to come through a small hospital in Kimberley, Texas."

"Yes, indeed."

"Would you say you are an expert at treating victims of violence?"

"Objection," said the defense attorney. "Leading question."

"Overruled," said the judge. "Answer, please."

"Yes. I would definitely say I'm an expert at that."

"And your responsibility, as a doctor in an emergency room, is what?"

"To determine, as quickly as I can, in seconds, if possible, what has occurred, what needs treatment, and in what order."

"Some things being more urgent than others?"

"Yes."

"Such as?"

"Well . . . The heart must be kept beating, first of all. Restarted if it has stopped, and stabilized if it is erratic. Breathing must be unobstructed, because lack of oxygen to the brain, for too long a time, causes irreparable damage. Bleeding, both external and internal, must be attended to before we turn to broken bones, for example."

"You are called on, then, in your work, to make decisions about what has happened to the patient you are seeing."

"Yes."

"You do this regularly?"

"Yes. Every time someone comes in through the door."

"And accuracy of judgment is critical, so that proper treatment can begin at once."

"Yes."

"So, would you say that, in addition to being an expert at treating wounds caused by violence, you are also an expert at determining how those wounds were inflicted?"

"Objection."

"Overruled. Answer the question."

"Yes. I believe I am an expert at that."

"What about blows to the head and body? Have you diagnosed and treated many of them?"

"Yes."

"How many?"

"Hundreds."

"On the night of October 19th, a young man was brought

by ambulance to your emergency room. Is that correct?"

"Yes."

"Only one such case that evening?"

"Yes."

"What time did this person arrive at the emergency room?"

"Ten twenty-three."

"How do you know that?"

"I checked the admittance records."

"Which you know to be accurate?"

"Our admitting nurses are extremely conscientious about things like that. By nature and by hospital regulation."

"Did you know who this young man was?"

"Yes. Once we'd washed the blood from his face, I recognized him right away."

"How?"

"Everybody there knew him. He was the grandson of the man who founded our . . ."

"Objection."

"Sustained. Jury will ignore that answer."

"Did the young man brought in by ambulance that night have identification on him?"

"He did. In his wallet."

"Which was found where?"

"In the pocket of his jeans."

"At the hospital?"

"Yes."

"And what form did this identification take?"

"Driver's license. Credit cards."

"Credit cards? Still in his wallet?"

"Yes."

"How do you know that?"

"Admitting records, again. The contents of his pockets were itemized."

"And, from this driver's license and these credit cards, still in his possession, the admitting nurse learned the name of the young man. Is that correct?"

"Yes."

"And what was his name?"

"James Arthur Davidson."

I winced. Up until then, I could pretend it was someone else. Some hypothetical patient. A character on a TV show. But no longer. Now it was Jimmy. They were talking about Jimmy.

"Having established his identity, let's go back to the moment when James Arthur Davidson came through the door into your emergency room, bleeding profusely, fighting for his life."

"Objection."

"Sustained. Facts, Counselor. Not descriptions."

"Yes, Your Honor. Let's go back, Doctor, to the moment when James Davidson was brought into your emergency room. Please tell us what happened."

"We'd gotten a call from the ambulance crew. That they were on their way. And giving us their initial assessment."

"Which was what?"

"Numerous blows to the head and upper body. Severe loss of blood. Patient unconscious. Pulse weak and erratic."

"And when you examined him yourself, what did you find?"

"Multiple fractures of the skull. Concussion. Fractures of the left clavicle, scapula, and humerus."

"Which are?"

"His shoulder—collarbone and shoulder blade—and the bone of his upper arm."

All of them broken. Battered. My chest was so tight I could hardly breathe. My head felt light, dizzy. Livie was trembling beside me.

"Anything else?" the prosecutor asked.

"Fractures to four of his ribs."

"On which side?"

"The left."

"And what was your initial analysis of the cause of these injuries?"

"Beating. With a blunt, not a sharp-edged, instrument."

"Based on the location of the injuries, Doctor, in which hand would the instrument that inflicted them have been held?"

"Right, definitely."

"Because?"

"Because the injuries were all to the left side ..."

"Of the victim."

"Yes."

"Could the victim have been facing away from his assailant, in which case a left-handed person could have been beating his left side?"

"No."

"You're sure."

"Yes."

"Because?"

"Because of the angle of the blows. Clearly to the front of his body."

"Thank you, Doctor. Please be patient ..."

She caught herself and smiled, just slightly. Several members of the jury nodded appreciatively. Had she done it on purpose? To lighten the moment, thereby making this testimony that much more horrifying? With her, shrewd as she was, I couldn't be certain.

"Please be patient for a moment, Doctor, while we give each of our jurors some photographs of Jimmy Davidson"— *Jimmy* now, I noticed—"taken by Deputy Sheriff Norris soon after the attack."

A clerk began passing out large brown envelopes to the jurors. The photographs the defense attorney had tried to keep them from seeing. The reason was quickly apparent. I heard a few small gasps as jurors opened the envelopes and took out the pictures. One woman reached into her pocket for a handkerchief to wipe her eyes. A man turned quickly away and put his hand to his head. Others stared at the photographs, transfixed.

The defense attorney leaned over to say something to Carey Plummer. The killer nodded. The prosecutor handed a set of photographs to the witness.

"If you would, please, Doctor," she said, "help the members of the jury to understand what they are seeing."

"Well . . . In the photo labeled One-A, you can see a deep crease near the top of the . . ."

Oh, dear god, I thought. I can't listen to this. A clinical analysis of the destruction of that lovely head. The cracking open of what enclosed all that had been Jimmy. His wit. His intelligence. His talent. His love—for his parents, for Livie. For me. I tried to keep it out, I tried hard, but a stark image of Jimmy's bloody face came into my mind and lodged itself there. I was glad for one thing: the grief and horror I was feeling were beyond tears, far beyond, so my eyes stayed dry. My mind and my heart, though, were racing.

Images. So clear they could be happening now. A dark road. One man holding Jimmy. The other hitting him. Again. And again. And again. I wanted to scream. I *had* to scream. But I couldn't. Livie reached over and squeezed my hand. Hers was trembling.

"Thank you, Doctor," the prosecutor was saying.

The jurors were passing the photographs back to the clerk.

"I have no more questions for you at this time."

The judge turned to the defense attorney.

"Counselor?" he said.

The defense attorney got up slowly. Walked slowly over to where the witness was sitting. Not a sound in the courtroom. Not a hint of a sound.

"Dr. Murray," he said at last. "We have established, at some length, that you are an expert in injuries caused by beating and other forms of violence. Is that correct?"

The doctor looked at him warily.

"Yes. I believe it is."

"And is part of your expert knowledge an ability to estimate the amount of force behind a blow?"

"I think . . ." Dr. Murray hesitated. "Relatively speaking, yes."

"Relatively speaking. I see. So . . . You, an *expert*"—he rolled the word around in his mouth—"an expert in these matters, are more certain about some things than others."

"Objection."

"Sustained. Careful, Counselor."

"Yes, Your Honor. So . . . You are *relatively* comfortable estimating the force behind a series of blows, based upon the effect they have had on the body you are examining. Is that correct?"

"Yes."

"And how much force would you say was behind the blows that hit James Arthur Davidson?"

"Quite a bit."

"Are you speaking relatively or absolutely?"

"Absolutely."

"Quite a bit of force. Which, in your *expert* opinion, could mean the person delivering the blows was in the grip of a powerful emotion?"

"Objection."

The judge leaned forward. "Is this line of questioning important to your defense?"

"Essential, Your Honor."

The judge thought for a minute.

"I will allow it, then. Overruled. You may proceed."

"In your expert opinion, Doctor, might the person who struck James Arthur Davidson have been in the grip of a powerful emotion?"

"Either that, or he was a strong person to begin with."

"Or both."

"Or . . . both."

"Thank you, Doctor. I have no more questions at the moment, but I reserve the right to recall this witness at a later time."

'Powerful emotion,' I thought. I could feel myself nodding. Yes. I bet I know where he's headed with this.

10

Dr. Murray came toward us up the aisle. He waved at Livie, Henry, and Mary Beth as he passed. They waved back.

The prosecutor called a Dr. Willoughby. A middle-aged man with glasses, a mustache, and a goatee was sworn in.

"What is your job, please, Dr. Willoughby?" the prosecutor asked.

"I'm an examiner with the state coroner's office."

"That's it," I heard Livie say. "Enough."

She leaned over and whispered to Henry and Mary Beth. They both nodded.

"I'm goin'," Livie whispered to me. "I can't take any more of this."

"I'll stay," I said. "I don't want to, but I will. See you at home."

She smiled. A weak smile. She was still trembling. For the first time, she looked old to me. She stood up, kissed the top of my head, patted my shoulder, moved past me into the aisle, and left. Heads turned to watch her go.

"... asked to examine the body of James Arthur Davidson?"

"Yes, I was," the witness said.

"And what did you determine to be the cause of death?"

"Massive hemorrhaging of the brain. The result of a number of blows to the head."

"How many?"

"Five, for sure. Possibly six."

"Was a specific one of those blows the direct cause of death?"

"That I cannot say. More likely a combination of one or more."

"What kind of instrument was used to inflict these injuries?"

"Something blunt, round, long."

"A baseball bat?"

"Smaller diameter. And ... we found traces of metal, not wood, on the body. In the area of the wounds."

"Small diameter. Long. Round. Metal. A tire iron, perhaps?"

"Objection. Hypothetical question."

"Not at all, Your Honor. Quite specific. I am trying to determine if, from a forensic standpoint, a piece of evidence in our possession could have been the murder weapon."

"Objection overruled. You may continue."

"Dr. Willoughby. Is the use of a tire iron consistent with the injuries you found on the head and upper body of Jimmy Davidson?"

"Yes."

"With which hand would you say these blows were administered?"

"The right hand."

"Why do you say that?"

"The victim was facing his assailant, and the blows were to his left side."

"Thank you, Doctor. And do you believe that anything else—anything beyond these blows from a long, round, metal instrument—contributed to Jimmy Davidson's death?"

"No. Nothing else."

"No further questions."

The defense attorney rose, stood looking at some papers on the table in front of his chair, stood a bit longer. Someone coughed. A rustle as people began to stir. Was he deliberately building tension? If he was, it was working. *I* was certainly tense.

He looked up from his papers and walked over to the witness stand.

"Dr. Willoughby. Since you can tell us so precisely that the instrument had a small diameter, the indentations in James Davidson's skull must have been deep." I winced. Henry looked over at me. "Deep enough for you to gauge this diameter."

"That is correct."

"Would you say that a great deal of force would be necessary to make such indentations?"

Again? For god's sake, do we have to hear this again?

"Yes," said the doctor. "A great deal of force."

"And would you say that, in order to cause such a deep indentation with such an instrument, the person holding the instrument was likely to have been in a highly emotional state?"

"Objection."

"Overruled."

"Doctor?"

"My work is scientific, not emotional. I can tell you *what* happened, to the best of my knowledge. I could not speculate as to why."

Score one for the prosecution.

"Thank you, Doctor. No further questions."

The prosecutor called a Dr. Armstrong, who turned out to be a staff physician at Davidson Memorial Hospital.

Doctors. Doctors. Doctors. They should be talking about healing. Getting well. Long lives. Bright futures. But no. Fractures. Clavicles and scapulas. Indentations in the skull. Death.

That's what this doctor was here to tell us. About death. Jimmy's death. When. Exact time. Circumstances. Making it all official. He was attacked. He suffered. He lingered a bit. He died. Methodical. Precise. Unassailable. I had to admire the way she'd done it, this prosecutor, but I hated having heard it. The details. The impersonal nature of it all. It would color my memories of Jimmy from now on. When he came into my mind, so would all of this. Would I have been better off not coming down here? Not hearing it?

No. Of course not. I owed it to Jimmy. And to myself? My vindictive self?

But all of that was irrelevant, I realized. If I hadn't come back, I would never have gotten to know Livie. I wouldn't exchange that for anything.

The doctor finished his testimony, and the prosecutor sat down. The defense attorney had no questions. The judge said we would take a brief recess.

And brief it was. Just time for a run to the men's room, ahead of the crowd. Into a stall where I wouldn't have to talk with anyone. A gulp of water from the fountain in the hallway and back to my seat. Martin, Mary Beth, and Henry came in after me. The others in the family had left for the day. The four of us nodded. Smiled. Sat.

The prosecutor recalled Sheriff Wright.

"The morning after Jimmy Davidson died," she asked, "what did you do, Sheriff?"

"Petie an' me, that's my deputy, we went on over to the scene of the crime..."

"Objection."

"Sustained. Jury will disregard that answer."

"Where exactly did you and your deputy go that morning, Sheriff?"

"To the place out there where the car Jimmy'd been drivin' was found. Mother's car, we'd learned by then. We'd had it hauled away, a course, already, over here to Bainbridge."

"Why was that?"

"Check it over to see if there was anythin' in it we needed to know about."

"Was there?"

"No."

"And why did you go out to the place where it had been left?"

"Take a look around. See what we could find out there might be helpful."

"Did you find anything?"

"We did."

"And what was that?"

"Tire iron."

A buzz rippled around the room.

"Where did you find this... tire iron?"

"Off in the scrub brush other side a the fence."

"You found it yourself?"

"I did. Sorta up beside a mesquite tree, in amongst some weeds."

"Could this tire iron have been thrown there from the area where Jimmy Davidson was attacked?"

"It could."

"How do you know that?"

"Took my own tire iron outa the backa my car. Same size. And throwed it that direction. Went on a bit further'n the other one had."

"I see. Did you find anything else in that area, Sheriff?"

"Few empty beer cans. Couple McDonald boxes. An' a ol' soda pop bottle. 'Bout all."

The prosecutor walked over to a table at the front of the room and picked up a clear plastic bag with something heavy in it. She walked back to the witness stand and handed the bag to the sheriff.

"Is this the tire iron you found near the place where Jimmy Davidson was attacked?"

"Yes," said the sheriff.

"How do you know that?"

"We put it in this bag an' marked it soon's we found it."

"And what did you do with it then?"

"Sent it right off to state forensics to be analyzed."

The prosecutor took the bag and put it on the table. She walked back to the witness stand.

"Tell me, Sheriff. What did the analysis by the state forensics lab discover on the tire iron you sent them?"

"Blood. Grease. Dirt. Fingerprints."

"What sort of analysis was done on the blood they found there?"

"DNA. Latest stuff."

"And did this test match the blood on the tire iron to that of any known person?"

"It did."

"And who was that person?"

"Jimmy Davidson."

Murmurs and a few gasps filled the courtroom. The judge tapped his gavel lightly.

"Order," he said.

The courtroom was quiet again.

"And the tests for fingerprints on this same tire iron. What did they find?"

"Two sets."

"Fingerprints from two different people?"

"Yes, ma'am."

"Please name those two people whose fingerprints were found on the tire iron."

"Well . . . There was Leroy Curtis."

"And the other?"

"Carey Plummer."

Noise erupted around me. Henry put his arm around Mary Beth and held her close. The judge banged his gavel, hard this time. Then again.

"Order," he said loudly. "I will have order, or I'll clear this courtroom."

The noise subsided.

"I will not caution you again," the judge said. "You will keep your reactions to yourself—all of them—or I will remove you. That sort of disruption has no place here. I hope I've made myself clear. Counselor?"

The prosecutor took a deep breath.

"Sheriff Wright," she said. "Let me just clarify this. The

tire iron on which the forensics lab found the blood of James Arthur Davidson was also found to have on it the finger-prints of two men. Leroy Curtis . . ."

"Yes, ma'am."

"And Carey Plummer, the defendant in this case."

"Yes, ma'am."

"I have no further questions, Your Honor."

The defense attorney looked up.

"No questions at this time, Your Honor. I reserve, as always, the right to recall this witness."

"Of course," said the judge. "It's nearly four-thirty. We will recess until ten o'clock sharp tomorrow morning."

He tapped his gavel, and we all stood.

Noise again filled the courtroom, everyone, it seemed, talking at once. Mary Beth was talking to Martin. Henry was talking to a man in the row behind us. I was dizzy, shaky inside. I wanted to be gone, away from here, without having to say a word to anyone.

Henry turned and caught my eye.

"I'll be going now," I told him. "See you tomorrow. I . . . Thanks for . . . keeping me a place. And for the lunch. For everything."

He nodded. "Only doin' what's right."

Mary Beth turned. I waved to her and Martin. They both waved back.

11

I made supper for us—chicken cacciatore, steamed broccoli, and fresh pasta I'd found at the Bainbridge Mall. Livie still looked drained and weary, but she was delighted with the meal. I was glad I could do something to cheer her up, at least a little. And cooking for her made me feel a little less desolate, too.

But . . . What could we say? She'd left the trial so she wouldn't have to hear those awful things, and I wasn't about to bring them up. We ended up talking, desultorily, about the courthouse, when it was built, the judge, fine man, according to Livie, moved to Bainbridge from Amarillo twenty years ago, lovely wife, pillars of the community, both of them. Even the weather, for god's sake. How fine the day had been. A strange conversation. I felt removed from her, at a distance, and I was sorry.

She finished the last of her second helping, wiped her

mouth, and put her napkin on the table. I stood up and took away our empty plates.

"Lord a-mercy," she said. "When you told me you wanted to help out with the cookin', I had no idea what a treat I was lettin' myself in for. That was truly delicious. Reckon the Chat-'n'-Chew won't be seein' much of us. Not if you can keep *this* up."

I put the plates in the sink. "I certainly can. And it's the least I can do, after you were good enough to take me in, like an orphan from the storm. Coffee?"

"Love some. To heck with whether I can sleep or not."

I poured us both a cup and sat across from her. We were at the old oak table in her kitchen. Imagine the conversations *it's* heard, I thought. I looked around, at the carved oak cabinets, the heavy cast-iron stove, the shelves lined with jars full of canned vegetables. Beets I could make out. And carrots. And lots of green things. It was a big room, but it seemed cozy to me. Comfortable to be in.

"So," said Livie. "That's that. Great meal. Now tell me how you're feelin'. After the day we've had."

"All right, I guess."

She sat looking at me, nodding, waiting.

"That the best you can do?"

I felt myself tensing involuntarily.

"What do you mean?"

"I *mean*, look at you. Every time I try to get through to you, I bump right smack into a wall. I've never met such a closed-up person in my life. Easy to be with. Likable. Can't help bein' fond of you. But you are sealed up tighter'n a drum. That a Northern trait—or one of your own?"

I laughed. She really *was* wonderful.

"Both, I think."

"You plannin' on keepin' it that way? Or you willin' to get underneath it some?"

I wasn't sure. I thought maybe I liked things the way they were. But . . . She'd been so honest with me. Told me such intimate things about her life. How could I justify holding her at arm's length from mine? I couldn't.

"Get underneath it, I *suppose*," I said. "Although . . . I don't know . . . I haven't had much experience with that."

"Why ever not? You got no family?"

"No. Practically none."

"Bless your heart. Poor lamb. What do you mean by 'practically'?"

"No brothers or sisters, for a start. I had an older sister—would've had. But she died. When she was three. Just after I was born. Rheumatic fever. My mother was never the same, so they tell me."

"Course she wasn't. How could she be?"

"She sat all day and stared out the window, is the way I understand it. Now we'd call it a major depression. I don't know what they called it back then. Anyway, they were scared to death I'd get the fever, too, so they sent me off to stay with my mother's sister. In Rhode Island. For almost a year, seems to me. Could've been longer. I was six months old when I went, and don't remember a thing about it. But maybe I . . . They say now, all these researchers, that those first months are the really formative time for a child, so maybe . . . Maybe a part of me *did* think I'd been abandoned. I do remember feeling, as soon as I could understand what feelings were, that my mother was . . . unapproachable.

"Oh, she loved me, there was no question about that. My father had been killed during the last days of the war. Okinawa. May of 1945, when I was two. I don't remember anything about him either. Just his picture. I wish I could have known him, but . . . I was all my mother had left, so of course she loved me. She just never . . ."

Where was all this coming from? I hadn't thought of any of it for years.

"Never what?" Livie asked.

I hesitated. Could I stop? Retreat and protect myself? No. Not now.

"Never . . . *talked* to me," I said. "Never sat with me and held me. At some point, I began to think that . . . That *I* was all I had to really depend on. That if I loved myself enough, took care of myself, I'd be all right. I wasn't going to abandon *myself*. Then . . . when my mother died, the year I turned fifteen, I knew I'd been right. You let yourself believe in people, you rely on them, and they leave you. Not intentionally, not always, but they leave you all the same."

It was coming out in a flood now. I couldn't have stopped if I'd wanted to.

"And Jimmy was the hardest of all. He was so young. He *couldn't* die before me. How could he? And I . . . It took a while, but I finally believed he loved me. I really did. I believed he wouldn't be changing his mind anytime soon, so I could . . . *count* on him."

She nodded. "You were right. You could."

"But he's *gone*."

"Which has nothin' to do with whether you could believe in him or not. Now does it?"

I looked at her, looked away, looked back.

"No," I said.

"It's *you* that's doin' the abandonin', now," she said. "Tryin' to tuck yourself away where life can't get at you."

I stared at her. Echoes in my mind.

"You said that to Jimmy, didn't you? At some point in his life."

She smiled. "At *several* points in his life. He was a lot like you, you know. Felt cut off from things. Had the idea he wasn't ever gonna . . . fit in. Difference was he'd come over here, stay all night, and we'd talk about it. At this very table. Hot chocolate, though, 'steada coffee."

"He talked to you . . . about being gay?"

"Course he did. Land sakes. It was too important *not* to talk about."

"And you didn't mind?"

"I loved him, Ian. What was there to mind?"

I nodded. "He was lucky. To have you."

She shrugged. "*I* was lucky. To have him. So . . . What about *your* grandparents?"

"Never knew any of them."

"Aunts? Uncles? Cousins?"

"One uncle was killed in a skiing accident. Freak thing. Another moved to Argentina, and no one ever heard from him again. So far as I know, I have one aunt left and two cousins. One in Florida and one in Vermont."

"Where's the aunt?"

"Rhode Island. I suppose."

Her mouth flew open.

"The one that took you *in*? When you were a baby?"

"Yes."

"And you *suppose* that's where she is? Don't you ever see her?"

"Not often, no."

"Uh-huh. 'Not often' in a pig's eye. You're fudgin' with me here. How long since you've seen her?"

"Maybe . . . twenty years."

She nodded, sadly.

"That's what I figured. And it seems mighty ungrateful of you. After what she did."

"I guess . . . it is. But that was a long time ago. A *long* time. And I can't imagine what we'd have in common, now."

Livie slapped the top of the table. The coffee cups jumped. So did I.

"That's a Yankee comment if I ever heard one. No Southerner'd ever say such a thing. The blood that runs through your veins is what you have in common. She's your mother's *sister,* for cryin' out loud."

"But what would we find to talk about? I doubt she knows anything about the theater. Travel. Good food."

Livie leaned back and raised her eyebrows.

"You are a pure *snob,* Ian McBride. As if those were the only things that mattered. You could talk to her about her *own* life. Her own disappointments. What it was kept her from knowin' about theater and good food and travel, if in fact that's the case. She's worked hard, I'll bet you anything, to get wherever it is she's gotten to. You could talk to her about *that.*"

I felt ashamed of myself. For the first time in . . . what? Fifty years? Forty, certainly. I *was* a snob. I did care more about my Aubusson rugs than my aunt Charlotte.

"You start in bein' this snooty when you were a kid?" Livie asked.

I smiled. What *was* it about her bluntness that endeared her to me rather than offending me?

"Actually," I said. "I think I did."

"How come?"

"That's . . . a good question. I . . . Maybe I thought . . . if people were going to look down on me for what I was, I could . . . I don't know. Preempt all that, I guess, by looking down on them first. Before they got a chance."

"Doesn't have to be one or the other of those, does it? You're better off, seems to me, figurin' out a way to look straight across at people; not up *or* down. How 'bout friends? You a snob there, too?"

I thought about that for a minute.

"Yes," I said.

"And how's it worked out?"

I thought again.

"Mixed, I'd say."

She nodded.

"And what about that first man you loved?"

"Trevor?"

"Did you look up, down, or straight across at him?"

This was striking too close to home. I felt myself wanting to avoid it. I got up and went to get the coffeepot. I looked at Livie, who laid her hand across her cup and shook her head. I poured myself a cup, put the pot on the counter, and sat back down. I surprised myself by starting to answer.

"A little of all three, I think. Mostly straight across, I guess. Although it's hard to say since we really didn't talk much. Certainly not like this. We did things together and talked about *that*. But not . . . this."

"And Jimmy?"

"Well . . . Jimmy was a kid. I kept trying to tell *him* what was what."

"He might've surprised you."

"Oh, he *always* did that. But . . . I understand what you mean. And yes. He might've. If I'd been more . . . aware. I'll never know, now. Will I?"

"Nope. We don't get to go back and change things. We don't have that luxury. All we can do is keep movin' forward."

I took a sip of my coffee.

"I do talk to him," I said. "To Jimmy. Sometimes."

She smiled. "And does he listen?"

"He does."

"And what do you tell him?"

"Oh . . . Things that are happening."

"And how you're feelin'?"

"Not so much."

"Try it. Next time. You might learn somethin', yourself."

12

The next morning at breakfast, it was Livie's turn to thank *me.*

"I'm glad you were able to let your walls down some," she said. "Real glad. Took some pesterin' on my part, for sure, but it was worth it, I think. I like bein' in closer to you."

"I like it, too," I said. "It feels good. A little threatening, I have to say, but . . . good."

We took both cars to the courthouse again, just in case. Martin came over with his parents. His wife had gone back to Houston the afternoon before, Henry told me, to see about their children. And Cinco had gotten a call during the night, some labor dispute, so he and Rosalind were flying out to El Paso that morning. Maybe it was selfish of me, but I was glad they were gone.

We sat as we had on Tuesday—our assigned seats, I thought with a smile. Martin farthest in, then Mary Beth,

Henry, Livie, and me. Fewer people in the courtroom that day. I could see some empty seats here and there. No one standing.

The trial began exactly at ten. I felt reassured by that, somehow, as if promptness and justice were neighbors on the scale of virtues. The first three witnesses had all been at the Bainbridge Cineplex on the night of October 19th. Each had seen Jimmy there. Each had seen Leroy Curtis and Carey Plummer there as well. The last witness, an extremely thin, extremely nervous woman, had been waiting in the parking lot for her daughter and two of her friends to come out of the movie.

The prosecutor's tone was soothing.

"While you were waiting there, Mrs. Vaughan," she asked, "what did you see?"

"Well . . . I saw Jimmy Davidson come out the door, get in a car, an' drive away."

"Are you sure it was Jimmy Davidson you saw?"

"Course I'm sure. Known him all his life. Used to come into my dad's pet shop a lot. Over in Kimberley. Look at the puppies an' play with 'em there. Loved dogs, but . . . couldn't have one at home, for some reason."

I heard a sound and looked down the row. Mary Beth had bowed her head. Punishing herself again, I guessed.

"In which direction did Jimmy Davidson go when he left the parking lot?"

"Out the back way, leads to what we call the shortcut, over to Kimberley."

"And did you see anything else, while you were waiting?"

"Sure did. Few minutes later, Leroy an' Carey came out the same door."

"Leroy Curtis and Carey Plummer."

"Yes."

"You know them, too?"

"Absolutely. They were in the same class as my oldest girl."

"What did they do after they came out of the movie house?"

"Both got into a car, Leroy drivin', an' went off after Jimmy."

"Objection."

"Sustained. Jury will ignore that answer."

"When Leroy Curtis and Carey Plummer left the parking lot, in which direction did they go?"

"Out the back way towards the shortcut."

"The same way Jimmy Davidson had gone a few minutes before?"

"That's right."

"Thank you, Mrs. Vaughan. I have no more questions at this time."

The defense attorney was on his feet immediately.

"What you are saying, Mrs. Vaughan, it seems to me, is that three people, all of whom had come from Kimberley to see a movie in Bainbridge, chose to go back to Kimberley on the same road. Is that correct?"

"Well, I . . ."

"Is that correct?"

"I guess it is."

"And you have no reason to think that the second car was actually *following* the first, other than that they went off in the same direction. Is that correct?"

"I . . . I guess so."

"No more questions."

Next came a woman named Phillips, on duty as admitting nurse when the ambulance crew brought Jimmy in. We established the time once more—10:23 P.M. Then she read from the itemized list of what had been found on Jimmy's person and in his pockets after he got to the hospital. Gold watch, brown leather band. Gold ring with small ruby. Ticket stub. Handkerchief. Comb. Car keys. Eighty-seven cents in change (mercifully not broken down further). Wallet.

Ah, yes. The wallet. Brown leather. Driver's license. Three photographs, not identified. Social security card. Library card for the Kimberley library. Membership card for a health spa in Washington, D.C. Card warning of an allergy to penicillin. Two twenty-dollar bills. One ten. Three ones. An AT&T calling card. Two credit cards—one American Express, one gold MasterCard.

Was that all?

That was all.

Was the nurse certain that the gold ring with the ruby, the gold watch, the $53 in cash, and the two credit cards were on Jimmy's person when he arrived at the Kimberley hospital?

Yes, she was certain.

The itemized list she had made that night was entered into evidence.

The defense attorney had no questions.

A man named Larson was sworn in. He stated that he was a baseball coach at Kimberley High School. Yes, Carey Plummer had been on his baseball team for two years, tenth and eleventh grades, before Carey dropped out of school. What position did he play? Pitcher. Which hand did he pitch with? Right. Did the coach ever see him pitch with his left hand?

Never. Did Carey Plummer bat right-handed or left-handed? Right-handed. Did the coach ever see him bat left-handed? No.

The defense attorney asked a few questions about ambidexterity, but his heart wasn't in it, I thought. He just didn't want all of these verifying witnesses to go by without his asking them *any*thing.

Henry had pulled some strings and gotten permission for us to have lunch in the courthouse cafeteria in the basement. We went down the back stairs and had soup and sandwiches in among the courthouse employees. Henry and Martin were soon engrossed in a problem that was upsetting Martin at work. Something about accusations of underpayment of royalties. All beyond me.

Mary Beth still looked pale and drawn. She was so upset about the reference to the puppies she could hardly eat. Livie tried to console her.

"You can't keep frettin' about what's past and gone," Livie said.

"But it's just one more thing that makes me know I failed him," said Mary Beth. "I knew how much he wanted a puppy. How happy it would've made him to have one to take care of. But I just . . . didn't want to be bothered. Too noisy. Yippin' around all the time. And the *mess*. That's what really did it for me. I just didn't think I could put up with the mess. So he never got to . . ."

Livie patted her hand.

"Don't do this to yourself," Livie said. "You did the best you could. I know that. And it's all anybody can ever do."

"My *best*," said Mary Beth. "What I did was fail my kids.

Just look at Rosalind. As unhappy in that marriage as she can be. Not that she'll talk about it with us. Not right now, in the middle of all this. Which is a shame. Poor Rosalind. Just can't ever seem to get a grip on bein' happy."

And never will, I thought. But I didn't say that.

Mary Beth took a tiny bite of her sandwich, then put it back down.

"Everything's in such a muddle," she said. "Martin's got to go on back to Houston tomorrow mornin'. Can't put it off any longer. So I was hopin' . . . Could you both come over for supper tonight? Spend a little time with Martin before he goes?"

"That would be great," I said.

"Don't forget now, Wednesday's my duplicate bridge night," said Livie. "And if I ever needed to clear out my brain with some good bridge, this is the time. Besides, Bernice'd never forgive me if I didn't show up. We been on a roll for weeks now, rackin' up those points. Plus . . . I just know all the others are dyin' to get a real close look at me. See how I'm holdin' up. I reckon I'll just go give it to 'em. You'll understand, won't you, Martin? If I go to my bridge 'steada comin' by for supper?"

He interrupted his conversation with his father long enough to say, "Course I will, Livie. You go on ahead and play. Jonelle and I'll be bringin' the kids up here to see everybody in a week or so anyhow. They couldn't understand why we wouldn't let 'em come this time, so we said we'd come back real soon and bring 'em along."

Coffee. Pie for dessert. Back to the courtroom.

———

The afternoon brought a series of Plummer's friends. Frightened young men and women. Boys and girls, really. Uncertain of what was expected of them. Awed by the courtroom and the judge and the power of the law.

Each time, the questions from the prosecutor were the same. Have you ever heard Carey Plummer make derogatory, disparaging remarks about homosexuals? The defense attorney objected the first time around. Said Plummer's opinions about homosexuals had no bearing on the case. The judge ruled for the prosecutor, and she continued.

A pattern emerged. Each witness had heard Carey Plummer call other boys names, like "faggot" and "homo" and "queer." Often? Pretty often.

One young woman, whose name was Brandy and who had dated Plummer for a while, said yes, she had seen him push a boy he'd been taunting. Push him? Yes, up against the schoolhouse wall.

Did he hit the boy? the defense attorney asked.

No, Brandy said. Just pushed him.

The last witness of the afternoon was the most devastating. A young man named Mark. A longtime friend of Plummer's. He definitely didn't want to be here. Looked everywhere but at Plummer himself. The prosecutor was gentle but firm.

"How long have you known Carey Plummer?" she asked.

"Long time."

"When did you first meet?"

"Fifth grade."

"How did that happen?"

"I moved here. My family did. From New Braunfels."

"And were you in the same class with Carey Plummer?"

"Yes, ma'am."

"Did you live close to his house?"

"Yes, ma'am."

"How close?"

"Next block over."

"Did you and he do things together after school?"

"Yes, ma'am."

"How often?"

"Every day, got to be. For a while."

"Weekends?"

"Yes, ma'am."

"What kinds of things did you do?"

"Baseball. Fishin'. Messin' around."

"Just the two of you, or with other boys?"

"Sometimes others. Sometimes just us."

"When you were with other boys, did you ever hear Carey Plummer say unkind things to any of them?"

"Yes, ma'am."

His voice was barely a whisper.

"Please speak a little louder. What did you say?"

"I said, yes, ma'am."

"Did you hear him say these things a few times, a lot of times, or all the time?"

"A lot of times."

"What, specifically, did he say?"

"Little black boy, we didn't play with him much, just saw him now and again. He'd call him 'nigger' when he'd see him."

"What else?" Still in that gentlest of tones.

"Couple boys—at our school?—acted like sissies, he'd call 'em 'queer.' "

"And?"

" 'Faggot' sometimes."

"And?"

He looked embarrassed. " 'Cocksucker.' "

"Did you also call those boys these names?"

"No, ma'am."

"Did other boys?"

"Some."

"Who did it the most?"

"Objection."

"Overruled."

"Who did it the most, Mark?"

"Carey did."

"And did Carey Plummer ever hit any of these boys he was taunting?"

The young man hesitated. Looked pleadingly around the room.

"Did he, Mark?"

"Yes, ma'am."

"Are you and Carey Plummer still friends?"

"No, ma'am."

"When did you stop seeing him frequently?"

"Tenth grade."

"Why did you do that? Stop being his friend?"

"I was afraid."

"Of what?"

"That sometime, he was gonna . . ."

"What?"

No answer.

"What, Mark?"

"Hurt somebody."

It was a long afternoon, and I was glad when it was over. Livie had stayed through it all this time, and it had clearly taken a toll.

"I'm wiped out," she said. "Let's go get ourselves a nap, before we have to head off for the evenin'."

We walked to our cars together, but when she roared away, I didn't even try to keep up with her. She was upstairs—sleeping, I hoped—when I got home.

13

We sat for a while in Henry and Mary Beth's huge den. The air conditioner was working overtime, and the room was very cold. Strange, I thought. They can't imagine living through a Northern winter, and yet they spend a fortune freezing themselves all summer long. Good thing Livie likes open windows.

Henry poured me a glass of the single-malt Scotch he and Martin were drinking. It was excellent, and helped to warm me up. Mary Beth sipped at a glass of wine.

"I really do hate to leave," Martin said. "Seems disloyal, somehow. To Jimmy. But . . . I just can't be gone any longer. Complicated business, oil and gas. Things come up need tendin' to, and I'm the one has to do the tendin'."

I nodded. What could I say? I didn't know a thing about the oil business. Nor about Martin and his feelings of loyalty, what they might or might not be. What I did know was that nothing in *my* life was important enough to make me leave. Nothing.

"You know what I wish?" Martin said. "More than anything else?"

"What's that?" I asked.

"That I'd had a chance to know Jimmy better. Well, I had the chance. But that I'd made better use of it. Had the sense to try to understand him."

"None of us did that, I'm afraid," said Henry.

"Except for Livie," said Mary Beth. "She's the best thing that ever happened to him."

She looked quickly over at me.

"Oh, I didn't mean . . ."

"It's okay," I said. "I didn't take the time, or have the sense, to understand him very well either. And I regret it now, too. The same as you."

"Even so," said Martin, "you knew him better than we did. More recently anyhow. So could you . . . ? Could you tell us about him a little? What he was like, after he left here?"

"I'd love to," I said.

Henry poured the three of us another glass of Scotch, and in the comfortable glow it produced, I reminisced. About Jimmy's talent. His wit. His love of life. I told them about Granada and the Alhambra and the astonishing impression Jimmy had made with his flamenco. Right there where it all began.

Mary Beth smiled, sadly, and shook her head.

"We tried to get him not to take those lessons," she said. "Over at Velma Skinner's little 'school of the dance.' But he just insisted. Rode off on his bicycle three times a week.

Right after school. Didn't really care whether we liked it or not."

"I was the worst one about that," said Henry, "I'm ashamed now to admit. Embarrassed the hell out of me, if you want to know the truth."

"Yeah," said Martin. "Me, too. All my friends razzed me about it somethin' fierce. And I never defended him. Not once. But . . . He just kept right on."

"I remember how he'd look at us," said Mary Beth, "when it'd come up. What was he . . . all of nine? Ten, maybe? And he'd look at us like he just couldn't comprehend why we didn't *get* it."

"Well . . . ," I said. "Other people did. They got it, all right. Seasoned professionals who've seen the best saw him and . . . knew what he had inside."

"He must've known it, too," said Martin. "All by himself, without anybody else to back him up."

"He did," I said. "He definitely did."

A middle-aged black woman came to tell us supper was ready. We went to the dining room, where bowls of soup, cream of asparagus, Mary Beth told me, were waiting for us. A very good wine—merlot, I thought—added to the mellowness I was already feeling.

"I loved hearin' you talk about Jimmy," Mary Beth said. "Made me wish I'd been a better mother to him."

"Mom!" said Martin. "You were a *good* mother."

"No. I wasn't. I wanted him to be what *I* expected of him. Not what he was. And now I see that what he *was* was so much more than I could ever've imagined for him. So . . . I got it all backwards. And I feel awful about that."

"You shouldn't," I said.

She looked over at me.

"You need to forget about what you didn't do and concentrate on what you *did*. You raised an extraordinary son. Maybe two, for all I know, but I'm sure about Jimmy. He was a fine young man, and you had to've had something to do with that. What you gave him. The way you loved him. My own mother had a really rough time, and I used to blame her for that. But not anymore. I loved her in spite of it all, I see that now. And Jimmy loved you."

She blinked her eyes and ducked her head.

How'm I doin', Livie? I thought.

The black woman, without a word, took away the empty dishes and brought in a standing rib roast and bowls of mashed potatoes and fresh peas.

"What do you think of the trial so far?" Henry asked me as he sliced into the rare roast beef, blood running out onto the platter.

"The prosecutor's terrific," I said, "that's for sure. I've never watched one in action before, but I can't imagine anyone doing it much better."

"That's what we were thinkin'," said Henry. He had finished serving the meat and sat back down. Mary Beth started passing the vegetables.

"I have to say the defense attorney's no slouch either," I said. "Which makes me wonder . . . How'd a kid like him ever get such a good lawyer?"

"Court appointed him," Henry said. "Volunteered, so they say. Likes to defend difficult cases. My *own* opinion is, high-profile case like this, he's after the publicity. But that's just me."

"Well . . . Whatever his motivation, he makes me very nervous."

"Why is that?" Martin asked.

"I'm afraid he'll find a way to play on the jurors' sympathies."

"And you're not feelin' any sympathy, yourself?" asked Mary Beth.

I turned to her, stunned.

"For *him*? After what we've heard these past two days? None. Absolutely none."

She took a sip of her wine.

"I'd feel better, I guess," she said, "if I didn't either."

"You mean you *do*?" I asked.

"Maybe it's 'cause I know him. Well, know *about* him. His family and all."

"What on earth are you talkin' about, Mary Beth?" said Henry. "You've never mentioned a word of this to me. Here I've been thinkin' you were as upset about it as I am."

She put her glass down hard on the table.

"Up*set*," she said. "Let's not get into a contest over who's the most up*set*. I'd run circles around the rest of you in *that* department. I'm the one made him come down here, don't forget."

"Fine," said Henry. "We're perfectly willin' to grant you that. You're way up there on the pinnacle of sufferin'. Fine. We know that. But where in the name of all that's holy is this *sympathy* comin' from?"

"From the fact that if they *do* convict him, if this terrific prosecutor does her job as well as it looks like she's goin' to, then they'll kill that boy. He'll be dead, just as sure as Jimmy is, and what will that have gotten us? Two dead boys instead of one. Two mothers who'll never know another day of peace instead of one. What's the good of that?"

"I can't believe this, Mom," said Martin. "He did a dreadful thing. To Jimmy. *And* to us."

226

"He did. And he should be punished. Lock him up so he can't ever do such a thing again. Take away his freedom. Let him think on what he's done every mornin' and every night for as long as he's got left. Fifty years? Sixty years of that? Day after day of regret and remorse? That would satisfy me."

"But what about justice?" Henry asked. "What about that?"

"Don't talk to me about justice," she said. "If there was any justice in this world, Jimmy would be alive, and we wouldn't be havin' this conversation."

14

I left Henry and Mary Beth's confident I knew how to get back to Livie's. It was soon apparent that I didn't. I took a wrong turn somewhere and found myself out on a dark road headed away from town. Two cars were coming along behind me, so at least it wasn't completely deserted. I was looking for a place to turn around when the first car sped up and pulled alongside me. I slowed down to let it pass, but it kept edging toward me.

Oh, my god, I thought. I swerved to the right, and it swerved toward me, almost touching my fender. I stepped on the brake and swerved some more, off the road onto the shoulder. The car parked at an angle in front of me. The other, which I could now see was a pickup, pulled up close behind me. In its headlights, I saw that the car blocking my way was green. A Camaro, no doubt.

Holy sweet Jesus, I thought. It this it? Is it my turn?

In that instant, terror took complete control of my mind

and my body. Terror and a feeling of utter helplessness. These were my last moments on this Earth, and I had no control over them.

Not true. I could at least prolong the inevitable. I pressed the buttons beside me, rolled up the windows, and locked all the doors.

Two men got out of the car in front. I glanced in the rearview mirror. A third was getting out of the pickup. They all had bandannas across their faces. They looked ludicrous. Kids playing Jesse James. I wished I could laugh, but I couldn't. My insides were churning, and my heart was beating so fast I thought it would burst. I almost wished it would. Surely that would be less painful than what was coming.

I watched the three men come closer to the car. I would have given anything for a magic staff I could wave and stop them in their tracks. But the staff was gone. Broken and buried deep in the ground. I was on my own.

They were at both front doors, rattling the handles, knocking on the windows. How on earth was I going to get through this? The knocking grew louder, angrier. Then, through the window on my side, I saw the end of the barrel of a pistol.

"Git on out here an' we'll talk," the man with the gun shouted. "Stay in there, an' I'll blow your head off. Don't think I won't."

As I looked at that cold dark circle pointed at me, instead of intensifying, my terror began to subside. My heart continued to race, but my mind steadied. I thought of Jimmy—what he had faced and how I was sure he had faced it—and a strange, almost otherworldly calm settled over me. If this *is* the end, I thought, so be it. I was still frightened, I was too much of a realist not to be, but I was no longer stricken with terror. I knew, somehow—from where?—that I wasn't going to let this fear defeat me.

How much time had passed? Seconds? Minutes? Hours?

"Don't try my patience now," the man said. "I'm not gonna tell you agin. Git on outa there, or I'll shoot, I swear to Christ I will. Straight through the window."

I unlocked the door and opened it. As I got out, slowly, I realized I'd been wrong. I wasn't helpless. I couldn't control what was going to happen. But I *could* control how I would face it. Take what they were planning to give. A beating, I now thought, since their faces were covered. If they were intending to kill me, they wouldn't care if I knew who they were.

Those ridiculous bandannas gave me courage somehow. I wasn't going to grovel, the way they expected. I wouldn't beg for mercy. That's what they wanted, and I wouldn't give it to them. They thought they were about to confront a sissy. I'd show them they were dealing with a man.

As soon as I was out of the car, two of them shoved me over onto the shoulder, off the road toward the fence. The glare from the lights of the pickup was blinding.

"We been followin' you ever since you got back down here," said the man with the pistol. "Just keepin' a eye on you, like. Mighty cooperative of you to come off out here by yourself like this, finally. At night, without old lady Davidson. You lost? Or out lookin' fer more queers to play aroun' with?"

"Lost," I said.

They chuckled.

"We wadn't sure," the man continued, "whut we oughta do 'bout you. Grown man seducin' a young kid like that. Settin' 'im off down the road to perdition. We just wadn't sure. Then when we seen you in the courtroom, sittin' right there with the fam'ly, big as you please—actin' like you thought you belonged . . ."

"Don't keep runnin' off at the mouth like that," said another. "Jesus! No need to talk so damn much. Just git on with it, 'fore somebuddy comes by."

"Ain't nobuddy comin' by out here," said the first. "Not this late. An' course there's a need. Whole point is to teach 'im a lesson, an' we gotta make sure he knows whut the lesson *is*. That he *don't* belong. Not down here, corruptin' decent people with his heathen ways."

I was shaking in spite of myself. Nobody coming by? My courage was waning. Damn! What in god's name was I going to do? What could I say? I had no idea what might set them off, so I decided I'd better say nothing.

The big talker with the gun turned back to me.

"All's we gotta work out now," he said, "is how hard to hit you, an' how long. To make sure that lesson's been learned. You two grab aholt of 'im."

They moved toward me.

"I don't think I'd do that if I was you," said a voice behind us.

"Holy shit!" one of them said.

Sheriff Wright stepped into the area illuminated by the headlights, his pistol in his hand. His deputy was behind him, carrying a rifle.

Oh, thank god, I thought.

"Words by themselves are what's known as a threat," the sheriff said, slowly and quietly. "Puttin' hands on somebody is called battery. Much worse offense. Aggravated by the fact you been wavin' a gun around. Now, which is it you want me to charge you with?"

No one answered.

"Put that pistol down, Tommy Joe," said the sheriff. "An' git those damn fool bandannas off your faces. All a you."

No one moved.

"You know better'n to mess with me," the sheriff said. "You waitin' for me to remind you why?"

The man laid his pistol on the ground. They all took the masks off their faces. None of them was the man from the motel. Why was I glad?

Sheriff Wright nodded.

"Elmer. Sammy Lee. Damn buncha useless, ignorant bums. Drunks an' loafers, ever' one a you. You the ring-leader, Tommy Joe?"

The big talker ducked his head and looked at the ground.

"Course you are," said the sheriff. "Don't know how to keep yourself outa trouble, do you? Don't have the least idea. Well, you're in it now, all right. The bunch a you. This, an' a little matter of a car-burnin'? I'm gonna make real sure you don't screw aroun' with people anymore for a long time to come. Petie?"

"Yessir?"

"Pick that pistol up off the ground an' then go call for the van. Mr. McBride an' I'll keep a eye on these idiots."

When he got back, the deputy took the key to the green car and moved it so it no longer blocked mine. In a few minutes, the van arrived. The driver and a man with him loaded the three assailants, now subdued and vaguely pathetic, into the back and drove away.

"Don't forget to read 'em their rights," the sheriff said. "Soon's you get 'em inside."

The deputy nodded and got in his car. He drove off after the van.

I turned to the sheriff.

"I can't tell you how glad I was to see you," I said.

He smiled. "I can just imagine."

"It was certainly a surprise, to all of us. I don't think anyone heard you drive up."

He nodded. "Practice."

He looked at me hard. "You okay?"

"Better now," I said. "Thanks."

"What on earth you doin' off out here, anyways?"

"Took the wrong road, looks like. And then couldn't find a place to turn around."

He nodded again. "We been watchin' those fools watch you. Just waitin' for a chance like this, I reckon."

"Good thing you were."

He smiled. "Only doin' my job. Sorry we had to let you go through as much as you did, though. Had to radio for Petie, first off, to come back me up. Then I wanted to wait till they'd actually threatened you, verbally an' with the gun, while we was there to listen in. But . . . It's over now."

"I hope so."

"Oh, I'd say it is. We'll keep on keepin' our eyes open, though, just to be sure. An' you stop by my office tomorrow, when you get a chance, so we can take down a statement from you. About what happened here."

"I could come over during the noon recess. I'll be right across the street."

"That'd be fine. Want me to show you the way back to Livie's?"

"Please."

After I had parked in the driveway, I waved to Sheriff Wright, who drove on off. As I walked up the steps to the back porch, Livie came out through the kitchen door.

"I just heard about it," she said. "Are you all right?"

I was astonished.

She put her hand on my arm.

"Lord have mercy," she said. "You poor man. You hurt at all?"

"No," I said. "I'm not hurt. I'm fine, really. But . . . *How* could you have heard? We just left there and drove straight here."

"You're *sure* you're all right. You're not backin' off from me again, now, are you?"

"No. I'm fine. I promise. Not a scratch. Still pretty twitchy inside, but they didn't get around to hitting me. Thank god. I . . . How could you possibly find out so fast?"

She smiled. "These Internet people think they're the ones invented instant communication. Ha! They just never lived in a little Texas town. Gerald Finney heard it on his CB radio, called his wife, who checked with Wanda over at the jailhouse in Bainbridge and then called me. I'd just that minute gotten home from my bridge game. Mighty efficient, wouldn't you say?"

I shook my head. "Very."

"I got some cocoa heatin' up on the stove. You come right in here and tell me all about it."

Much later, as I went from the bathroom back to bed, I glanced out the front window. Across the street, I could see a car parked under the streetlight, the word SHERIFF in bold letters across the side.

15

I slept well and woke refreshed, the opposite of what I would have expected. I looked out the front window. There, across the street, was the sheriff's car. I felt well taken care of. The queasy sense of uneasiness that had surrounded me as I went to sleep was not gone entirely, but going. My courage in the face of danger had surprised me. I hadn't expected it, but was glad.

When I got downstairs, Henry and Mary Beth were in the kitchen with Livie, sitting at the table. As I walked through the door, Mary Beth got up and came over to hug me.

"We're *so* sorry," she said. "What an awful thing. I just feel so . . ."

"Please don't worry," I said. "Your sheriff was great. Came to my rescue, just like the cavalry."

She went back to her cup of coffee.

"Ernie been out there all night?" Henry asked.

"Looks that way," I said.

He nodded.

"Thought we'd all go over together this mornin'," he said. "The four of us."

I smiled. "Fine with me. If it's all right with Livie."

"You bet it is. I'm not lettin' you outa my sight today. Nor tonight. Like it or lump it."

I smiled again.

"Like it," I said.

"Besides," said Henry, "that son of a bitch . . ."

"Henry!" said Mary Beth.

"Leave me alone, Mary Beth. I'm in no mood for niceties. That son of a bitch Leroy Curtis'll be testifyin' today, so they tell me. Streets all around'll be packed. No one'll be wantin' to miss *that*."

"Why would he be willing to talk about it like this?" I asked.

"Nothin' to do with whether he's willin' or not," said Henry. "*Has* to. Part of his 'plea bargain' with the state. Bargain with the Devil, if you ask me. The bastard."

Mary Beth clicked her tongue.

Sure enough, the courthouse square was mobbed once again, demonstrators for both sides waving their placards. The eerie chaos I was becoming accustomed to. We pushed our way through—reporters crowding around, shoving microphones at us, hoping for a comment—went into the courtroom, and took our seats.

Just after ten, the prosecutor called Leroy Curtis. He was ill at ease sitting there in the witness stand. Uncomfortable in what looked like a new sport coat and tie. He was in *prison* now, for god's sake. For life. Why didn't he come in stripes, like the skunk he was?

I could barely look at him. Young. Fresh-faced. A little

cocky. Well, why not? His future was set, bleak though it might be. At least he knew *he* wasn't going to die anytime soon.

I hated him.

The prosecutor walked over and stood beside him.

"On the night of October 19th of last year," she asked, "what did you do?"

"Got off of work, there at the fillin' station, 'bout five, an' went by to get Carey."

"Carey Plummer?"

"That's right."

"Where did the two of you go?"

"Over here to Bainbridge. Burger King first, for a hamburger, french fries. Then to the picture show."

"Which one?"

"Which place, or which picture?"

"Which place."

"Cineplex, out at the mall."

"What time did you arrive there, you and Carey?"

"Little after seven. Picture s'pose to start at seven twenty-five. Somethin' like that."

"What time was the movie over?"

"Nine-thirty. Round there."

"What happened as the two of you were leaving?"

"We seen this faggot walkin' out through the lobby."

A wave of whispers hissed around the room.

The judge tapped his gavel.

"Order," he said.

"Whom did you see walking through the lobby?"

"Jimmy *David*son. Back in town. Been a few years ahead of us at school, but everbody knew he was a fairy. Didn't *mind* people knowin', seemed like. Like he was *glad* about

237

it, 'steada bein' ashamed like he oughta been."

"When you saw Jimmy Davidson in the lobby after the movie, how did it make you feel?"

"Objection. This witness's feelings are irrelevant to the case being tried here."

"Overruled. Please continue."

"When you and Carey Plummer saw Jimmy Davidson in the lobby of the Cineplex, how did it make you feel?"

"Pissed. Good an' pissed. Way he looked, first of all, struttin' aroun' like that. But that wadn't the worst of it."

"What was the worst?"

"Had the nerve to *flirt* with us, Carey an' me. Tried to pick us up."

"The hell he did." I only realized I'd said it aloud when heads started turning toward me. Including the judge's. He looked stern. The others look startled.

"I've warned you before," the judge said. "I will not have outbursts like that in my court. The next person who ignores my warning will be removed from this courtroom. Proceed, Counselor."

She nodded.

"Why did you think Jimmy Davidson was trying to 'pick you up'?" she asked.

"Way he smiled at us."

"Did he say anything to you or to Carey Plummer?"

"No."

"He only smiled."

"Yeah."

"Did he smile at other people in the lobby?"

"I didn't notice."

"But he may have."

"He might. Yeah."

238

"So his smile to you and Carey Plummer may have been one of greeting, nothing more."

"No. It was more, all right. More like a come-on. An' it pissed us off."

"You've had experience with looks like that? These 'come-ons'?"

His face flushed a bright red.

"No! Course not. No."

"Then you may have been mistaken."

"No, I wasn't. He . . ."

"Let's move on to what happened next. You and Carey Plummer were there in the lobby, feeling 'pissed' at Jimmy Davidson for whatever reason. Is that correct?"

"Yeah."

"And what did you do then?"

"We seen 'im walkin' out the door . . ."

"Jimmy Davidson?"

"Yeah."

"And?"

"An' we said, 'Less go get 'im. Show 'im he can't do that to us.' "

" 'We'? You both said the same thing at the same time?"

"Well . . . No."

"Then, one of you said it first."

"Yeah."

"Which one?"

"I did."

A buzz all around the room. A tap from the judge's gavel.

"And did Carey agree with what you said?"

"Yeah, he said, 'Less go git 'im.' "

"What did you do then?"

"Went through the door he'd left out of . . ."

"Jimmy Davidson."

"Yeah."

"And then?"

"We seen 'im gettin' into a car. Fancy one. Pissed us off even more. So we went over an' got in my ol' clunker an' took off after 'im."

I glanced at the defense attorney. He bowed his head and rubbed his temples.

"Which way did Jimmy Davidson go?"

"Out the back way. Shortcut over to Kimberley."

"What happened then?"

"We waited till we got to this long dark stretch, between the towns like, an' then I come up fast behind 'im an' blinked my lights. Sure enough, he pulled over to see what was up. Big mistake."

If I could have pointed my finger at him and struck him dead, I would have done it in a second.

"He pulled over. Just pulled right over an' got on out. 'What's wrong?' he says. 'You need some help?' "

Did *they* need help? Dear lord in heaven. I loved Jimmy more at that moment than I ever had before. Did *they* need help?

"And then?"

"Me an' Carey we walked over towards 'im. 'You all right?' he says. 'We're *fine*,' I say. 'But you ain't.' 'Whadya mean?' he says. An' that's when I told Carey to grab 'im."

"Did he?"

"Yeah. He did."

"And what did you do?"

He hesitated.

"What did you do, Leroy?"

"Made *my* big mistake."

"What was that?"

"Shoulda just socked 'im a couple times. With my fists, but . . ."

"But what?"

"I was . . . How could I explain it? Somethin' just took over inside, you know? Seein' 'im there. Scared look all over 'is face. I liked that. Seein' 'im scared. *We* was in control, you know? We could do anything we liked with 'im. So I . . ."

He hesitated again.

"You what?"

"I opened up my trunk an' got out the tire iron I keep there. For fixin' flat tires? Just reached in an' got it. I'll never know why I did that. Shoulda just smacked 'im some. With my fists. But I didn't."

"What did you do with the tire iron you'd taken from the trunk of your car?"

"Hit 'im in the side first, while Carey was holdin' onto 'im. Then in the . . ."

"Go on."

"Then in the head."

I thought I was going to faint.

"Once? Twice?"

"I don't know. Few times. Then Carey says, 'Let me.' "

"Carey Plummer said to you, 'Let me.' "

"Yeah."

"Meaning?"

"Meanin', 'Let me hit 'im, too.' "

The courtroom was absolutely silent, as if no one were breathing. I was outside myself, disconnected. Able to hear, but too numb to feel.

"What did you do when he said that?"

"I give 'im the tire iron an' then hung on to . . . Jimmy,

best as I could, he was kinda slumpin' by then. An' Carey give 'im a few whacks."

"On the head."

"Yeah."

"Do you know how many?"

"Not for sure. Two or three."

"Was there a reason Carey stopped hitting Jimmy Davidson?"

"Yeah."

"What was it?"

"We seen a car, headlights comin' down the road. From Bainbridge goin' towards Kimberley. Way off. I dropped . . . Jimmy, an' he fell on the ground. Carey flung the tire iron over the fence into the cow pasture other side. We turned out the lights in both cars real quick, an' then hid behind mine."

"And?"

"Car went right on by. Didn't even slow down."

"What did you do next?"

"We jumped in my car an' tore off home."

"Thank you, Mr. Curtis. I have no more questions at this time."

The prosecutor sat down, and the defense attorney stood up. He walked over to the witness stand.

"Mr. Curtis," he said. "Let me just double-check a couple of things you said here. When you saw James Davidson in the theater lobby, you realized that you were angry. Is that correct?"

"Yeah."

"Please say 'yes' or 'no'."

"Yes."

"And you assumed that Carey Plummer was angry as well."

"Didn't assume nothin'. He was pissed. Same as me. I know he was."

"How did you know that? Did he say to you, 'I'm pissed'?"

"No. But I . . ."

"Did he raise his fist? Make an angry gesture?"

"No. But I could tell."

"How?"

"I could just tell."

"Based on no word or gesture, you could tell. I see. And sometime after that, you told us, you suggested that you and Carey Plummer 'go get' James Davidson. Is that correct?"

"Yes."

"And it was only after you had suggested it that the thought occurred to Carey Plummer. That he agreed to go along with you."

"No. It was both of us. We both said, 'Less go git 'im.' "

"But you said it first."

"Yeah."

" 'Yes' or 'no,' please."

"Yes!"

"And after you had said it first, Carey Plummer then said, 'Okay. Let's go.' "

"Yes!"

Very clever, I thought. Just 'Let's go' this time. Not 'Let's go get him.' *Very* clever.

"The two of you had gone to the theater in your car. Is that correct?"

"Yes."

"So you drove that car from the mall across the shortcut toward Kimberley."

"Yes."

"It was your idea to catch up to James Davidson's car, blink your lights, and try to get him to pull over. Is that correct?"

"Yes."

"Did Carey Plummer suggest any of these things? Did he say, 'Let's try to catch up with him'? Did he say, 'Blink your lights and see if he'll pull over'?"

No answer.

"Did he?"

"He didn't. No."

"After James Davidson had stopped and you were all out of your cars, *you* told Carey to grab James Davidson. Is that correct?"

Told, not asked.

"Yes."

"Did Carey say, 'I'm going to grab him so you can hit him'?"

"No."

"No. *You* said, 'Grab him so *I* can hit him.' Is that correct?"

"Yes."

I almost felt sorry for the boy. Confronted with a mind that could run circles around his own.

"Only after all of this—only after you had first suggested that the two of you 'go get' James Davidson, after you had driven up behind him, pulled him over, gotten him out of his car, told Carey to grab him—only after you had gotten a tire iron out of the trunk of your car and severely injured James Davidson yourself—only then did Carey Plummer say, 'Let me.' Is that correct?"

"Yes."

"Was Carey Plummer upset when he said, 'Let me'?"

"Yes! Yes, he was upset."

"Because *you* were. Because of the emotion created by *your* actions. By *your* own anger."

"Maybe. Yes. I don't know."

"Thank you, Mr. Curtis."

The defense attorney turned and walked to his seat. The prosecutor was on her feet instantly.

"A few more questions, Your Honor, if I may."

"Certainly, Counselor. Proceed."

"Mr. Curtis, was there any time during all of this when Carey Plummer said, 'Let's *not* do this'?"

"No, ma'am."

"When you said, 'Let's go get him,' meaning Jimmy Davidson, did Carey Plummer ever say, 'No, let's *not* go get him'?"

"No, he didn't."

"When you were all standing beside the road, and you said, 'Grab him,' meaning Jimmy Davidson, did Carey Plummer ever say, 'No, I don't think we ought to grab him'?"

"No."

"And after Carey Plummer had grabbed Jimmy Davidson and you had gotten the tire iron out of your trunk, did Carey Plummer ever say, 'Don't hit him with that'?"

"No, he didn't."

"No. He didn't. Instead, he continued to hold Jimmy Davidson while you beat him and then he said, 'Let me.' Meaning, '*You* hold him and let *me* beat him now.' Is that what happened?"

"Yes."

"Thank you, Your Honor. This concludes the prosecution's case."

A sigh, like air escaping from a punctured tire, moved around the courtroom.

"We will adjourn for lunch," the judge said. "The defense will begin promptly at one-thirty."

16

I told the others about my appointment with Sheriff Wright. This reminder of the previous night's events distressed them all.

"Want me to go over with you?" Livie asked.

"No," I said. "Thanks anyway, but I'll be fine. It's just across the street. You go on down to the cafeteria with Henry and Mary Beth."

The square was packed with people, many of them waving placards. For both sides. I pushed my way through the crowd, grateful that no one seemed to be recognizing me. It was a different story at the sheriff's office. Reporters swarmed around the door.

"Mr. McBride!"

They all shouted at once.

"We've just heard about . . ."

"Can you tell us . . . ?"

"When did you . . . ?"

I'd learned my lesson well, so I took their questions as calmly, patiently, as I could.

Yes, I was fine.

No, I had not been hurt.

No, I didn't think I could discuss anything more about it until after I had talked with the sheriff.

Did I know who the men were?

I thought I'd better not comment on that.

What was my reaction to the trial so far?

That I was pleased with the professionalism of everyone concerned. And if they would excuse me, I had an appointment with the sheriff.

He wasn't there, but an efficient young man, wearing a suit not a Stetson and boots, wrote down all I could remember about the night before.

"What should I say to those reporters outside?" I asked him.

"As little as possible," he said. "You don't want to jeopardize the case in any way."

I laughed. "No. I sure don't."

"Just refer 'em to us. We got people here know what to say."

I thanked him and left. Outside, I was polite but firm. Can't say much right now. Sorry. You'll have to ask the sheriff's office about that. I appreciate your being so understanding. Now if you don't mind, I've got to get back to the trial.

No hope of grabbing any lunch on the way, but I wasn't really hungry.

We settled in, and the other attorney began presenting his case for the defense. He called teachers, a Boy Scout troop leader, a coworker at Wal-Mart, a couple of neighbors. They all said the same thing: Carey Plummer was a good boy. Not a brilliant or an especially gifted one, by any means, but a good boy who tried hard. Temper, yes. But he usually kept it under control. Usually? the defense attorney asked. Yes. Unless he was provoked.

A frustrated prosecutor kept pleading irrelevance, to no avail. The judge was being *very* lenient, it seemed to me. Giving the defense the same leeway he'd given the prosecution. In the process, my worst fears were being realized. This attorney's strategy wasn't to challenge the facts, which were pretty near irrefutable. He was going for the heartstrings instead. Well, he wouldn't get anywhere close to mine.

Late in the afternoon, he recalled Mr. Larson, the baseball coach, who said yes, he remembered Carey Plummer well.

"Carey was a pretty good pitcher, you know," he said. "Really was. Some real ability there. But . . . there was others that were better, those years. Another year, Carey mighta *been* a starter, yeah. But . . . not then."

"How long did he play on your team?"

"Two years. Tenth, eleventh grades. Didn't come back his senior year, though. No word about it to me. Never did know why."

Henry and Mary Beth dropped us off at Livie's house. A few reporters were gathered out on the sidewalk.

"Don't they ever give up?" Livie asked.

"Apparently not," I said. "Why don't you go on in, and I'll see if I can get rid of them."

"All right, I guess. But . . . you holler if you need me."

I was cordial—it didn't cost me anything—but noncommittal. I wished I could help, but the sheriff's office had said no. Not just yet. They made notes, took pictures, filmed me as I talked, and left.

Supper was easy. I poached a piece of fish Livie had defrosted, and we sat for a long time talking. About my career—New Haven to Seattle to Chicago to Washington. Her childhood. A lot about her father, the department store owner.

Memories. So many memories.

After a while, I excused myself and went upstairs. I stood for a few minutes beside the telephone in the hallway near my bedroom. I picked up the receiver and dialed. Calling card number. Directory assistance for Providence. Then the number they gave me.

"Aunt Charlotte?" I said.

"Y-e-e-s?"

"It's Ian McBride."

"Oh, my heavens. I couldn't think who that was calling me 'aunt.' "

"Your nephew."

"Of course it is. I know that *now*. But . . . Wait a minute till I can sit down. Get off of there, Clarissa." I heard a scrape and a rustle. "Cat was on the chair. Well, now, Ian. You'll have to forgive me if I'm a little bit rattled here, but . . . It's the most amazing coincidence. I just saw you on the news, not two hours ago. Some men tried to beat you up, they said. In *Texas,* was it?"

"Yes. And they didn't succeed."

"Even so, you must have been terrified."

"Oh, I was. But the sheriff came riding to the rescue."

"Sheriff!" she said. "Right out of John Wayne. But it's all terribly sad, really. That fine young man, murdered like that. I've thought about you so often. And him. Ever since last fall, when I first started hearing about it. It seems . . . Even though these things keep happening, this one was especially shocking. That people could *do* such a thing. And you're down there, I guess. For the trial?"

"Yes. I just . . . had to be here."

"I understand. Someone you loved. It must be quite an ordeal, though. For *all* of you."

"His family's been wonderful to me. They've sort of taken me in. Like you did, right after I was born."

"Imagine your remembering that. It was a happy time for me, I hope you know that. And you've been very important to me ever since."

I felt a twinge of pain. She'd loved me, and I'd gone away.

"It seems inappropriate somehow to say this," she continued, "since the circumstances are so sad, but I've been glad to have a chance to see you. On the television. Hear about your career. They showed some more of it, just the other night. After the trial started."

"Did they?"

"They did, and I have to say, it was impressive. All the things you've done, and how well you've done them."

I laughed. "Big fish in a small pond, I'm afraid."

"If you say so. But that's not what it sounded like to *me*. All those awards."

"Three. Only three."

"Never mind. To be told you're the best there is at what you do—three times—is something to be proud of. And so good-looking. Distinguished, just like your father. From what I could see, you look a lot like him."

"I do?"

"More mature, of course. He was only twenty-seven, you know, when he . . . But I do see a lot of him in you."

"I'm glad. I wish I could've known him."

"He was a fascinating young man, no question about it. Smart. Ambitious. A number of us thought he was quite the catch. Not just your mother."

"Do you think . . . ? After this trial is over, could I come see you? Talk about him some? And about Mother? And you, of course. How you've been. There's so much I don't know."

"I'd love that, Ian. You come stay as long as you like. There's an apartment for guests here at the retirement home. I don't have the room myself, you understand. I'm in an efficiency now, just big enough for me. But you could stay there, close by. Would that be all right?"

"Yes. Of course it would."

"Just let me know when, so I can call for a reservation."

Livie was in the parlor, reading. She looked up as I walked through the door.

"I've just talked to my aunt in Rhode Island," I said.

She actually applauded. Clapped her hands and smiled.

"And?"

"She was charming. Delighted to hear from me. I told her I'd come up and see her after I leave here."

"Well, now, isn't that the best news I've heard in a long, long time."

"Thanks to you."

"No, indeed. Thanks to *you*. People can give all the advice they like. It's the ones that act on it deserve the credit. I'm proud of you, Ian. Mighty proud."

17

Friday morning, I looked out the front window. No reporters. Just the sheriff's car in its familiar spot across the street. Before going back to the kitchen for breakfast, I went over to say hello. He rolled his window down all the way.

"Good morning," I said.

"Mornin'." He touched the brim of his hat. "Nice one, too, looks like."

"Yes, it does. Are you getting any sleep at all?"

He smiled. "Some. You okay?"

"Oh, yes. Knowing you're on the job, I've been sleeping like a baby."

He nodded. "Good," he said. "Glad to hear it. Makes one of us, at least."

I laughed.

"Anything else I need to do?" I asked. "About the . . . other thing?"

"Not right now. We'll let you know."

"I just want to thank you again. For everything."

"No need," he said, but he was smiling. "No need a'tall. We got our problems down here, can't say we don't. But shirkin' our responsibilities isn't one of 'em."

"Not where *you're* concerned, that's for sure. Well . . . I'll go on in and eat now. Nice to see you."

He touched his hat again.

"You, too."

The fickle press paid little attention to me as Livie and I pushed our way up the steps and into the courthouse. My story was old news by now, I guessed, and they were stampeding off in another direction. Henry and Mary Beth were already in their seats when we got there.

The first witness for the defense that morning was Norma Plummer, Carey's mother. After she was sworn in, she waved to her son. He waved back.

"How many children do you have, Mrs. Plummer?" the defense attorney asked.

"Six. There's Alma, Carey, sittin' over yonder, Sadie, Nellie, Bert, an' Jo-Jo. Joseph. He's my baby."

Oh, god, I thought.

"The oldest is . . . ?"

"Alma. She's twenty-three."

"And how old is the youngest?"

"Jo-Jo's five now. Well, five and a half."

"And Roy Plummer was the father of these children?"

"Yes, sir. Every one."

"Where do you live, Mrs. Plummer?"

"Trailer park. Out on the West Bend Road."

"In Kimberley?"

"Yes, sir. Just outside."

"Do your children still live with you there?"

"All but the oldest one, Alma. She's livin' with a man down south of Bainbridge now."

"How many rooms does this trailer have?"

"Four. Kitchen, livin' room, two bedrooms. Plus the bathroom."

"One bath?"

"Yes, sir."

"Seven people in four rooms, with one bath?"

"Just six of us now, with Alma gone. My husband died. Little more'n four years ago."

"What was the cause of his death?"

"Tied in to his drinkin', they said. Somethin' about his liver."

I was growing more irritated by the minute. What possible relevance does this have to Jimmy's death? I wondered. Why isn't the prosecutor objecting? Doesn't want to seem unsympathetic, I'll bet.

"What kind of work did your husband do, when he was alive?"

"Odd jobs, when he could get 'em. None of 'em ever lasted for long."

"Was what he made enough to support the family?"

"Not hardly. We barely scraped by, most of the time. Kids doin' paper routes, baby-sittin', stuff like that."

"Did you work yourself, Mrs. Plummer?"

"Couldn't. *Can't.* My back's real bad, you see. Don't get around too good. An' sure can't stand for long."

"Weren't there places you could go for help? Especially after your husband died? Disability benefits? Child support?"

"In *this* state? Ha! You gotta be kiddin'. They give me chicken feed. I needed it if anybody ever did, an' they give me chicken feed."

"So who supported the family, after your husband died?"

"Carey, mostly."

"Part-time jobs?"

"At first. After school an' weekends. But that wasn't nearly enough, so he had to quit school an' go to workin' full-time."

"Where was that?"

"New Wal-Mart's. Here in Bainbridge."

"Doing what?"

"Stock clerk. Cashier. Buncha different things."

That's what this was about. A campaign to make us feel sorry for the little bastard. Sad life. Hard times. Savior of the family. Oh, my goodness. I was irate. Why in god's name wasn't the prosecutor objecting? I would've been happy to, but I knew the judge would throw me out of the courtroom.

"Did your husband and Carey get along, Mrs. Plummer?"

"Not too good, no."

"Ever?"

"No, sir."

"Why was that?"

"Well . . . Roy was real fond of Alma. Thought the sun rose an' set in her. So maybe . . ."

"Maybe what?"

"Maybe he just used up all his patience—an' affection—on her. An' didn't have much left over for Carey."

"How about the other children?"

"Liked some. Didn't like others."

"Which of them did he dislike the most?"

"Carey. Hands down."

"How did your husband demonstrate his dislike for Carey, Mrs. Plummer?"

"He'd pick on 'im somethin' awful. All the time. Criticize

'im. Nothin' Carey ever did was good enough. Now Alma, he'd praise her to the skies. Her cookin', her grades, everthing she did, seemed like. But never a good word for Carey."

"Did you ever ask your husband why he did this?"

"A little. At first. Said he had to make a man outa Carey. Toughen 'im up, like. Couldn't go easy on 'im or he'd never be able to make his way in the world. Said the world was a tough place. Showed no mercy to anybody weak."

"What was Carey's reaction to this treatment?"

"Never gave up tryin'. Always kept hopin' the next thing he did'd be the one made his daddy proud."

"And did he succeed? Did he ever make his father proud?"

"No."

"What about Carey's temper? Did he lose it sometimes?"

"Oh, yes. Like his daddy in that respect. He'd go along, doin' his best, gettin' wound up tighter an' tighter all the time. An' then he'd explode. All of a sudden."

"What did he do when that happened?"

"Throw things mostly. Dishes, a lot. Smash 'em up against the wall. Thank god for yard sales. I had to always be on the lookout for plates an' things at two bits, buck apiece."

"Did Carey ever hit anyone when he was angry, Mrs. Plummer?"

"Not in the fam'ly, no."

"Outside the family?"

"Sometimes, yes. Got into fights at school, in the neighborhood. Just regular growin'-up stuff for boys, I always thought."

"Did your husband ever hit his son, Carey?"

"Some. For punishment, you understand. Spanked Carey whenever he was naughty."

"Was that often?"

"Could be."

"More when your husband had been drinking?"

She hesitated.

"Mrs. Plummer?"

"Yes, sir. More when he'd been drinkin'."

"Did your husband call Carey names?"

"Yes, sir."

"Quite a bit?"

"Pretty much all the time."

"What sorts of things did your husband say?"

"Called 'im useless. Lazy. Incompetent. He liked the sound of that one. Incompetent."

"What was your reaction to all of this?"

"Learned to stay out of it."

"Why was that?"

"Didn't want 'im turnin' on *me*."

"And he would have, if you'd defended your son?"

"Oh, yes. He surely would."

"Did your son Carey ever talk with you about the way his father treated him?"

"Talk? Whadya mean? I seen Roy doin' it. Carey didn't have to tell me about it."

"No. I mean, did Carey ever say how he *felt* about it?"

"Felt?"

"He didn't tell you if he was angry, or sad, or upset?"

"Heavens no. He wasn't no whiner. He'd just take it like a man an' go on about his business."

"I see. Thank you, Mrs. Plummer. Thank you very much for your help. I have no more questions for you at this time."

The prosecutor got up slowly. Walked slowly to the witness stand.

"Mrs. Plummer," she said, her voice soft and kind. "Do you know how Carey felt about homosexuals?"

Mrs. Plummer narrowed her eyes. "You're not on Carey's side," she said. "Are you?"

"I work for the state of Texas, Mrs. Plummer." Still soft. Still kind. "And I'm on the side of truth. All I'm asking you to do is to tell me the truth. Nothing more. Nothing less."

"Oh, well then, in that case . . . Indeed I *do* know how he felt . . . about those people."

"Objection. This is a secondhand opinion."

"It is her opinion that is being asked for, Counselor. Overruled."

"Mrs. Plummer?"

"What does 'overruled' mean?"

"It means the judge would like you to answer the question. How did Carey feel about homosexuals?"

"Oh. Couldn't stand 'em. Course not. Healthy, God-fearin' boy in that respect."

"How do you know he felt this way?"

"Well! He'd point 'em out to me when we'd be goin' someplace, an' tell me how he couldn't stand 'em."

"What did he call them?"

"You mean, what were their names?"

"No. What words did he use to describe them?"

"Oh. 'Faggot' usually. That was his favorite. An' the longer one. The one I tried to get 'im to stop usin'. Told 'im it wasn't nice to say in mixed company. But he kept right on."

"What word is that?"

Her eyes got wide.

"You don't expect me to *say* it!"

"Just this once. Just so we'll know what it is, for sure."

"Well . . . 'Cocksucker.' God forgive me."

"And would Carey appear to be upset when he would see these people and call them these names?"

"Well, course he was upset. They was sinners, if what he said about 'em was true. An' I had no reason to doubt it was. They was sinners, with no right to be out walkin' around among decent folks like that. Course he was upset. I was, too."

"But not upset enough to call them names."

"No. That isn't my way. That's more how the menfolk do. I just think it."

"You . . . just think it. Thank you, Mrs. Plummer."

The defense recalled Leroy Curtis. Same sport coat. Same tie. Same cocky smile.

"Let's go back," the defense attorney said, "to the night you and Carey Plummer were in the lobby of the Cineplex out at the Bainbridge Mall. When you saw James Davidson there, what was he doing?"

"Walkin' past us."

"And what did he do as he walked past you?"

"Flirted with us."

So *what*? I thought. Jesus, Mary, and Joseph! What if he did? This is *it*? *This* is the defense? Making Jimmy a participant in his own destruction? So he smiled. Maybe he flirted. So what?

"And this made you and Carey Plummer very angry. Is that correct?"

"Objection. He cannot speak for Carey Plummer."

"Sustained."

"But James Davidson's flirting with the two of you made *you* very angry."

"Royally pissed."

"And would you say this anger took control of your actions?"

"Objection."

"Overruled."

"Please answer, Leroy. Did this anger take control of your actions? Cause you to do the things you did later?"

"Course it did! We couldn't let 'im do somethin' like that to us."

"Thank you very much. I have no more questions at this time."

The prosecutor walked over to the witness stand.

"You say, Mr. Curtis, that Jimmy Davidson was walking *past* you. Did he stop?"

"No."

"Did he say anything to you? Anything at all?"

"No."

No, I thought. He's stuck there. He can't say Jimmy talked to them. Witnesses could deny that.

"All he did was walk by and smile."

"It was the way he smiled. We both knew what it meant."

"You *assume* you knew."

"We knew, all right."

"Based on the experiences with being 'picked up' that you say you've never had. Is that how you knew?"

"We knew, all right."

"No more questions."

The defense attorney called a Dr. Carruthers. Tall. Thick glasses. Supremely self-assured.

"What is your profession, Doctor?" the attorney asked.

"I am a psychiatrist."

Deep, resonant voice. The result of training, I was willing to bet.

"And where do you work, Dr. Carruthers?"

"I am head of the Center for the Study of Sexually Based Criminal Behavior. Executive director actually."

"Where is this center located?"

"In Richmond, Virginia."

"How long have you been its executive director?"

"For nine years."

"And what is the mission of this organization?"

"We gather together the best minds in our field in order to study the relationship between sex—feelings about it, past experiences, repressions—and behavior that is criminal in one way or another."

"Have your studies found that there *is,* in fact, such a connection?"

"Most definitely."

"Is one of the aspects of sex that you have studied in this way homosexuality?"

"Certainly. It is a large and growing part of our group of concerns."

A tight, purse-lipped almost-smile flickered across his mouth.

"What, in your opinion, is making this area 'grow,' Doctor?"

"The fact that, in recent years, the homosexual agenda has been thrust so forcefully into the public arena."

"By whom?"

"By all these homosexual activists. The so-called 'gay rights' lobby."

"What has been the effect of their activities?"

"To stir up the very strong, very powerful feelings against homosexuality which had lain dormant for so many years. That was a more peaceful time. A time of 'live and let live.'

Of respect for the sensitivities of those who would prefer not to be confronted with this kind of thing, so foreign to their own lives. Now, everywhere you look, there is 'gay' this and 'lesbian' that. Right in everyone's faces."

I was shaking so hard I could barely continue to sit there. Livie reached over and patted my arm.

"And you believe, Dr. Carruthers, that this increased activism is reflected somehow in criminal behavior?"

"It certainly is. Young men just beginning to explore their sexuality, looking for ways to guide it into proper channels, are bombarded with all these disturbing images of men holding hands, kissing each other, parading down the Main Streets of America. The less mature, less . . . steady among them are too often provoked, beyond their control, into acts of violence against the ones who are stirring up these feelings, which would otherwise have been left to lie undisturbed deep inside them."

"Your center has conducted studies that verify this connection?"

"We have indeed."

I could see the prosecutor busily making notes.

"Have you talked with the defendant in this case, Dr. Carruthers? Carey Plummer?"

"I have."

"And what were your conclusions?"

"This is a young man from a difficult home, emotionally unsteady as the result of cruel, at least verbally abusive, behavior on the part of his father. A young man with a temper he has tried, sometimes unsuccessfully, to control. Then, one evening, he was faced with what he considered to be the ultimate insult. A known homosexual, a 'gay' man, flirted with him in a public place. Implied that he thought Carey

Plummer himself would be interested in this kind of activity. Later, when Carey and his friend found themselves alone beside the road with this homosexual, something inside Carey snapped. His deep feelings of revulsion were heated to the boiling point, and he lashed out. With tragic consequences."

'Found themselves'? 'Tragic consequences'? Where did this man come from, anyway? Out of a cave somewhere?

"Would you say, Dr. Carruthers, that this 'lashing out' was premeditated?"

"By no means. No, no, no. He was provoked. By an action that threatened his view of his own masculinity. His was a violent act, yes. But not a premeditated one. It was not carefully planned and carried out. It was an action of the moment. Stirred to life by forces he could not control."

"You believe, then, Dr. Carruthers, that had James Davidson not flirted with Carey Plummer, the events that transpired that evening would not have occurred?"

"Yes. I do believe that."

I closed my eyes. This man was a horror. I wished I could bring his smug world, full of smug theories, crashing down around him. Bury him under piles of rubble. But I looked again, and he was still there, that maddening smirk still fluttering around his mouth. *He* was more dangerous than Carey Plummer any day.

"Thank you, Doctor," the defense attorney said. "We appreciate your coming here to help us in this way."

He went to his seat.

The prosecutor sat for a moment, staring at her notes. She got up finally and walked over to the witness stand.

"Dr. Carruthers," she said. "I am, for once in my life, practically speechless. I hardly know where to begin. But I must, so . . . May I ask what your organization's 'studies' are based on?"

"Certainly you may. On reviews of the literature. Conferences. Symposia."

"But *not* on actual clinical examinations. Rigorous, comprehensive, impartial analyses of real people. Extensive interviews, evaluations, testings of hypotheses. This is not what you do at your . . . 'center'?"

He looked at her almost pityingly.

"If you understood the workings of academia, you would know that the sorts of things you describe are done in other places. It is our job to evaluate the results of these widely scattered activities."

"Through the lens of your own preconceptions."

"I beg your pardon?"

"Tell me, Doctor. Do you have a particular bias against homosexuality yourself?"

"No, not at all. I view it quite objectively, as I do all things."

"I see. You will forgive me if I failed to notice that. Let me ask you then, objectively, are there other criminal behaviors that you believe to be 'provoked' by the actions of the victim?"

"Oh, yes."

"For example?"

"Well . . . rape, of course."

"Of *course*, Doctor?"

"Yes, the . . ."

"Objection. This line of questioning is immaterial to the facts of this case."

"Overruled. This is an unusual case, Counselor, requiring patience on all our parts, if we are to arrive at a just conclusion. The prosecutor was patient with your examination of this witness. You will now be patient with hers. Please proceed."

"Thank you, Your Honor. How, in your opinion, Doctor, do women provoke those who attack them?"

"By their actions. Their way of dressing. Their . . . air of availability."

The defense attorney put his head in his hands.

"The women are, in some way, 'asking for it.' Is that what you're saying?"

"In layman's terms, yes."

"Thank you, Dr. Carruthers," the prosecutor said. "I believe that will be all."

Atta girl, I thought. You're a genius. Quit while you're ahead.

The defense attorney stood up.

"Just a few more questions, if I may, Your Honor," he said.

"Certainly," said the judge.

"I'd like to go back to the *important* part of your testimony, Doctor, for a minute. The crucial question here is one of premeditation. Whether Carey Plummer planned ahead of time to abduct and murder James Davidson. Remind us, Dr. Carruthers, what you have concluded—after a rigorous, comprehensive, impartial, *personal* analysis of Carey Plummer—about this crucially important matter."

"On the night in question, Carey Plummer's actions were most definitely not premeditated. They were the unfortunate result of the accumulation of a lifetime of disappointment and neglect, aggravated by what we must call a 'proposition' that offended him."

"Thank you, Doctor. This concludes our presentation of the defense in this case."

"Thank *you*, Counselor," said the judge. "We will recess until one-thirty sharp, at which time we will hear the closing statements of both sides."

18

Everyone else stood up, but I couldn't move. Livie bent down and kissed the top of my head. Henry pulled me up and put his arm around me. Mary Beth held my hand.

"If that's a sample of what you an' Jimmy've had to face all your lives," said Henry, "then I admire you both more than I can say. For carryin' on in spite of it."

He squeezed me and took his arm away.

"Didn't you feel like *strangling* him?" Livie asked.

I laughed.

"Oh, yes," I said. "But he'd've just come back from the grave to tell me I was living proof of how psychotic gay men are."

They all smiled, relieved.

"He met his match in your 'terrific' prosecutor, though," said Mary Beth. "Didn't he?"

"He sure did," I said. "*Her* I could hug."

"Look," said Henry. "There's a little Italian place out east of town. Far enough away it shouldn't be too crowded. Let's go out there."

A smooth Chianti calmed us all down. Livie, her dead-eye intuition in full swing, got us off on a discussion of bridge, a game we all played. The strategies that worked best when she played duplicate. How splendidly she and her partner were doing lately. The excitement of a game well played.

Henry described, in detail, a slam he'd made at a friend's house a couple of weeks before. So difficult, and therefore so satisfying, that he remembered every card. He told the story well, and we all nodded and laughed. He paid the bill and drove us back to town. I was glad to have avoided all discussion of what Jimmy may or may not have done that evening.

Soon after one-thirty, the prosecutor began her closing statement.

"Your Honor. Ladies and gentlemen of the jury. The very able defense attorney has tried hard to shift our attention—away from Jimmy Davidson as the victim of the violence that led to his death over to Carey Plummer as a victim of the harshness of life. Those of us who are the least bit aware learn very early that life *is* harsh, sometimes uncaring, often unfair."

As with her opening statement, she walked up and down in front of the jury, looking each of them in the eye. Her delivery was calm and measured.

"If Carey Plummer had a hard life, we can all feel pity for that. But if everyone who had a hard life lashed out each time he saw someone who was different from or better off than he, none of us would be safe. Ever. The fragile bonds of civilization would be ruptured, torn asunder, and we would sink back into chaos and anarchy.

"But we will not sink." Her voice rose. Became more impassioned. "We are protected by the glory of the rule of law. And what the rule of law says is that when someone does what he knows he must not do, he will be punished. Swiftly, surely, in accordance with the severity of his unlawful act."

She stood for a minute, looking from one juror to the next, then resumed her walking.

"Civilization. The rule of law. Learning to live together. We *must* learn, if life as we know it is to continue. However harsh our upbringing, however bleak our surroundings, we must learn to see that there are things in our lives we can control, and things we cannot. We must learn to live with the things we *cannot* control, and to take responsibility for those we can.

"Here again, the defense has tried to divert our attention. To subtly shift the responsibility away from the act itself to the 'provocation.' You had only to listen carefully to hear that there *was* no provocation. Jimmy Davidson smiled. That is all anyone has said that he did. He was not responsible for his own death, Carey Plummer was responsible. The word 'provocation' cannot be stretched so far as to include killing someone because he smiles at you.

"No. Carey Plummer is responsible for what he did. And because he is, he must be punished to the fullest extent of the law. For that to happen, he must be convicted of the crime with which he has been charged—murder in the first degree.

"What this means, in plain language, is that Carey Plummer intended to murder Jimmy Davidson. And this is, in fact, the case. He saw Jimmy at the movie theater, he was offended by what he saw, he had a lifelong habit, as you have heard, of lashing out at what offends him, and he proceeded to do just that.

"And *why* did he do this terrible thing?" The emotion in her voice was intense. "Why did he hit this gentle, generous-hearted young man—who, after all, had stopped to see if he could be of help? Why did Carey Plummer feel he needed to beat Jimmy Davidson so brutally? Not for any kind of material gain. As our witnesses have told you, he didn't touch the watch, the gold ring, the cash, the credit cards Jimmy Davidson had with him.

"So it was not for what Jimmy Davidson *had*, but for who he *was*. Carey Plummer lashed out the way he did because he had an uncontrollable hatred of homosexuality, and Jimmy Davidson was a gay man. An open, honest, unapologetic gay man. This hatred had festered inside Carey Plummer for years, as you have heard. It consumed him to such an extent that, when an opportunity presented itself, an opportunity for which this hatred had been preparing him for years, he committed the act he had been moving toward for so long. He struck at what he hated—and killed it.

"This was murder with intent, ladies and gentlemen. Murder in the first degree. The verdict I ask you to return in this trial. If you do that, you will give yourselves a choice, something Jimmy Davidson did *not* have those last hours of his life, from the time he stopped on a dark, deserted road to see if the people signaling him were in trouble. Returning a verdict of guilty—of murder in the first degree—gives you, the jury, two options. Life imprisonment. Or what I will ask for in the sentencing phase of this trial, the death penalty. The punishment this vicious act deserves.

"Why will I ask for the death penalty? To keep the concept

of responsibility alive. To demonstrate to all of us—the accused, the jury, the spectators here in this courtroom, the world at large—the essential link between cause and effect. 'If I do this, then that. If I kill, I must pay the price set by the society in which I live.' And in this state, the price for the willful, brutal taking of another person's life is death. Set by our duly elected legislature, approved by our federal Supreme Court, enforced by our governor. This penalty is not a vindictive act on society's part. It is a punishment that fits the crime. Death for death. Cause and effect. Do not kill, and we will not kill you. Take another person's life, and we will take yours. Equal, almost poetic justice.

"So does this case warrant that ultimate punishment? Oh, yes, it does. This act was willful, and it was brutal. Carey Plummer struck. The man he struck died. We call this murder.

"I ask you—for the sake of Jimmy Davidson's family, for the sake of Jimmy himself, for the sake of justice—I ask you to find Carey Plummer guilty of murder in the first degree."

She stood for a minute, then went and sat down. The defense attorney walked over to the jury box.

"Your Honor," he said. "Ladies and gentlemen of the jury. Please take a moment to look at the defendant in this case. He has been sitting at that table, day after day, so you have surely glanced at him from time to time. But look at him now with particular care.

"This young man, Carey Plummer, started out with the same hopes and dreams we all have—for people to care about him, for some freedom from want and anxiety, for a life that seems to matter. As the years went by, he had to watch those hopes and dreams wither and die. Pushed far beyond his reach by an uncaring world he could never quite comprehend.

"He loved baseball. Wanted more than anything to be a famous big-league pitcher. This wasn't an entirely foolish dream on his part because he *was* good. Just . . . not good enough. Not even good enough to be a starter for his high school team.

"He knew he needed an education to have any hope for a worthwhile job, a way out of the grind his family had been caught in all his life. And his grandparents before that. And *their* parents before that. He applied himself and did all right in school. Not brilliantly, but . . . all right. Then that dream faded, too. Like all the rest. His father—the father who had always denigrated his abilities, put him down every chance he got, told him he was no good—this father died, of acute alcoholism, and left a hole that Carey had to fill, as breadwinner for his family. And what job was he able to find? Something interesting? Something fulfilling? He ended up as a clerk at Wal-Mart. No more school. No more baseball. No more dreams of a way out of this rut. No more hope.

"This was his life. Day after day. Month after month. The 'better' young people in town saw him as a loser. Someone going nowhere. And they weren't interested in being his friend. Those who *were* interested were other losers like himself. Aimless, undisciplined, angry young men.

"Then one night, purely by chance, someone came into this bleak, monotonous, hopeless world. And that someone was James Arthur Davidson. Handsome, well-dressed, confident, driving his mother's expensive car. A Mercedes convertible. As far from anything in Carey's world as the moon. This privileged, talented young man could go anywhere, do anything. Everything was ahead of him. What was ahead for Carey Plummer was more of the same.

"So he snapped.

"But—please remember—after, and *only* after, his friend had set the chain of events in motion. It was his friend who suggested they follow Jimmy Davidson, stop him, beat him. The friend initiated all of these actions. Carey Plummer only went along.

"Still, at the time of the beating—not before, but at the time—Carey was indeed greatly disturbed. Not because Jimmy Davidson was a homosexual. Or not *only* for that. But because Jimmy Davidson's life was everything his own was not. Angry? Oh, my, yes, he was. And that powerful emotion took over and led him to do something he would never have done if he'd been thinking clearly.

"Carey Plummer did not set out to kill Jimmy Davidson—or anyone else. He didn't think about it, plan it, lie in wait for him. None of the evidence you've heard here has shown any kind of premeditation. What it does show is a young man stretched by fate and an unkind world beyond his capacity to endure. So he lashed out at what he couldn't have—comfort, ease, privilege, a bright future.

"What he did was awful. He knows that and regrets it. Regrets it with all his heart and will continue to do so for as long as his life lasts. As long as you permit it to last. He should be punished. Yes. He should be made to pay. He knows that. But he should not be put to death. *His* death is not the way to heal the wounds of the death he helped to cause. Let him live. Let him learn what he can as he matures. Let him become a better person.

"He is not innocent. How many of us are? He, specifically, is not innocent of the death of James Arthur Davidson. But he is not guilty of murder in the first degree. Ruthless, cold-blooded, premeditated murder. That's not what we are talking about here. We're talking about a young man overcome by anger, loss, hopelessness, who, while in the grip of that powerful, blinding emotion, did a terrible thing.

"That thing has a name—a very specific legal name. Manslaughter. 'The unlawful killing of a human being without malice aforethought.' *This* is the key. The crucial, vital key to this case. 'Without malice aforethought.' There was none.

"Think about this carefully. Think about this young man—tossed around by the vagaries of fate, made to feel worthless by a harsh, even cruel father, misunderstood. Try now, while you still can, to understand. Give him that, at least.

"Give him a chance, now. Show him the compassion we all are capable of.

"Let your decision be manslaughter, not murder in the first degree.

"Let Carey Plummer live."

The courtroom was hushed as the defense attorney went back to his seat. The prosecutor rose. Walked toward the jury.

"I am allowed a rebuttal to the defense attorney's statement," she said, "and I am glad. It gives me the opportunity to remind you of a few things.

"Compassion? Carey Plummer showed no compassion to Jimmy Davidson. None.

"Let him live? Would that he had let Jimmy Davidson live.

"No malice? The malice was in his homophobia. His hatred, nourished for years, of people who are gay. We don't know *why* he felt this way. But we do know, from testimony you have heard here, that he surely did. And when the opportunity arose for him to act on that hatred, he did so, ruthlessly and without mercy.

"And no premeditation? Of course there was. The murder of Jimmy Davidson was not premeditated in the sense that Carey Plummer identified him, resolved to kill him, and then lay in wait for him. No. Jimmy appeared as a target of opportunity. But the premeditation had been building for a long time. Through all those years of aggressive behavior against people he knew, or suspected, to be homosexual. The taunts, the name-calling, the physical blows. *This* was the premeditation.

"None of the emotional pleas you have heard just now can change the cold, hard facts. Carey Plummer saw Jimmy Davidson, he followed him, he beat him, he killed him.

"Intent. Brutality. Death.

"First-degree murder.

"Nothing less."

19

Months of planning. Days of drama. And now it was over. The two attorneys were packing up their briefcases, the defendant was on his way back to jail, the jurors, now filing out, would begin their deliberations on Monday morning. They were not to talk with anyone about the case, the judge had reminded them before he left the room. They must avoid newspapers, television, radio. Into a kind of vacuum for the next two days. Lucky them. I needed something like that, too.

I had decided, just before I went to sleep the night before, that I would drive down to San Antonio for the weekend. I'd heard it was a beautiful city, only three hours away, and I was eager to put some distance between me and these two odd little towns—for a while, at least. Get away from TV cameras and reporters and sheriffs parked outside. All of it too much. I was willing to bet Livie could use a break as well.

It was still early, not quite four o'clock, when we got back to the house, so I packed a few things and told Livie good-bye. She said she would call the sheriff, let him know he could skip his all-night vigil for a while.

I stopped for supper along the way and arrived in San Antonio around nine. I checked into a hotel right on the river downtown. Very elegant. Very expensive. Part of the river flowed across one corner of the lobby. Amazing. From the balcony of my room on the third floor, I could look down at the river, moving majestically along on its way to who-knew-where. Walkways on both sides of the river were illuminated, and the lights of the city twinkling above me were reflected on the surface of the water. I could hear the unmistakable brassy harmonies of mariachi. The hotel behind me was flashy and modern, the river and the music timeless.

I went back into the room and called Zena. She asked immediately about the car-burning and my narrow escape. She'd seen both on the newscasts and in the papers. She'd been horrified, she said, almost distraught, but hadn't known how to reach me. I apologized for my self-absorption, and had to assure her over and over that I hadn't been hurt either time. That I was all right. We spent most of the next hour talking about the events of the past week. Only a week? More like a lifetime. I told her all about the trial, much of which she already knew. About Livie. About the rest of Jimmy's family. She was sympathetic, interested in everything, concerned about how I was holding up. She was a good friend, and I missed her. I began thinking I'd be glad to get home.

The next morning I woke early and took great pleasure in rolling over and going back to sleep. I got up, eventually, and went out to look around. The city *was* beautiful. I found the Alamo interesting, the old Spanish missions scattered around even more so. But what I loved most was the river, down below the level of the city and its tall buildings. A quiet, shady, tranquil other world, cut off from the noise and bustle and mundane concerns of the crowds rushing by up above. Down here, people moved more slowly, in harmony with the gentle flowing of the river. Here there was peace. And a chance to think.

I spent hours wandering along the riverwalk, sitting now and then on benches I came upon, watching the boats, the ducks, the people. I saw flickers of recognition in a few faces, but no one came near me, for which I was enormously grateful. I had dinner at a restaurant that served Mexican food but played Spanish music. Flamenco. I thought at first it was going to be too painful, that I would have to leave. But gradually I began to enjoy it, to appreciate once more the unquenchable passion at its heart—and in its soul.

On Sunday, I took a longer, more meandering route back to Kimberley. Through hilly country that had a beauty all its own. Stark and haunting, but inviting. I stopped often to get out and walk and listen to the wind.

When I finally got to Livie's house, it was nearly five. I took her out to the Hook, Line, and Sinker for supper, read for a while after we got home, and went to bed.

20

Monday was a disjointed, trying day. Livie and I drove over in my car around nine-thirty, parked, and walked to the courthouse. We were shown to an anteroom, where Henry and Mary Beth were waiting. More strings, I decided. The jury was deliberating, Henry said. No idea how long they would be. Mary Beth had brought her needlepoint. Henry paced. Livie and I flipped through the stack of magazines we found on a table. A dispiriting selection. Teenage beauty tips. Hot vacation spots. Old *National Geographics*.

Henry stuck it out for about an hour, then went off to see some people. Mary Beth was to call him on her cell phone the second we heard any news. The three of us just waited.

Around noon, we went down to the cafeteria. We sat at a table, almost immobilized. They both seemed to be feeling the way I was, completely wrung out. We'd been through too much, heard too much, said as much as we could say about it.

Back upstairs, we waited, wandered around the room, read. A little after two, a man came to tell Mary Beth that the jury was on its way. We could take our seats in the court-room. Mary Beth pulled her cell phone out of her purse and dialed as we walked.

"Henry," she said. "Get over here quick. They've decided."

Word was clearly spreading outside. People were pouring in, finding seats. We went and sat in ours.

A clerk entered and said, "All rise."

We did. Henry came rushing in and stood beside me.

The judge walked to his chair. He sat. We sat. The judge spoke to the clerk, who nodded, went to the door on our right, and opened it. The jury began filing in—slowly, sol-emnly. They sat.

The courtroom was utterly silent. I seemed to be holding my breath.

"Has the jury reached a verdict?" the judge asked.

A man stood up. "We have, Your Honor," he said.

He handed a piece of paper to the clerk, who took it over to the judge. The judge looked at it, handed it to the clerk, who took it back to the foreman.

"What is your verdict?"

"Guilty, Your Honor. Of murder in the first degree."

Noise all around me, the judge banging his gavel—in vain. Henry raised his fist and said, "Yes!" Mary Beth bowed her head. Livie simply nodded. I felt . . . glad, but not elated. What was wrong with me?

As the judge continued to bang, loud and hard, the noise subsided.

"We will recess until Wednesday morning," he said, once the room was reasonably quiet. "Ten o'clock sharp. At which time we will begin the sentencing phase of this trial."

We stood up. Mary Beth walked past me and put her arms around Henry. He held her close and laid his cheek on the top of her head. She moved back and looked over at Livie and me.

"I'd like to just go on home now," she said. "If you don't mind. We'll talk tomorrow."

Livie patted her arm, I leaned down to kiss her, and they left.

Outside was pandemonium. Demonstrators shouting, placards waving, reporters shoving.

"We have to talk to them," I said to Livie, "or they'll just follow us home."

She nodded.

I said a few words to every reporter who approached me. Yes, I was satisfied. Yes, it was a relief to have this part of the trial over. Yes, I was glad the men who had accosted me had been arrested. No, I had no idea if they were involved in the burning of my car. No, these events had not given me a bad impression of Texas. Things like this could happen anywhere.

Did I believe that? I wondered. Probably not.

I looked around. I couldn't see Henry or Mary Beth anywhere. Had they gone out through another door? To avoid all this? If they had, they'd be sorry when they got home. I remembered the scene at their house that night, so long ago, when I had tried to see them.

Livie was being dignified and charming. Of course. I couldn't hear what she was saying. More microphones were shoved in my face. Yes, I would be staying for the sentencing. Yes, I hoped it would be the death penalty.

Exhausting and maddening as the ordeal had been, it was the right decision. We gave them what they wanted as they swarmed around us. Then, like a school of fish responding to some mysterious communal signal, they all turned and rushed away. I looked back up the steps. The prosecutor was coming out the door of the courthouse. The mob surrounded her. Livie and I were able to walk, unmolested, the three blocks to where I'd parked my car.

"How are you feeling?" I asked her on the way.

She smiled. "Like an old dishrag been through too many scrubbin's."

Back home, we were glad again for having faced up to the monster. No reporters. No vans. Not even a sheriff. Just the quiet, peaceful street.

I heated up some leftovers, and Livie drove off to a meeting of her hospital auxiliary.

"The sooner I can get back to a normal life," she said, "the happier I'll be."

I took a book off the shelf in the library and sat down to read. *Lord Jim*. Guilt and regret. It was hard going. I had a feeling the doorbell had rung a couple of times before I actually heard it. I went through the front hall, turned on the porchlight, and opened the door. A young woman was standing there.

"Mr. McBride?" she said.

"Yes."

"I'm Alma Plummer. Carey's sister?"

I wanted to close the door. Not slam it in her face, maybe, but certainly close it. Shut her off from my life. She looked so tired and sad, though, I couldn't do it.

"Yes?" I said.

"I saw the car was here and some lights on, so I kept on ringin'. Hopin'..." She was twisting her hands together. "I'm sorry to bother you like this, but... Could I talk to you, just for a minute?"

Say no, I thought. Say no, close the door, leave all this alone. Too much pain. I've already had enough pain. I don't need any more. But there was pain in her eyes, too. Oh, my god, I thought. He's her brother.

"Yes, of course," I said. "Please come in."

I opened the screen door, and she walked into the hall. I was suddenly embarrassed. I remembered the home she'd grown up in. Eight people in four tiny rooms. What must she be thinking about *this* enormous place?

"Let's go out on the side porch," I said. "Should be a nice breeze out there."

And no expensive rugs or leatherbound books.

We sat on two of the wicker chairs.

"I...," she said. "I just came from seein' Carey. At the jailhouse. He wanted me to ask you... if you'd come by to see him tomorrow. Over there at the jail?"

"*What?*"

She couldn't have said what I thought she'd said.

"What does he want?"

"For you to come by, if you would. He says there's somethin' he's gotta tell you."

"Gotta tell me? What on earth does he think that might be?"

284

"He didn't say. Just asked would I drive over here, and see if you'd come."

"Why me? Why not someone else? Why not Jimmy's parents? If he has something to say, why not to them?"

"I don't know. He said you. He said you could arrange it at the jailhouse. They're lettin' him see a few people. Mama's goin'. And the older ones of the kids. It has to be soon, though, 'cause right after they decide on . . . what to do about him, they'll be takin' him away."

She was twisting her hands again, barely hanging on. How hard must it have been for her to come here, alone? I didn't need to make it any harder.

I smiled, but shook my head.

"I can't do that," I said. "I appreciate your coming by. It was kind of you to do this for him, but . . . No. I can't go see him. It's too much to ask."

She closed her eyes for a minute, then nodded.

"All right," she said.

She looked up at me.

"But . . ." She opened her purse and handed me a piece of paper. "Here's the note I wrote in case you weren't here. It's got my phone number on it. You can call me if you change your mind."

I took the paper, looked at it, put it in my pocket, and smiled again.

"I won't be, but . . . I do understand your trying."

After she left, I took my book up to bed and dozed off. When I woke up, the house felt dark and silent. A cool breeze was coming in through the windows. I heard my old friend the solitary dog bark, once, off in the distance. I looked at the clock. One-thirty. Livie was home long ago and in bed herself.

285

I took off my clothes, turned off the light, and stretched out on the bed. Jimmy was there beside me. I felt comforted—and unbearably sad.

"I'm glad you're here," I said.

I felt him nod.

"It's almost over, I guess. By the end of the week, they'll decide. Whether to kill him or not."

Did he wince, or was that me?

"I'd give anything if I could hold you," I said. "But . . . I'm afraid if I try, you'll go away."

He didn't answer.

"I'd like to just . . . talk to you awhile, though, if that's all right."

He nodded again.

"You'd be surprised at how much I've been learning." I laughed. "No, you wouldn't. *You* wouldn't be surprised a bit. But I am. I see so many things now I never saw before. Most of all, that I've been very foolish—for such a long time."

I felt him smile and nod.

"About you. About my life. So many things."

Not your work.

Did he say that? Or did I imagine it?

"No," I said. "Not my work. But pretty much everything else. I didn't start closing myself off after Trevor died, you know. Not at all. I've done it all my life. I've just looked for excuses to justify it—and found them easily enough. I kept thinking I was safe. All tucked away with my books and my performances. And my Aubusson rugs. But I wasn't. You knew that . . . right away. As soon as you met me. You tried to teach me to reach out. Be a part of things. But I wasn't listening. Too busy thinking I knew best."

My sense of his presence beside me was stronger than ever.

"I see now that . . . what? How can I say it? That it's our separation from each other—those distances we let grow up between us and other people—that allow these things to happen. Your death. My isolation."

He nodded.

"And I've been as guilty of that as anyone, keeping my distance. Especially with you."

He shrugged. That wonderful shrug.

"No, it's true. I should've loved you more while I had you with me. Listened to you more. But . . . I was far too busy concentrating on myself—*my* wants, *my* fears—instead of you. I'm sorry for that now, but . . . I didn't know.

"I thought we had time, you see." I chuckled. "Even at my age, even on what is clearly the downhill slope, we keep thinking we have all the time we need. But we don't. We don't have time. All we have is now.

"You knew that, though, didn't you? You knew we needed to not waste our time on misunderstandings. It isn't ours to waste. It's not ours at all. We belong to it, not it to us. I see that now."

He seemed to be telling me, it's all right.

"It's *not* all right," I said. "No. It's not. I should've known better."

How? he asked.

"I don't know how," I said. "I didn't have anyone like Livie. Someone honest and forthright and uncompromising. So . . . I don't know how. I just hope it's not too late. I hope there's still a way."

This, I felt him say.

"What do you mean, this?"

This, he said again.

Yes, I thought.

Loss. And through loss, understanding.

It was my turn to nod.

2 1

When I woke the next morning, alone in my bed, I heard echoes in my mind of the night before.

'All we have is now.'

I went to the phone in the upstairs hall and called Alma Plummer. She gave me the number at the jail. Ten-thirty, they said.

Livie had left me a note on the kitchen table. *Gone to the dentist in Bainbridge. Back by noon.* I fixed my breakfast, ate it out on the side porch, and watched as heavy gray clouds gathered in the west. Without warning, the rain was there, coming down fast and hard, blowing in through the screens of the porch.

I ran through the house closing all the windows. I wouldn't have believed there could be so many. After I'd washed my breakfast dishes, I showered, shaved, dressed, and sat by the big bay window in the living room watching the downpour. Lightning lit up the room. Thunder rolled past, shaking the house. Sheets of water beat against the glass. I could barely see as far as the street.

Good, I thought. I can call and cancel. I went out into the hall and picked up the phone. I put it down. That was too easy. Unworthy. Retreating again. I went back to the window, watched the rain—even heavier now—for a few minutes, put on my windbreaker, pulled up the hood, ran for the car, and headed for Bainbridge.

As I walked into the room on the second floor of the jail, I saw him sitting on the far side of a Plexiglas partition. He looked so young. From my seat in the courtroom, halfway back, he'd looked older, harder. Up close he looked young and vulnerable.

Twenty-one. That's all. I knew his age because the papers always mentioned it: "Carey Plummer, 21, faces trial in the slaying of..." "Carey Plummer, 21, has been found guilty..."

I wanted to turn around and walk out—I had no intention of feeling the least bit kindly toward him. But just as I was about to go, he raised his hand and waved.

Why did I stay? I'll never know for sure. What I do know is that I went over and sat in the chair on my side of the partition. Two guards sitting back near the far door were chatting quietly.

"Hi," said Carey, his voice a bit muffled as it came through the grate in the partition.

"Hello."

He seemed hesitant. I wasn't about to make things easy for him.

"Bad storm out," he said. "I thought you might not come."

"I almost didn't."

"I'm glad you did, though."

I couldn't think of a way to respond to that.

His eyes wandered around the room. Then he looked directly at me.

"You hate me, don't you?" he said matter-of-factly.

At that moment, for some incomprehensible reason, I wasn't entirely sure I did, but I said 'Yes' anyway. I didn't need the complications involved in any kind of alternative.

He nodded. "Will you listen to me anyhow? Just for a minute?"

"Why?" I asked. "I can't imagine what you might have to say to me."

"No. I guess you can't. But it's just . . . It's really hard when you realize you might not be around for too much longer. You start thinkin' about . . . tidyin' things up."

"Such as?"

"Such as . . . All that talk about how Jimmy came on at us? Leroy an' me? I didn't like to think about you bein' . . . hurt by that. Made me feel bad somehow. So I wanted to tell you, while I still can, that it . . ." He shook his head. "That's not how it was."

"No?"

"No. That lady lawyer was right. Jimmy *did* just smile. Like he was glad to see us, even if he didn't know who we were. Not like . . . that other stuff."

"Then why did Leroy say Jimmy 'flirted' with you? Why did he say that in court if it wasn't true? And why did you tell it to your lawyer?"

" 'Cause we were scared. Leroy'd opened his big mouth an' bragged about it—about us hittin' him, before we'd heard that he was dead—so we knew we were gonna get caught. Just a matter of time. Leroy said we oughta tell that story. Said it was sure to work. Said if we told 'em we did what we did cause *he* came on at *us,* everybody'd believe it. I mean, us bein' regular guys an' him bein'... like he was. But... it didn't work out that way, did it?" He shrugged. I winced. "So... I just wanted you to know. It's too late to matter for me, but I... I didn't want you to go on thinkin'... that other thing."

"Thank you," I said. And I meant it. "I didn't believe it. Not really. But I might always have wondered—just a little bit. So... thank you."

"You're welcome."

"This was a very... generous thing for you to do," I said. "What made you think of it?"

"I'm not a rotten person," he said. "Not clean through, like you think. An'... this is the only life I've got. What's left of it. So, like I said, I figured I better do what I can to make things right. Don't you see?"

I felt my head nodding and forced it to stop. I *did* see. That was the problem.

"Then...," I said. "If Jimmy didn't 'flirt' with you, what made you so angry that evening?"

He looked away, stared at his hands, looked back up at me.

"It was... The way he looked. So handsome. An' clean. An'... comfortable with himself. An' then, my goddam temper kicked in, like it sometimes does, an'... just ran away with me."

"But... I still don't understand. Why would the way Jimmy looked have made you angry enough to do... what you did?"

He stared at his hands again. So did I. They were strong, tanned. Hands that had worked.

"No," he said. "You're right. It was more than that. It was . . ."

He looked up at me, his eyes pleading.

"I just need somebody to understand. *Some*body, for god's sake. Just once, before I . . . Will you try?"

"Yes," I said. "I'll try."

He rubbed the back of his neck.

"An' will you not tell on me? This is somethin' I never said to another soul. An' never will again. So . . . please. Let it just be between us. All right?"

"All right."

He stared at his hands. I waited. He glanced at the guards, leaned forward, and said quietly, "I wanted things. We *all* do. Not just fancy people. We *all* do. Problem for me was . . . mine were filthy things. Evil, sinful things."

He hesitated.

"My friend Mark? You saw at the trial? The way I felt about him. Scared me to death, so I . . . I never *did* anything about it. Never said anything. Least of all to him. *God*, no. But I felt it, all the same."

He looked up at me and back down.

"I read in the papers, while back . . . What you said at the funeral? About what Jimmy'd meant to you an' all. How you'd miss him every day for the rest of your life. You said that?"

"Yes."

"You mean it?"

"Absolutely."

He nodded. "Good. 'Cause it was when I read those things you said that it all came clear to me."

He kept staring at his hands.

"What did?" I asked.

"That I wisht . . . Oh, god, I can't say it."

"Try."

"That I wisht somebody—somebody like you—coulda loved *me*. You know?"

He glanced up and back down.

"I reckon it all woulda come out different."

I gripped the arms of the chair, so tightly I thought they would snap off. I saw what had been trying to break through for days. I didn't have to hate him. Be the next link in that never-ending chain. I could turn away from it. Rob it of its power to regenerate itself in me.

He looked up, his eyes searching mine.

"I wisht now . . . so much . . . it coulda been that. Insteada . . ."

"So do I," I said.

Dear lord in heaven.

"So do I."